Praise for Bernice L. McFadden's debut novel, *Sugar*

"Hauntingly memorable . . . clings to one's mind long after the last page has been turned . . . In this touchingly written story, Bernice L. McFadden goes to the heart of her characters, challenging one to empathize and reevaluate conscious and unconscious judgments upon fellow human beings."
—Akosua Busia, author of *The Seasons of Beento Blackbird*

"Strong and folksy storytelling . . . Think Zora Neale Hurston . . . *Sugar* speaks of what is real."
—*The Dallas Morning News*

"*Sugar* is sooooo good! McFadden tells a story that leaves you satisfied."
—Eric Jerome Dickey

"Bernice L. McFadden grabs the reader's attention immediately and doesn't let go until the last sentence. Pearl and Sugar touch your heart and linger in your mind long after the final page is read. *Sugar* is moving, tragic, and hopeful in equal measure."
—Sharon Mitchell, author of *Sheer Necessity* and *Nothing but the Rent*

"A stunning tale of love and loss . . . Bernice L. McFadden erupts on the scene with a literary explosion . . . Reveals amazing talent and promise."
—*The Chicago Defender*

BERNICE L. McFADDEN grew up listening to family stories of Southern living. The roots of the South became her touchstone and the inspiration for *Sugar*. She lives in Brooklyn, New York, where she is at work on her second novel.

SUGAR

Bernice L. McFadden

A PLUME BOOK

PLUME
Published by the Penguin Group
Penguin Group (USA) Inc., 375 Hudson Street, New York, New York 10014, U.S.A.
Penguin Group (Canada), 90 Eglinton Avenue East, Suite 700, Toronto,
Ontario,Canada M4P 2Y3 (a division of Pearson Penguin Canada Inc.)
Penguin Books Ltd., 80 Strand, London WC2R 0RL, England
Penguin Ireland, 25 St Stephen's Green, Dublin 2, Ireland
(a division of Penguin Books Ltd.)
Penguin Group (Australia), 250 Camberwell Road, Camberwell, Victoria 3124,
Australia (a division of Pearson Australia Group Pty. Ltd.)
Penguin Books India Pvt. Ltd., 11 Community Centre, Panchsheel Park,
New Delhi – 110 017, India
Penguin Group (NZ), 67 Apollo Drive, Rosedale, North Shore 0632, New Zealand
(a division of Pearson New Zealand Ltd.)
Penguin Books (South Africa) (Pty.) Ltd., 24 Sturdee Avenue, Rosebank,
Johannesburg 2196, South Africa

Penguin Books Ltd., Registered Offices: 80 Strand, London WC2R 0RL, England

Published by Plume, a member of Penguin Group (USA) Inc.

First Plume Printing, January 2001
20 19 18 17 16

 REGISTERED TRADEMARK—MARCA REGISTRADA

The Library of Congress has catalogued the Dutton editioin as follows:

McFadden, Bernice L.
    Sugar : a novel / Bernice L. McFadden.
    p. cm.
  ISBN 0-525-94531-8 (hc.)
        978-0-452-28220-9 (pbk.)
  1. Afro-Americans—Arkansas—Fiction.   I. Title.
  PS3563.C3622S84   2000
  813'.54—dc21   99-35589
                                            CIP

Printed in the United States of America
Original hardcover design by Eve L. Kirch

PUBLISHER'S NOTE
This is a work of fiction. Names, characters, places, and incidents either are the products
of the author's imagination or are used fictitiously, and any resemblance to actual persons,
living or dead, business establishments, events, or locales is entirely coincidental.

For Mommy & Daddy

ACKNOWLEDGMENTS

I ask God for so many things on a daily basis, I must acknowledge him first and foremost, because if not for him where would I be?

Thank you, God, for supplying me with the strength, wisdom and creativity to begin, continue and complete this book.

My mother and father, Robert and Vivian McFadden, for coming together and giving me life and love. My daughter, R'yane Azsa Waterton, my greatest, most beautiful work of art. My grandparents, those living and those who watch over me from the great beyond: Thelma and Wilfred Nettles, Gwendolyn and Harold McFadden. My siblings, Reggie, Misty and Kris. My niece, Shania Simon, nephew, Myles McFadden, and sister-in-law, Maritza Barzey-McFadden.

My Sister-Friends & Soul Brothers, for their consistent encouragement, love and support, Robyn Roundtree, Quovardis Banks-Lawrence, Pascale Villate-Jacques, Cicely Peace-Edouard, Wanda Toney, Charlette CeCe Jimbes, Elizabeth Warren, Sonia Rillera, Lionel Crichlow, Dean Henry and J. R. McNeil.

My creative writing teacher, Professor Margaret Lamb of Fordham University, for teaching me the art of storytelling and encouraging me to push forward.

My agent, James Vines, for recognizing my talent and sharing my vision. My editor, Laurie Chittenden, who also shared my vision and worked tirelessly on this project to make it a dream come true. Anita Diggs of Warner Books, for recognizing the possibilities and guiding me to the rainbow.

To family and friends, who are special to me and let me know that they care and are concerned about my well being, Dolly Green, Diana Crichlow, Anita Miles, Kathleen and Laura Taylor, James Griffin, Cheryl Bernard, Margaret Bernard, Fay Nurse, Bentley "Rooney" Green, Carlo Lawrence, Laura Smiley, Anthony Lloyd, Stephanie Pearson, Lisa Ford, Sheridan Abraham, Estela Olivier, Eustace Thomas, Errol Ellis, Ian Chandler, Pierceson Fenty, Wayne Alleyne, Richard Small—where are u now?—and Tonya Bodison.

To the women writers who paved the way, Nella Larson, Zora Neale Hurston, Maya Angelou, Toni Morrison and Alice Walker. A special Thanks to J. California Cooper, who took the time to verbally respond! *Thank you.*

Aretha Franklin and Nina Simone, thank you for providing my background music.

The ones who made my life extraordinary and remain with me in spirit, Rebecca Hopkins, Ruby Nelson, Virginia Cummings, Richard May, Rose Tyler, Peggy Ann Williams, Menyon "Minnie" Nettles.

And finally a special thanks to the new people in my life who added additional support and encouragement through the final part of this particular journey, Dawn Nedd, Sophia Black, Donna Trotman, Jackie Quidort, Marsha Cox, Marie Rosemond and Elton Andrews.

God Bless Us All.

"There's a little bit of hooker in every woman.
A little bit of hooker and a little bit of God."

—Sarah Miles

BEFORE

SPRING 1940

*J*UDE was dead.

On a day when the air held a promise of summer and people laughed aloud, putting aside for a brief moment their condition, color and where they ranked among humanity, Jude, dangling on the end of childhood and reaching out toward womanhood, should have been giggling with others her age among the sassafras or dipping her bare feet in Hodges Lake and shivering against the winter chill it still clutched. Instead she was dead.

She'd been taken down by the sharp blade of jealousy, and her womanhood—so soft, pink and virginal—was sliced from her and laid to rest on the side of the road near her body. Her pigtails, thick dark ropes of hair, lay splayed out above her head, mixed in with the pine needles and road dust. Her dress, white and yellow, her favorite colors, was pulled up to her neck, revealing the small bosom that had developed over the winter.

The murder had *white man* written all over it. (That was only a half truth.) But no one would say it above a whisper. It was 1940. It was Bigelow, Arkansas. It was a black child. Need any more be said?

No one cared except the people who carried the same skin color. No one cared except the parents who had nursed her, stayed up all night soothing and rocking her when she was colicky. Applauded her when she took her first steps and cried when the babbling, gurgling sounds that came from her sweet mouth finally formed the words Mamma and then later, Papa.

They cared. The parents of sweet, sweet Jude, who would never hurt a fly, no less a human being. Look at what they did to her!

Word first came via the Edelson boy. He'd run all the way and was breathless when he arrived. Black John, the blacksmith, had found her about a mile down the road and covered her body with a Crocker sack while he put himself in the right frame of mind to start coming. He had to pop the boy upside the head, twice, this just to get him moving instead of gawking.

Black John remained behind, gathering the broken child into his arms and placing her gently in his wagon among the bags and crates of field provisions. He stood looking at the beaten body of this almost woman. In life, she was a tall child, strapping, like her father, but in death, she seemed so small. Perhaps it was because of her broken bones and the way her skin sank in the places between the breaks that made her look so tiny and uneven.

He shook his head in pity and looked up into the heavens for an answer. An arrow of blackbirds blinded the sun and then moved on. If that was clarification of why and what lay ahead, Black John never said, but he would think back on this day again in fifteen years' time.

His wife had helped birth this child, as she had most of the Bigelow children. She would take it hard, like she'd lost one of her own. He looked back at the child again and a heavy sigh escaped him. "No rest for the weary," he muttered and then couldn't think of why that would come to mind at all.

He was procrastinating. Standing there behind his wagon of potatoes, turnips, cabbage, yam and Jude, he was stretching the space between his arrival and the scene that would follow. Crying eyes and screaming mouths. He'd seen plenty of grief in his life. But grief let loose from a woman who lost a child—that was the worst type of grief of all. If you could, you'd try to avoid that sort. Because grief that comes from loss of child just took a piece of you away each time you met up with it.

And if you found yourself among it too often for too long, you'd certainly die way before your time.

No, Black John was in no hurry to go.

The sun sat watching curiously on its perch, delaying its descent into late afternoon. It was long past three and Black John's shadow stood stout before him, watching and waiting. He removed his straw hat, the one that belonged to his daddy before him. The one that he inherited when his uncle handed it to him with a quiet word. Black John could never remember the exact word that was spoken, but it left an emptiness in him. The strawberry-colored stain stiffening the center part of the hat's hump confused him more than scared him because his daddy hated strawberries.

Black John fingered the stain and looked back at the dead child, her dress blotched with her own strawberry stains. "Well," he muttered in resignation, as he pulled his handkerchief from his pocket and wiped the sweat from his brow and the back of his neck.

He moved to the cab of the truck and removed a second empty Crocker sack from the floor. Returning to Jude he looked her over once again and shook his head in pity and then tucked the Crocker sacks around her body and went to the left of the wagon. That's when he saw it. Glistening in the sun. His shadow stepped forward and shaded the glare. Black John knew immediately what it was, although he had never seen one without a woman's support, protection and guidance behind it; something like that, once seen, always known. He leaned down and with the sweat-soiled handkerchief retrieved Jude's womanhood. He would later recount (and he often did) how it quivered in the palm of his hand.

His mule closed the distance in a slow saunter that barely disturbed the road dust. Black John looked over and his shadow looked back at him. Ahead he could see the small pond of black faces, eyes big with wanting to know, eyes big with wanting to see. Black John rode right into the middle and when he stepped down from his wagon he was six years old again, his father's straw hat, with the strawberry stain stiff and dry on its hump, in his hands. He pushed through the worn and patched sea of skirts, fought through the tree-long legs of men and bit down hard on a hand that tried to cover his too-young-for-death eyes. When he made it to the clearing there was his father. Beaten so hard and for so long that his skin had bubbled up purple. The top of his head was open and there he saw precious memories and somehow-someday dreams wrapped in I Love You colors spilled out for all of Bigelow to see. Then came the wail and Black John lost a little bit of his time on earth.

That's what scared him now. The silence. The absence of that mournful homage that broke your heart, stole time from Black John and pushed the most pious to question God.

Pearl's mouth hung open, but no sound came. Her heart had broken into tiny pieces that rose up, plugging her throat, allowing only breath to pass.

She tried again when Black John laid Jude's battered body to rest at her feet, the beaten, brutalized, eyeless body of her baby girl; but all she could do was claw at her own eyes and scratch at her throat, drawing blood instead of sound.

Pearl was fighting. Fighting with the reality that there would be no more candy sweet kisses and hugs that could magically erase a problem, worry or fear. In the halls of their home, who would skip, dance and sing so loud that the dogwoods raised their branches in delight?

Who would call her "Mamma honey baby" in that teasing, innocent voice that only Jude possessed?

And there would no longer be a reason for her to answer: "Jude baby doll."

These thoughts ran through her mind until her head ached with grief. Searing hot tears fell heavy from her eyes and landed on her bosom, soaking through the black cotton dress and white brassiere, stinging her skin and scorching her heart. The pain. The pain!

Later, she turned her face toward the heavens, unable to bear the sight of the sorrow-faced men as they covered her baby's coffin with brandy brown dirt. She had prepared herself to be taken from the earth at the very moment she heard the muffled sound of the first shovelful hit the top of the small wooden box. She had asked the Lord to release her from this life and allow her to walk beside her sweet Jude as she entered the Kingdom of Heaven.

But with each shovelful of earth, the sound that marked where Jude lay, quieted, and with the last sprinkling Pearl swayed suddenly and was aware of being lifted from the ground. She smiled, believing the Lord had answered her prayers. She quickly opened her eyes to take in, for what she thought to be the last time, the faces of her husband and two sons.

And they were there, faces pinched with concern and grief, as they hoisted her up and carried her limp body away from graveside.

She lay in bed for nearly thirty days, taking in very little food or water. Calling for Jude and crying when her call was not answered and still, as she wallowed in grief and anguish, the sorrowful wail that was reserved for mothers who've lost their only daughters, remained locked in her throat.

Pearl eventually returned to her life. Now absent of Jude. People stopped talking about it and allowed the matter to slip into the space in their minds reserved for horrors like those. She attempted to do the same, putting her pain not behind her, but beside her, where her sweet Jude should have been, and prayed not for redemption, but for salvation.

No, the Lord would not answer her prayers on that day. Not as she had wished. She did not die. Not physically. Her soul and spirit had departed our world the moment she touched the cold, bruised brow of her child. But God would keep her walking and breathing for quite a few more years to come. He had work for her to do.

SPRING 1955

Chapter One

TWENTY-FIVE days of freezing rain and thirty days of below-zero temperatures found most of the population of Bigelow bedded down with fevers and pneumonia.

Five babies died that year. Their bodies were stored in the basement of the small church until the ground thawed enough to bury them. Plenty of tears fell that winter.

The people swore blind it was the beginning of the end, and those who hadn't seen the inside of a church for more than twenty years flocked in bright and early every Sunday.

Minnie Grayson warned the people of Bigelow, told them her head had itched something awful the previous summer. An itching head always meant death, destruction or devastation.

Her words came to pass when Bigelow lost the five small infants. The deaths of the "Bigelow Five," as they would be known, more than convinced the people to heed her words.

"Somethin' comin', time to save your souls 'for it's too late." People paid attention and grabbed worn (or brand-new) Bibles and asked the Lord for his mercy and forgiveness.

Come April the temperature soared. It felt like August in an oven. The lake dried up. Women refused to sleep with their men. Dogs ceased barking. The tulips that encircled the statue erected to the founder of Bigelow bloomed and died all in one day.

Everybody complained that it was hotter than hell. But only

one could say for sure and he was miles away. His reason for coming back to Bigelow was only just arriving.

Minnie Grayson started scratching again, and warned everyone she came across that "God's vengeance against their town wasn't near to being done."

Clair Bell sat on her porch, feet stuck in a tub of soothing hot water, soaking her bunions. This sealed what Minnie predicted. Clair Bell only suffered with her feet when something was near to going wrong, which usually meant a storm, drought or disease. Bigelow held its breath and waited.

They watched the sky for black billowing clouds. Licked the tips of their fingers and tested the air for a shift of wind. Waited for the first flash of light and thunderous bass.

They boiled roots and leaves and drank tall simmering glasses of murky, stinking liquids to cleanse their bodies and protect them from any maladies that could bed them and in time, kill them.

They cured meat, canned fruit and pickled pork, packing their sheds full, anticipating crops lost and animal deaths.

They waited.

A storm blew in. It wasn't what they expected, but some would say later that it was just as deadly as any twister or hurricane they had ever experienced.

The storm walked into their small town on two legs in spiked, red patent leather heels. She waltzed right through the main square, blond wig bouncing to the rhythm of her walk, a leopard print pocketbook slung over one shoulder, matching suitcases in each hand. Her eyes were covered with cat's-eye-shaped, white-rimmed glasses, mirrors to her soul, unavailable for view. A Lucky Strike hung from her red-painted lips.

She was tall, taller than any man in that town, except for Joe Taylor. Tall and black as the day was long. She walked with a confidence most people in Bigelow had never known. She swaggered along like a cat in heat, leaving swirling curtains of dust in her wake.

People named her right there and then. Named her without an introduction, without two words ever passing between them. Called her things they had only whispered under their breath, or in their bedrooms when the doors were closed tight and passion drove them into saying it. Words no self-respecting, God-fearing man or woman would ever use in public. But now they publicly stated it, because they had a right and reason to.

Slut. Whore. Bitch.

She made her way down the main road past the white-washed homes with their large wrap-around porches and picket fences. Past magnolia gardens and sweeping peach trees where young boys hung precariously from knotted limbs, watching her with large dark eyes.

She walked with purpose past the general store where the white man called Abraham gave out credit and charged a 2 percent interest if you didn't settle your bill with him by the first Friday of every month.

She came down Pleasant Way, where Anna Lee (said to be the illegitimate offspring of the general store owner) swept at the dirt that always seemed to need sweeping when word came that something interesting was happening outside the perimeters of her home. Anna Lee watched the woman with an even eye and stopped her lazy sweeping, not to tilt her head in greeting but to concentrate on the vision before her. When their eyes met, Anna Lee's did not smile or blink with shame; they stretched wide and shouted: Unacceptable! Unwanted! Get out!

Sugar turned the corner that held Bigelow's only school-house. It was small, white and unassuming.

She stopped short, dead in front of Fayline's House of Beauty, and peeked in at the women whose hair was in the process of being washed, dyed, teased, conked or pressed into the latest styles from New York, Detroit and Washington, D.C.

No one said hello, welcome or even invited her in for a Coke. No, they just sat, openly watching her, their arms folded defiantly across their breasts, hands resting in resistance on their hips, as she examined the chipped blue paint on the dusty storefront glass that separated them from her. The paint that used to be a brilliant blue and would have in the past screamed FAYLINE'S HOUSE OF BEAUTY, but years of winter wind and summer sun had faded the letters so that they barely whispered to you what and whose establishment you stood in front of.

She moved on, aware of the pandemonium that was brewing around her.

Sugar walked slowly down a narrow dirt road, sycamores on either side giving an eerie shaded feel to the walkway. The homes that lined the street were identical in every way except color. Small, neat, board-and-shingle houses, painted white, light gray or a watery sort of blue. Two floors, two windows to each of the five rooms. Fenced-in yards that held sleeping dogs or guileful cats and mulberry bushes that sat beneath open windows shading blooming azaleas.

A sign, rusted and bent nearly in half by a passing twister or unruly adolescent, swung around and around on the lone post, stopping briefly as the breeze that guided its frantic spin lulled. GROVE STREET.

Sugar stopped, set her bags down and pulled a damp, folded piece of brown paper from her bosom. The address, written in black ink, was now smudged, causing the 10 and Grove Street that were written there to blend into each other, becoming nearly indecipherable.

She looked from the paper to the sign post and back to the paper. Satisfied she was in the right place, she retrieved her suitcases and walked toward her new home and new life.

Behind her the people of Bigelow buzzed like flies around shit. The heat forgotten, all thoughts were on the woman that had just strutted her way right through the main square in front of their children, and more important, in front of their men.

They hated her immediately, not knowing of her childhood or the life that, after only one day of living it, would have had them calling out to the Lord for help.

They hated her and did not know that she had never loved in *that* way. *That* way—when a man and woman come together and the cost involved is one that no bank could ever lend out, no national mint could ever print, reprint or discontinue.

They hated her because it was clear that she had been one of them at some point, but had left before she would mature into a woman that tied her hair up in worn cloth at sunset and pushed her sleeves up around her elbows to begin an evening of toil after having toiled all day for the Man. Baking bread and churning sweet butter, growing butter beans and collard greens in the yard behind the small house that would (during her entire lifetime) belong to the bank even though she had a thirty-year mortgage that should have been paid off five years ago, but somehow the bank keeps telling her about interest that was miscalculated back in '46. And so now she owes for a few more years, but they can't say how many for sure, and she won't demand an exact count, because she's colored and they're not and this is the South, 1955.

At night she would kiss her children (never less than four offspring) good-night. If she was lucky and owned a radio, she could sit on her porch or in the tiny living room and listen to a radio show and chuckle at the humor, because a day of picking cotton, chopping wood or canning fish leaves you with little strength to out-and-out laugh. You save your laughter for real good time evenings, when the boss man is an extra day away. Blessings may shower her and that hot talent Ella Fitzgerald may come across singing "A-Tisket A-Tasket" and get her foot to tapping and maybe even humming along, but not too hard because she's darning a holey sock as she listens to this song about the basket, or hemming hand-me-down pants, and working with a needle by candlelight can be tedious. She's got drawers soaking in a bucket behind the house that have to be scrubbed and hung to dry in the night air, but her husband has bathed tonight and splashed a little of that drug store aftershave on his cheeks; that means he wants to do more than just lay beside her, he wants to lay up on her and inside her. So she leaves the drawers to soak for another hour or so, while she does her duty as Mrs. and pleases her man, because she can function on three hours of sleep. Keeping her man well fed and fucked are number one priorities that she can't slack on because you can never know when a woman dressed to the nines with a blond wig, long legs and a high fat ass that should have been equal to you in almost every way may decide to hop on the first southbound Greyhound and end up looking at you through whispering letters on a dusty storefront window.

Chapter Two

HE phone blared out and startled Pearl, causing her heart to skip a beat. She still had not grown used to the sound of it. The black speaking and hearing contraption that she had waited patiently nearly two years for while Ma Bell decided whether it was cost effective to put up telephone lines in a town full of coloreds with low-paying jobs was ringing for the first time all day. Pearl had picked up the phone at least twice that day and listened to the clicking sounds that traveled through the long snake-like cord that exited the bottom and disappeared into her wall. And now after watching it and tip-toeing around waiting for it to ring, it does just that and startles her breathless.

"Lord have mercy." Pearl jumped at the shrill sound of the phone and then moved quickly into the living room where the phone sat on its own table for easy viewing. Pearl was short and stout and her walk was more like a waddle than a stride. Her arms were thick and visibly strong from years of lifting heavy household objects and pushing a scrub brush back and forth over countless wooden and tiled floors. She was sixty, but her face was still very youthful. Her husband called her Bit, a nickname that carried over from the days when Pearl was short and petite. Pearl is still short, but *petite* is a word and a proportion long forgotten.

"Hello?" Pearl answered the phone in a labored voice.

"I think she here! She ain't too long passed my house . . . girl, she is a sight!" Shirley Brown was rattling a mile a minute. "She coming in your direction."

"Shirley, who you talking about—"

"The one the Reverend told you about. The one you suppose to welcome and all. She a sight. If that's her she a sight, Pearl!"

Pearl listened to Shirley ramble on excitedly as she vaguely recalled the conversation she'd had with Reverend Foster just two weeks ago.

"Pearl, you have been a faithful member of this congregation for years." Reverend Foster moved in close to her as they stood in front of Bigelow's First Baptist Church. He lowered his voice so that the congregation that was leaving Sunday service would not hear what he was relaying to Sister Pearl. He took her lightly by the elbow and guided her away from the crowd.

"Don't tell no one, but you are one of my favorite followers." He smiled at her and Pearl lowered her eyes away from his handsome face and soft eyes. He smelled like the air after a good rain. Him being so close to her made her feel light-headed.

"I hear we gonna have a new resident in our small town. A woman coming in from over in Short Junction, taking over the house next door to you."

"Hmmm," Pearl said and nodded her head.

"So I figure since you are such a dedicated member, and my favorite, you would be the perfect person to welcome her to our little community and eventually bring her into the fold."

Pearl looked up from his shiny shoes, which seemed a little too fine for a Reverend in a town made up of sharecroppers and factory workers. But she pushed the thought away and tried to concentrate on his words.

"Would you do that for Reverend Foster, Sister Pearl?" His voice was pleading.

"Of course, Reverend. When we expecting Mrs. . . . Mrs.?"

"Oh, it's Mizz Lacey, a niece, I believe, of some people over in Short Junction," Reverend Foster said, lowering his voice another notch and looking over his shoulder as he did. "We expecting her any day, I suppose, Sister Pearl."

"All right then, Reverend, I'll be looking out for her then." Pearl smiled and walked slowly toward her husband who was patiently waiting.

Now Pearl watched from her window as the woman walked up to and stopped right out in front of her house. "She's here," is all Pearl managed to say before she placed the phone back in its cradle, cutting off Shirley's rambling.

Was this the woman the Reverend spoke of? The woman Pearl had been asked to guide and help and eventually lead into the flock? Was this her? This woman didn't look as if she'd ever spent a second in a house of worship, much less knew what one was. But there was something else too. A slither of something familiar that Pearl was yet to put her finger on.

Pearl stood there in the shadows, half of her body in the living room, half in the hall. The woman leaned back on one leg, dropped her cigarette to the ground and smiled a knowing smile. Pearl held her breath. Did the woman see her spying?

A crack of a bat and the roar of the crowd from the secondhand radio sent Pearl scurrying into the kitchen like a frightened mouse.

The stranger laughed a low bitter sort of a laugh and walked the less than fifteen feet to #10 Grove Street. She walked slowly up the front steps, stooped and retrieved the key from beneath a worn mat that said: GOD BLESS THIS HOME.

Pearl held her breath as the woman unlocked the door and disappeared into the house, allowing the screen door to slam loudly behind her.

Afternoon moved to evening and the sun set slowly over Bigelow, leaving purple-orange streaks across the Arkansas sky. Pearl had settled herself at the kitchen table, taking up a silent vigil by the open window, hoping to catch sight of the woman in #10 with the familiar face.

"Bit? What you doing, daydreaming again, girl?" Joe, Pearl's husband, stood in the kitchen entrance. He was a towering man of sixty-two. Amazingly, the gray had just started to creep into the blackness of his temples. "I been calling you for dang near ten minutes, ain't you hear me call you, Bit?" Pearl met his questioning eyes. She'd been sitting there at the kitchen table, attempting to separate the peas from their pods, her attention totally consumed with the woman inside #10 Grove Street.

"Bit?" Joe was still waiting for an answer from his wife. Instead what he got was a dubious look topped with guilt.

"Aw, baby, I just been in here popping these peas," Pearl said timidly. They both looked down at the two lone pods that lay on the wooden table. "Well, I guess I was sorta daydreaming too," Pearl added shyly.

Joe's gaze moved from the pods to the open window that looked directly onto the closed living room window of #10 Grove Street. He knew from pure instinct (and from being with the same woman for more than 30 years) that she wasn't telling the whole truth.

"Oh really?" was all he said, and turned to move back into the living room. Pearl immediately felt bad. She was caught and too silly to admit it. She walked into the living room and realized that the light that stretched along the wooden floor for most of the day had disappeared. The heat had subsided enough for Joe to have turned off the fan. A cool breeze came in on the tail of the blanketing dusk.

"Joe, how's 'bout we go on down to the Rib Shack. It's Saturday, don't feel much like cooking. 'Sides, the heat done drained me dry."

Joe just smiled.

"C'mon, baby, what you say?" Pearl pushed. Joe got up from the couch and walked over to his wife, lightly tweaked her nose and shook his finger. "Let me get my shirt," was his reply.

*J*oe was a simple man, enjoying simple pleasures. A hearty card game with his friends, evening meeting with his Mason brothers or fishing alone on the edge of Hodges Lake. These are the things that pleased him and brought him quiet joy.

God-fearing and soft-spoken, all that mattered to Joe was his wife, family and leading a life worthy of entering Heaven. Nobody could ever accuse this man of raising his hand or his voice in anger. He understood things about life and women that other men just couldn't.

Joe was a tall man standing nearly six feet, three inches, with skin the color of amber. He had a strong presence about him, the kind that made people move two inches more than necessary out of his path. People felt most comfortable addressing him with a slightly bowed head, avoiding the eyes that seemed to see straight through to your soul.

Pearl had gazed into those very same eyes long ago and fell in love. She knew the first time he took her small hands into his own that this would be the man she would give herself over to until death parted them.

They met after the war. That's when Bigelow came alive again. Men returned home to their wives and sons returned to their mothers. The cannery, a main source of employment before the war, reopened. Word of this traveled far south and people that once held jobs there received it like a cool breeze to a heated brow. Men and women dropped their gunny sacks filled with cotton, oranges or watermelon, and stood tall for the first time in years. The sound of machetes cutting through the air could be heard for miles as they were flung high above the tobacco and wheat fields. And like an Old Testament exodus, hundreds of people left Jackson, Clearwater, Salem and Charleston on foot, by cart and donkey and if possible by train headed for Ashton. Headed for home.

Joe Taylor was one of those who came home; a soldier boy who'd fought alongside white men who wouldn't share the same toilet with him or drink from the same well back home, but in the end, before the last breath left their dying bodies, did not hesitate for one moment to turn pleading eyes on him.

And so Joe put aside his memories of an uncle, naked, beaten, burnt and lynched, left to die hanging from a branch of a pecan tree. He shook the vision of his mother slapped so hard by a white woman that she permanently lost the sight in her right eye. He erased from his mind the words: "coon," "monkey" and "nigger"—words a soldier had used hundreds of times during his lifetime and just moments earlier on Joe before the shell ripped through his body.

Now this white soldier lay clinging to the last threads of life, his insides scattered around him, war sounds echoing in his ears and turns to Joe. "Please," he utters, because he's scared of death and does not want to die alone among bombs and bullets. It no longer matters to the soldier that Joe is Negro or colored. All that matters is that he is there.

Joe has read the Bible and the Good Book says: Forgive and forget and love thy neighbor. With these words in mind, Joe lays his gun down and takes the dying man in his arms. Carefully, tenderly like a fragile newborn he rocks and shushes the man as the soldier whimpers at the sight of his blood running from his open wounds and seeping into the earth. Joe lulls the man into the afterlife, places his head gently on the ground, closes the lids over his empty eyes, retrieves his gun and continues to fight for a freedom he would never be fully entitled to.

It was back in the evenings, when Pearl made her way home from washing, ironing and cleaning all that wasn't hers and would never be hers, she'd stop and stand for hours as close to the men as possible to listen in on their talk.

They gathered in small bunches outside the Rib Shack, spitting distance from the hat shop where Pearl stood, pretending to admire the hats in the window, while eavesdropping on their conversation.

Pearl had listened to Bigelow's young men tell their stories of war and love. She smiled as they imitated the *oui oui*s and *Bonjour*s of the pale thin-lipped French women who would do what the colored women wouldn't.

She listened, while her stomach twisted and turned as Mickey Johnson described how they sawed off his ravaged leg while he watched, a block of wood clenched between his teeth.

Izzy Cox told of a man who fought for two days, his intestines hanging from his stomach like snakes. "How the hell did that boy fight like that, Izzy?" a doubtful voice from the crowd asked.

"That nigga put his guts in a bowl, took the nylons he was

gonna bring back home to his woman, and bound it tight around his waist." No one said a word. "That boy had some Indian in 'im," Izzy added, and used his finger to make a swirling motion near his temple. The crowd of men nodded knowingly. A man was bound to do anything once he had some Indian in him. Everybody knew Indians were crazy.

After that story, Pearl didn't go around them for a few days. She couldn't get the picture out of her mind and had a hard time eating out of a bowl.

It was during one of those late afternoons that she first heard Joe Taylor speak. She'd seen him standing tall. Always quiet, maybe brooding. She did not know.

He spoke with a voice so low and deep, it reminded Pearl of rolling thunder before a late summer storm. His voice, like the thunder, caught you off guard, and before you knew it lightning bolts were dancing among the clouds and painting the blackened sky with streaks of bluish gold. That's how Pearl remembered it. His voice shook her and she unfixed her gaze on a wide-brimmed black hat with white imitation ostrich feathers. She tilted her head slightly to the side and snatched a quick look at the man that caused her soul to quake.

"Yup, that sure was some pretty countryside. Rolling hills and all. When I was there it reminded me a little of right here. I had a mind to just keep on going after it was all done," he said while studying the palm of his massive hand.

"Black men ain't never been nothing but chattel to these here white folks. Always been that way, always will be that way." The men fell quiet around him, lost in the thoughts brought about by Joe's statement.

Joe continued, "I can't say that I was proud to fight for my country, not say it and be truthful 'bout it. But I can say I felt proud when I looked around and saw the white men fall, bleed and die just like the colored."

One of the men, Benny Parks, who'd lost an eye in the war, cocked his head sideways so he could take all of Joe in with that one good eye, and asked in total bewilderment, "Now why would that make you feel proud, Joe? How death gonna make you feel proud?" The rest of the men kind of leaned in closer in anticipation of his answer.

Joe started off in the slow easy manner he was accustomed to. "I felt proud because there was the proof right there on the battlefield that we was men just like them. Not monkeys or some ornery creature that hid its tail in its pants. But men that bled the same red blood." The men milled Joe's words around in their minds for a bit, digesting each syllable and allowing it to restructure itself within them. Each of these men would repeat these words in separate company, claiming them for their own.

"I guess that is something to be proud of, Joe. Yup, hadn't thought of it that way," Benny Parks said.

Their stories propelled her to approach the group. She knew most of the men. "How ya'll doing this afternoon? Benny. Charlie. Gibson." She called off the names she knew and nodded a greeting to those she didn't. When she got to Joe, she nodded and fixed her eyes on his for what seemed like an eternity. Gibson spoke first. He was a scrawny man, smallest one of the group. Only action he caught during the war was the hard sole of a soldier's boot making contact with his jaw as he bent to remove a slop bucket full of shit and piss.

"Why, Miss Pearl, 'bout time you stopped staring at them hats and come over and say hello. How's your mamma and daddy doing?" Gibson asked, taking in Pearl's Coca-Cola-bottle figure.

"Oh they just fine," Pearl said, glancing back at Joe. A wry, knowing smile briefly surfaced on Gibson's lips. "Pearl, you remember Joe Taylor, don't you? This Mike and Cora Taylor's boy from down round Hancock way . . . near Jessie's farm." Gibson turned to Joe and continued, "This here is Henry and Belle Mason's girl."

Joe squinted at Pearl. "Yup, sure do remember you. Your daddy drive for the McHenrys, don't he?" He continued, answering his own question, "Yup, I seen him in that shiny fancy car, carting them look-alike girls through here to wherever." His attention turned back to the palm of his hand. Just as Pearl was about to agree with him, Joe looked up to meet her gaze. "Yup, you the one usta come to church with all them pretty dresses on. I sure did think you all was rich. You and them fine dresses."

Pearl gushed with sweet embarrassment. "Oh, yeah. I mean, naw we ain't rich. But you remember that?" She sure didn't remember him.

"Yup, I remember when we was leaving, me and my family, going down to Florida, you know, for work and all. I remember you was standing down underneath that old maple tree that usta be near Boones Ridge. Whatever happened to the tree? Anyway, we was on our way out, and you was standing there trying to keep from getting wet, the rain was just starting to fall. Pink bows. Pink shoes. You sure was small. My mamma saw you, pointed you out to the rest of us. I remember she called to Papa, told him to look at that pretty little bit of a girl dressed in pink under that maple tree."

Soft chuckles floated up from the group of men like small butterflies. Joe just said whatever came to mind, didn't care who heard it or their thoughts or opinions on it.

"Uh-huh, I remember that day like it was yesterday." Finished, he turned back to examining his palm. Pearl was speechless for a minute or two. She could not even recall that day. She couldn't have been more than four or five years old. She could feel red warmth climb from her bosom up to her neck and then spread across her face. "Well," she said in a voice that sounded a bit too high. "I best be going. It was nice talking with ya'll," she said as she hastened to depart the company of the man that seemed to say all the right things.

"I believe you best be going." Joe agreed and looked up into the darkening sky. "Sun is dipping pretty low. I think it best if'n I escort you home."

He didn't ask, he just said it and there was no trying to talk him out of it. And Pearl didn't want to. He moved to her side and fell into step.

That was the first of many walks home. Joe claimed her. Claimed her petite build and brown skin. Full bosom and long lashes. The crease behind her knees and the scar under her chin. They all belonged to him. He didn't have to say it aloud. Everyone knew she was his and respected it.

He came to her one day with a bouquet of wildflowers, and handed it to her on their fourth walk home. He told her it was time for him to meet her parents and explain his intentions.

Joe took a job with the railroad to supplement the money he was making at the cannery. He wanted to marry Pearl and place her in their own home as soon as possible. The extra money would enable him to do just that.

He got down on his knees, right in front of Henry and Belle Mason, and asked for Pearl's hand in marriage. He pulled a pink silk ribbon from his pocket with a tiny gold band with a wisp of a diamond tied to the end. Belle Mason broke into tears and Henry Mason nodded his approval and with a big grin and wet eyes, he slapped Joe hard on the back.

They were married in the one-hundred-year-old Baptist church and celebrated steps away in the area where the old maple once stood that shielded Pearl from the rain and allowed Joe Taylor the first look at his future.

Chapter Three

*S*UGAR sat still in the darkness of her living room and looked through the window at the approaching dawn. She hadn't been able to sleep a whole night since she arrived in Bigelow, and for the past eight mornings she had sat smoking and watching the sun slip up and over the horizon and settle itself snugly into the sheltering sky. She would remain there long after noon, her mind wandering through a jungle of memories until sleep finally took her.

She shifted and lit another cigarette. The smoke danced in the thin stream of light that filtered through the window and Sugar felt self-pity slip into her soul as she reminisced on her life so far.

It seemed to her that getting ahead was something reserved for people that already had their feet placed one in front of the other. Sugar, well, she guessed she was just born with both feet turned backward, 'cause every step she took placed her one step closer to where she'd been instead of where she was trying to get.

Her mother gave her up before the cord had stiffened and fallen off.

She was born just thirty miles down the road, in Short Junction. A town not unlike Bigelow; tract houses, and a general store that carried everything you wanted and some things you didn't. A bank that was barely open twice a week since colored folk deposited their money in jars, buried it in their yards or stuffed it in their mattresses. They hid their money in a shoe or hat box and placed it on the top shelf of their closets, behind the box that held the family mementos. Most often, though, they placed it between the pages of their Bibles, believing God would watch over it. No, wasn't much need for a bank in Short Junction, but it was there anyway.

There was a church that doubled as a school during the week. Sugar never went there to learn or pray. But it was there just the same.

People in Short Junction grew their own vegetables and slaughtered their own hogs and chickens. They washed their clothes by hand in large tin tubs, scrubbing them clean with lye soap that ate at your skin long after your hands were through using it. People hung their clothes out on ropes that ran from their houses to the buckeye trees that could be found in everyone's backyards. The noonday sun bleached their whites and nurtured the spinach, tomato and potatoes that grew in their gardens.

Short Junction's residents traveled ten, fifteen and sometimes twenty miles a day to work. They worked in nearby Sunflower, Beacon and Jamison counties, cleaning white folks' homes and raising their kids. And at night they'd travel back to Short Junction to clean their own homes and raise their own children.

On Sundays, there was church service and a lot of whooping and hollering in the name of Jesus Christ and after service they would gather on the lawn in front of the church and devour fried chicken, macaroni pie, baked sweet potatoes and potato salad until the sun went down.

I guess you would say Short Junction was a family town, filled with people that cared about one another, but Sugar was never a part of that family.

Three sisters, the Lacey women (as they were known), took Sugar in and called her their own. Their history became her history.

They owned a big house that sat right outside the city limits of Short Junction. This house was willed to them by their mother, Gwen Lacey. Gwen was a half-breed, the product of her slave mother, Abbey, and slave master, John Lacey.

It was said that John Lacey purchased Abbey for eight hundred dollars, outbidding two others who also wanted the strong backed, ebony beauty. John Lacey had stood before Abbey, pretending to examine her teeth for decay and her gums for disease, but his eyes never once left hers. He was smitten immediately and his knees went weak at the closeness of her. His hands trembled as he passed them over her long, strong arms and down the sides of her thighs. To him, her skin felt like silk and her scent was like newly turned earth. His heart beat hard in his chest and his manhood, dormant for so many years, strained against his fine wool slacks.

He did not intend to fall in love with a Negroid woman; he had tried to find love in the simple smiles of the lily white virgins of Short Junction and the other surrounding towns. Tried until he could no longer stomach the gardenia perfume that rose like smoke from their cleavage. He feebly campaigned against other bachelors that matched his wealth and status (it was required, otherwise he might have been labeled a queer) for the arched wrists and dainty hands of blond-haired, blue-blood maidens whose mouths promised eternal love. But John knew their love would run gone if he could no longer provide the gold, silk and jewelry these women claimed were necessary for their survival.

He loved Abbey as a man should love a woman, no matter the color. He gave her his name, his seed and the left side of his bed for twenty years. And when he died, he left her and their daughter everything he'd ever owned.

Gwen Lacey was nearly grown when John Lacey died, and his relatives came and pillaged what they could. Fine linens, furniture and jewelry. They cussed Abbey and spit in Gwen's face as they tore the fine velvet curtains down from the windows and removed the silverware from the kitchen drawers.

They wanted the house too, but the will was legal and binding and they could do nothing about that.

I, John Lacey, give and bequeath to Abbey, a woman of color, formerly my slave but since emancipated and with whom I

*have had one daughter called Gwen, the sole and exclusive
right to the house and property it sits on as well as the horses,
cattle and all the monies of which I die possessed.*

John Lacey 1858

"Mark my words . . . that nigga better enjoy this while she can,
'cause she and that beast she calls a child won't be here for long!"
a cousin of John Lacey screamed after a lengthy and heated argument with Samuel Gittens, John Lacey's lawyer and confidant.
The cousin stormed out of the house, but not before grabbing
the silver candlesticks from their place over the fireplace.

Abbey Lacey was not illiterate; John Lacey had made sure of
that. She in turn taught their daughter, Gwen. Gwen Lacey, who
was high in color, with long tight curls that hung about her face
giving her a wild, seductive look, was a rebellious child and remained the same way into adulthood. Gwen was courted by
many men, black and white, but in the end chose a man named
Isaac Thorpe who was half Chickasaw and half black.

Isaac was a gambler and a hustler. He was a smooth-talking,
handsome man that wooed Gwen into allowing him to move
into her home. Abbey was completely against it, warning her
daughter that this man she thought she loved was something less
than genuine in his claims of love for her. Gwen fought her
tooth and nail, reminding her mother that this was her house
too and she had all rights to place under the roof any person or
persons she chose.

Abbey and Gwen argued even as Isaac Thorpe's heavy, muddy
boots announced his arrival.

Isaac turned the seven-bedroom house into a brothel, con-
vincing Gwen that this was good business by adorning her with
beautiful dresses and jewelry bought with the money he made
from the misuse of flesh. In return, over time, Gwen gave Issac
three beautiful, bright-eyed baby girls.

As the years passed, he brought in Creole women from
Louisiana and Seminoles from Florida to work. "Add a bit of variety for the customers," he said aloud. And for himself. But he
kept that thought secret.

The first time Gwen caught Isaac with one of the women, he explained to her that it was necessary for him to test each and every woman he employed. "Gwen, I need to make sure these here women are doing all the right things to keep the mens 'round here coming back for more."

Gwen dug her nails deep into her palms in order to control the anger that was growing within her.

"It don't mean nothing to me, baby. You know you the one I love," he said and then asked her very nicely to leave the room while he finished handling his business.

She did, her eyes full of hurt and tears.

"What kinda women you is? You gonna let a man lay up on another woman in your own house and not do nothing about it?" At first she thought her mind was talking to her, but then she caught a blurred shape moving past.

"It ain't none of your business," Gwen yelled at Abbey before storming away.

Time is something that changes all things and it is true in Gwen Lacey's case. Gwen had been sent to the edge of madness, but she did not step off into it. She let it mold her and clear the fog she thought was love from her mind. She warned him, as she had before, but her voice carried something other than pain this time. Had he listened, he may have lived his life to the end God had set for him, but he ignored it.

"Isaac, if you lay down with one more woman in my house I'll kill you dead!" Gwen screamed outside the bedroom Isaac was holed up in with whatever woman he had chosen for the evening.

Gwen took her three daughters and placed them in the barn with the horses. Kissed them all tenderly on their heads and told them to stay put and stay quiet and no matter what they heard, not to move from the barn until she came for them.

The house was full. Men coming and going. Satisfied that they had found some release, some companionship, someone to listen and agree. Gwen walked into her home, her beautiful home, and for the first time in her whole life asked God for forgiveness. She moved slowly up the large staircase, smiling at the men and women that passed her on their descent. She traced the smooth polished oak banister with the tips of her fingers and savored the coolness of the wood. She walked to the end of the hall, past Abbey's room, stopping to peek in to see her mother sound asleep. Abbey still slept on the left side of the bed, a habit she could not break even though John Lacey had been dead and gone for nearly twenty-four years.

Gwen quietly entered the room, walked over to the side of the bed, went down to her knees and pulled the shotgun from beneath it. Abbey stirred and moaned in her sleep.

Once back in the hall Gwen moved on, stopping only to press her ear against each bedroom door and listen for Isaac's sounds.

She entered her own bedroom, the one she had conceived and birthed her children in, hoping to find him straddled atop one of the Creole women; this would surely justify her blowing his head off as well as assist in quelling the guilt that was building within her with every step she took.

When she opened the door she found Isaac Thorpe, the father of her children, alone, his throat cut from ear to ear. Gwen looked on, fully understanding and quite disappointed that Abbey had beaten her to killing him.

So the story goes.

Long after Gwen passed away, her children, May, Sara and Ruby Lacey, raised Sugar.

They told her that her mamma just dropped her off one day on her way to some other place with some man that she thought would make her happy.

They said that she was in such a hurry that she didn't even have time to name her.

"Ya'll go on and call her anything you want! She belong to ya'll now!" She was said to say as she jumped into his fancy automobile and waved good-bye.

Only a wisp of truth lay in that story.

Sugar spent fifteen years in Short Junction. Her friends were the wind, sun and trees; her playhouse, the woods and the river that flowed through it.

Her memories, the ones she allowed to remain, often wondered on a day when she and Sara went to town to pick up a few things from the general store. Sara gave her a peppermint stick and told her to wait outside until she was done. Sugar did as she was told and amused herself by watching the comings and goings of the people that lived in Short Junction.

The women smiled sweetly at her as they passed in and out the store, the men ignored her. She knew most of the men of Short Junction; they visited the Lacey home and the Lacey women quite often. Sugar had a jar full of shiny pennies to prove it. The men always gave her pennies. Their way of buying her silence.

On that day, just as the wind was beginning to kick up the dust in the road and a horse brayed loudly in a nearby stable, another little girl joined Sugar outside the store.

She sucked contentedly on her own peppermint stick, watching Sugar shyly from the corner of her eye. Sugar had never been this close to another child, and at the age of five, this nearness caused her heart to clamor with excitement inside her chest.

"What's your name?" the little girl finally asked, in the way only a little girl can.

Sugar considered her. Her worn dress, bare dirty feet and uncombed hair.

"Sugar," she said and waited for her reaction.

"Hmmm," the little girl uttered and looked thoughtfully at her peppermint stick. "That your mamma in there?" she said, pointing in the store. There were only two women in there, Sara and the woman who'd come with the little girl, and neither one of them was Sugar's mamma. In fact, at that tender age, Sugar had no real sense of what a mamma was. She'd heard the word used in conversation, but its meaning was foreign to her.

She shook her head no.

"Where's your mamma at?" the little girl asked, her eyebrows raised in surprise.

Sugar shrugged her shoulders.

"She dead?" she asked and her eyes widened.

Again, Sugar just shrugged her shoulders.

The little girl looked into the store again and then back at Sugar.

"Ain't you got a mamma?" she said with shocked disbelief.

Sugar just stared blankly at her. She had a May, a Sara and a Ruby. She didn't have a "mamma."

"What's a mamma?" she asked, hoping the little girl would shed some light on this thing that seemed so important.

The girl returned the same blank stare.

"Don't be talking to the likes of her, Caroline." The little girl's mother came out and dragged her by the collar away from Sugar. Her bare feet skidded across the dirt, leaving squiggly lines behind. "She a Lacey and we don't fraternize with those type of people."

"Those type of people," Sugar muttered to herself and moved to reach for another cigarette. Her face was wet with tears, but she did not notice. She tried to distract her mind and focus on the dust that swirled in the thin stream of light that filtered through the window. But like a storm, there was no stopping these memories, no matter how painful they were. Sugar leaned back, inhaled, and let them come back to her.

They lived in a big yellow and green house surrounded by willow trees and wildflowers. Sugar spent hours out and about the flowers and trees, trying to block out the heavy breathing and moaning that sailed down to her on the evening breeze.

Friday and Saturday nights found men and women from all over the county sitting in and around the Lacey home, where the good times rolled as long as you had the money to keep it going.

They came for the conversation, corn liquor, catfish and Lacey pussy.

The Lacey women sold themselves a sliver at a time. Leaving some back to fill the years when there would be no lean hard body to press against theirs and whisper sweet syrupy lies into the swell of a breast.

Time stopped and stepped aside to allow Sugar to walk away from the trees, leave behind her wreath of wildflowers and put away the sweet songs she sang aloud to the meadow. Time made way and Sugar strolled right into womanhood.

You see, no one ever told her to keep her legs closed and crossed at the ankles. No one ever said: "Save it for the one you love" or "Good girls say no."

They'd been watching her for some time. The men. Watching the way her ass grew out and moved up and onto her back. The way her legs lengthened and the muscles strained hard against her skin when she walked. The tight knobs that once struggled against her blouse had suddenly blossomed to something full and buoyant, ready to be held, kissed and caressed.

Her scent told them she was ready.

She went with him into the empty room. Some nameless, faceless him. They went to the same room that saw Isaac die.

She did not get kind words or gentle kisses. What she got was callused hands and boots that were worn thin at the sole. A man who, after he was done riding her, sat on the edge of the bed, his face in his hands, and wept out his guilt.

Guilty—'cause he was laying with someone else besides his wife.

Guilty—'cause he was paying out money he was supposed to use to buy food for his family.

Guilty—'cause the smell of Sugar reminded him of his own twelve-year-old daughter.

It was done and over. Tears mean nothing in the Lacey home. Just the two dollars on the dresser.

A door slammed in the distance and jerked Sugar away from her memories. She looked at her wristwatch; it was ten past six. "He's running late today," she mumbled to herself. She got up and walked over to the window, parted the curtains enough to see the tall, dark man bound down the stairs and then turn on his heel and bound back up to place a quick forgotten kiss on the cheek of his wife. Seconds later he was gunning the engine to his old pick-up and was off down the road.

Pearl stood out on the porch, her thin robe pulled tight around her against the morning chill, until the truck faded in the distance. She then turned her attention to Sugar's house. She stood there for quite some time, straining her neck this way and that way, trying to see whatever it is she thought she would see. Sugar smiled in spite of herself.

Nosy people irritated Sugar, so she began to keep the curtains drawn. Little it did, they still kept coming.

The town women were the worst. A few had ventured over to #10 Grove Street on more than one occasion, sometimes with their children in tow, always with food; knocking at the door and peering in the windows, hollering hello. Sugar would just sit there listening and waiting for them to leave. She did not need nor did she want to be friends with anyone in Bigelow.

Nevertheless, they kept coming. The women of Bigelow in their dainty dresses and light makeup. Some even wore white gloves on their hands and veiled hats usually reserved for Sunday church, weddings, baptisms and christenings. Some even jiggled the doorknob. Pearl watched all of this from her kitchen window and waited to see if the mystery woman would appear, and if she did what would she say?

But she never did and the women would clear their throats, look around, set their baked goods wrapped in shiny tin foil down in the rocking chair, or tuck them back under their arms and walk swiftly away. Some would stop at Pearl's house, pretending they'd come all that way to see her in the first place. They'd sit and smile, speaking on small things. Family mostly, inquiring about Pearl's two sons. "How Joe Jr. and Seth getting on up North?" Pearl knew better and accepted their Corning Ware filled with peach cobbler or stewed pears, served them coffee or tea and told them her boys were doing just fine. The women really only wanted to know one thing, and that was if Pearl had met her yet. But they behaved like the Bigelow women they were raised to be and engaged Pearl in light conversation that involved everything and everyone except her neighbor.

"Oh, by the way . . ." they'd say as Pearl showed them to the door and thanked them again for the visit, "have you met your new neighbor yet?" They'd say it with such an air of mock disinterest that it made Pearl want to laugh, call them phonies and point an accusing finger at them. Instead, she bit the inside of her cheek, shook her head and said, "No, I haven't had the pleasure."

The women would transform then; their eyes would go wild

and they'd have to fight to control the froth that formed at the corners of their mouths. "Oh, I seen her in town. She look like a harlot if there ever was one. What she gotta dress that way for? And all that makeup! She wear wigs that them white women wear, long, blond or red! I tell you, Pearl, not in all my years have I seen a sight like her. Umph!" Their words would run in a fast stream that made Pearl's head hurt.

Pearl would just raise her eyebrows. "Really," she'd say with exasperation.

"Yes, really. You better watch yourself, living so close to her and all. Best you keep away from her, she don't look like she mean nobody no good. Coming through town without even a hello. Umph! Who does she think she is?"

Pearl would close her door to their backs and their two-faced attitudes. She didn't much like people like that, and didn't care to eat food made by people with such wicked hearts, so the pie, bread or cake would end up in the garbage.

Chapter Four

*P*EARL blushed mauve with embarrassment as she ascended the steps. They creaked loudly under her weight and announced her arrival to everyone in and around the house. She'd been reduced to following the example of the gossiping women that came to this very same door with the intention of weeding out this foul seed that was now living among them. Befriend her, find out who she was and what she was about and then run her off when they find that she did not meet with their requirements. She being the color of crude oil and maintaining its qualities, Sugar would not and could not mix. That was their only interest. Pearl's intentions were different.

From the first day Sugar arrived and Pearl laid eyes on her from the shadows of her hallway, she was struck by the familiarity of her face. Her heart had skipped an entire beat when the woman stopped in front of her house. It wasn't because of how she looked or the way she was dressed that threw Pearl for a turn, it was her profile that caused her to catch her breath and grab her chest. For a split second Sugar looked everything like her Jude. Sweet, sweet Jude, spending the rest of eternity in a pine box, six feet underground.

For a quick instant Pearl thought Sugar was Jude and had to control the impulse to run out through the front door and grab the woman in her arms. But then Sugar turned toward her and smiled and Jude's face melted away like lard left out in the hot sun.

Pearl had to, needed to see her without the annoyance of shadows. She wanted to make sure her mind wasn't playing tricks on her again.

For the first year after Jude died she seemed to see her face everywhere. In her dreams, looking up at her from a dish that rested in the sink waiting to be cleaned, in her own reflection in the mirror and peeking at her from behind the living room drapes. Sometimes she would call to her, "Jude? Jude, baby, is that you?" And walk over to where she thought she saw her daughter's almond eyes. Joe, if he was there, would grab her firmly by the shoulders and guide her back to bed or the couch. "She gone, baby," he'd say and sit and rock her until the tears and weeping were done.

It was the hardest time in her life and after fifteen years it was still hard.

The worst incident had come when she and Joe went to Short Junction to meet the train. Joe's nephew and his wife were coming in from Jackson to spend some time with them. It wasn't too long after Jude's death. Colored papers were still hot with the story. No one had been picked up as a suspect and the police had all but given up on their halfhearted efforts at finding the killer.

The wife of the nephew was a nurse in Jackson and Joe had felt it would be a good idea to have her around. Pearl didn't seem to be getting any better; he thought he would lose her to grief.

Pearl stood beside him, lifeless, shoulders slumped, giving her a hunchbacked appearance. Her dress hung slack from her body, which was growing thinner by the day. Her straw hat sat limp on her head and stiff gray strands of hair poked out from beneath it like wild weeds. Her eyes were small dull black stones that held vast emptiness. She was nothing more than a dead tree trunk in the middle of all the hustle and bustle of the station.

Joe was holding her hand and looking toward the train that had just pulled in. Joe Jr. and Seth stood restlessly behind them, tugging at their shirt collars. People rushed to the train, waiting anxiously for loved ones to appear. Children chased each other around and between the legs of grown folks, and porters moved like sleek, black wildcats to and fro, moving large steamer trunks through the buzz of people like rats through an intricate maze.

"Here they come, Pearl," Joe whispered to her and squeezed her lifeless hand. He was waving at them as they approached. Pearl lifted her head slightly and tried to offer a weak smile, but none would come. Jude had taken her smile with her. And then her head bounced. She caught sight of a girl, just the same age as Jude, dressed in a dress that was too mature for her. Her face was painted, hiding the last threads of innocence. She turned to say something to the man that was with her, excitement swirling all over her face. Pearl saw her. Saw Jude. And began to walk toward her, slow at first, pulling Joe along with her. He followed, believing she was walking to greet his nephew, but she blew straight past them, her speed increasing to a run, leaving them standing, mouths agape, in shock. "Pearl?" Joe had yelled above the throng of the people. "Wha—" and then he saw what Pearl was rushing toward. He saw the girl that looked so much like his dead daughter and his heart thumped hard in his chest. He gripped Pearl's hand and jerked her sharply backward; she slammed into his chest and then turned eyes on him that reflected such savagery it made him shudder and he smelled his own sudden fear break out on his body in tiny beads of sweat.

She spoke to him between clenched teeth and quivering lips. Pearl looked like a trapped animal. "Turn me loose, Joe Taylor." And he did, without thinking of the consequences, he turned her loose and with the agility of a child, Pearl raced through the station toward the young woman and she screamed her dead daughter's name as she went, "Jude! Juuuudeeee!!!!"

Thank goodness it was too late. The girl had boarded the train. "All aboard!" was yelled one final time and the whistle was sounded. Steam bellowed out from beneath the cars and then the train started its steady movement as it pulled slowly out of the station. Pearl was running alongside it, her hands reaching out to touch the steel cars that were now swiftly whisking past her. She called Jude's name one last time and collapsed onto the platform.

A year passed before Pearl smiled. Another year before her laugh, high and gay, was heard again.

Not a day went by without her thinking of her daughter, but she kept the vision of her mutilated body buried deep in a section of her mind reserved for horrible things that scared and frightened her.

Pearl reconstructed her life, bit by tiny painful bit and now a woman, just the profile of her Jude, was slowly fragmenting what she had spent fifteen years putting back together.

*P*earl balanced the sweet potato pie in one hand and knocked on the chipped and peeling screen door with the other. The window to the right was open and the curtains pulled aside revealing the misty gray-black within. She resisted the urge to tilt her head to peer inside. That's what someone else would do, she told herself. She waited and then knocked again, the sound of her knuckles making rapid contact with the wood echoing loudly up and down the street.

She shifted on her feet and looked at the rocking chair that moved gently back and forth in the warm spring breeze. Small clay pots filled with mint and jasmine lined the base of the partition that encircled the porch area. The plants were in full bloom and enveloped the house with their fragrant soothing aromas.

Ivy crept silently along the side of the house and stretched over to run the length of the banister. Pearl was amused; she'd never noticed the ivy before. Not even when Old Mrs. Wilks was living there.

Pearl knocked again. Still no answer. She sat down in the rocking chair and rested the warm pie on her lap. "I'll just rest a bit," she lied to herself. She was actually lying in wait. She rocked slowly back and forth, the yielding sounds of the chair and the smells of mint and jasmine easing away any apprehensions she may have arrived with.

The previous owner, Beulah Wilks, had been dead and gone

for more than ten years. She'd been a nice old woman, pint-sized and frail with dull brown eyes and hair like snow, soft and white. Pearl and Beulah had made small talk over the years; neighborly chit chat that unfolded their lives to each other.

Beulah Wilks moved to Bigelow from Waco, Texas, with her husband and infant son. The husband died not too long after they settled in and she raised her son alone, supported by her deceased husband's war pension and her tailoring skills. She never remarried and never mentioned to Pearl any desire to marry. "Men are like children. They need too much time and attention. I ain't had the patience to go back to mothering two men instead of one, so's I stayed alone and liked it." Pearl was taken aback by the old woman's candor—talk like that was nearly alien coming from a woman who was raised in a time when they believed a woman needed a man to survive and the man made the woman complete.

Beulah watched Pearl's sons, Joe Jr. and Seth, move from boys to men and then North. She was there when Jude was found, and sent casseroles of food over daily for three months.

During that time Pearl had never met the son Beulah spoke constantly about. She glowed with delight whenever she said or heard his name mentioned: "Clemon."

He was her pride and joy and although she didn't see him often, he faithfully sent her a letter with money the first of every month. "Had a little trouble 'round these parts some time ago," Beulah confided. "He don't feel safe comin' 'round here no more." The old woman never mentioned what type of trouble and Pearl didn't ask.

The one and only time Pearl had laid eyes on him was about ten years ago when Beulah passed away, fell down dead among the beloved flowers, fruits and vegetables she spent all her time tending.

Pearl remembered he was a slight man, built like his mother, so small that a strong wind could come by and lift him from the ground and carry him up into the treetops. Pearl addressed him as "Mr. Wilks."

She held his small hand in hers and stared solemnly at the

bald spot on his head that so perfectly reflected the sun, and said her condolences: "She was a mighty fine woman, your mother was." Joe squeezed his shoulder and nodded in agreement. She had approached him after the funeral as he was preparing to leave. His mother's body lay waiting inside her coffin on a wagon. He was taking her body back to Texas for burial.

"Thank you," he said without looking at them and walked away.

The house had stood empty for all those years, no FOR SALE sign in the front yard, the fruits, flowers and vegetables dying from lack of love and attention.

Pearl rose from the rocking chair, her eyes wet with the memory of loss, and turned to knock one last time. The pie was cold now and her heart had cooled along with it. A tall dark woman stood in the doorway staring directly at Pearl, an off-white towel wrapped loosely around her head and short blue robe cinched tight around her long body. Her thighs glistened wet with water.

She looked annoyed, her face was twisted to one side with irritation and she watched Pearl through her slanted eyes.

Pearl was startled and stumbled back, her behind hitting sharply against the banister, causing her to cry out with pain and surprise.

"Yes?" Sugar said as she eyed the woman and at the same time reached into the breast pocket of her robe, pulling out a crumpled pack of Lucky Strikes and a book of matches. Pearl could not respond; she was staring intently at the woman's face. She wanted to reach out and touch it, scrape away the features that weren't Jude's, leaving behind the ones that were.

Sugar lit the cigarette and it dangled loosely from the corner of her mouth. She squinted her eyes against the rising smoke. "Yes?" she said, louder now, more intense.

"I—I . . ." was all that Pearl could issue. She was stunned stupid and had forgotten her very reason for being there.

Sugar stood back on her long mahogany legs and adjusted the towel around her head. "You just come by to use my rocker?" Sugar said. It was more an accusation than a question. She inhaled deeply on her cigarette and let the smoke out in tiny puffs of white.

Pearl found her voice. She opened her mouth and allowed the words to spill out in a senseless jumble, hoping at the end they would combine and become something intelligent. "I'm s-sorry for rocking in your chair. I just came by to introduce myself—I mean, welcome you to Bigelow." Pearl looked again at the glistening thighs and then down to the small puddle that was forming beneath Sugar.

"Did I—I come at a bad time?" she said a bit too loudly. She jerked a bit at the volume of her voice and then halted her babbling, breathlessly awaiting a response.

Sugar smirked at the short, wide woman in her starched blue dress and stiff white collar. So much perfection in one place was unsettling to her. "Yes, yes you did," she said, her voice chilled and stiff.

"Shoot, I sure am sorry, Miss," Pearl uttered and shifted her eyes away from Sugar. She wanted so much to stare into her face, but pulled her eyes away from those familiar features and concentrated instead on the staircase just behind her. As an afterthought and after a short period of silent awkwardness, she shoved the pie out before her. The movement was hard and fast and it slammed into the half open door that Sugar held ajar with one hand. The impact startled Pearl and she released the plate; it went crashing to the floor, sending bits of crust and sweet potatoes across the porch.

They stood there looking stupidly at the mess that had been made. Pearl went down effortlessly to one swollen knee, picked up the pan and began gathering up the broken pie bits, apologizing as she did.

Sugar did not move, but continued to draw on her cigarette as she watched the old woman's head bob up and down and listened to her *Lord have mercy*s and *For goodness' sake*s.

Sugar shook her head in surrender. "C'mon in 'for I catch cold. Leave it be, the ants will take care of it," Sugar said and walked into the house, leaving Pearl to catch the closing door before it slammed and bounced back on its rusty hinges.

She followed Sugar into the gray darkness of the foyer and then the living room. Pearl was uncomfortable with the dim lighting and the heavy smell of stale cigarette smoke. The room needed sunlight and a good airing out, but she sat down without comment where Sugar had indicated she should sit.

Sugar took a seat directly in front of her. An old wooden coffee table, its polish long gone, separated the two women.

Pearl recognized the furniture. It had belonged to Mrs. Wilks. A battered green sofa, its cushions not looking as if they could withstand another heavy dust beating, and two wingback chairs made of the same material of putrid green.

Nothing much had changed, except the cross that once hung directly over the fireplace was gone, although a clean imprint of it remained. It seemed to glow in the gloom of the room.

"Will you replace it?" Pearl asked, knowing full well she'd started the conversation off ineptly.

"Replace what?" Sugar asked, bewildered.

"The cross," Pearl said and pointed to the empty space on the wall.

Sugar looked in the direction of Pearl's pointing finger and stared at the space for a while. She hadn't noticed it before. "No, I don't think so," she said as she smashed the finished cigarette into an ashtray that held what looked to Pearl like hundreds of butts. She glanced again at the space and then absently pulled another cigarette out of the pack and lit it. She turned her attention back to Pearl just as the yellow and blue flame from the match illuminated her face. Pearl caught sight of Sugar's almond-shaped eyes, high cheekbones and smooth dark skin. Her heart leaped from her chest and to her throat.

My God, she looks like Jude in so many ways, she thought to herself as she fought to retain her composure.

"Well," Sugar said in a long drawn-out exhale of breath and smoke. The "well" came as an interlude to a lulling conversation, but there had been no real conversation so far.

Pearl shifted uncomfortably in her seat. "I'm real sorry 'bout that mess. I really wish you would let me clean it up." Her voice was uneven and she wanted to leave that dark, cigarette-choked room and return to the sunshine and clean fresh air outside. She wanted to move away from the face that looked so much like her Jude's.

"Ain't nothing," Sugar replied in a long lazy drawl, and then she took another long drag on her cigarette.

"Well it sure is nice to finally meet you. I been trying to get over here for a while, but you know how it is, you get caught up doing one thing or another and before you know it, it's bedtime." Pearl laughed at the end of her sentence, a small girlish giggle that she hadn't heard herself use since her youth.

No, Sugar didn't know. But she shook her head yes anyway.

"Well I best be going, I done taken up too much of your time already." Pearl stood abruptly and pushed her hand out toward Sugar. "Nice meeting you," she said without looking directly at her.

Sugar stared at the hand that was extended before her. She didn't offer her own. "You didn't tell me your name," Sugar said quietly and drew again on her cigarette.

"What?" Pearl said stupidly, her hand beginning to ache from its suspended position.

"Your name?" Sugar said, making sure each word came out crisp.

"My name?" Pearl was confused. Hadn't she given her name? She tossed it around in her mind. She realized she did not know the woman's name and evidently had not given her name either. Or had she?

"Oh dear! I'm Pearl. Pearl Taylor," she said all flustered and took a step closer to Sugar, her hand still extended, now in greeting instead of good-bye.

"Sugar. Sugar Lacey," Sugar responded and lightly took the old woman's hand in her own.

There was electricity when one hand enfolded the other. It caused both of them to jump and they snatched their hands apart.

"Damn static electricity," Sugar mumbled and wiped at the palm of her hand. She pointed down to the old faded section rug that at some point had been a bright rose, but now had been walked on and spilled on so many times it was more like a ragged maroon.

"Sugar? Well, that's an interesting name. Is it a nickname?"

Pearl asked, finding a conversational tone now. The shock had done something to her insides, jump-started her voice and quelled her nervousness. She could look into the woman's face for longer moments, and although she still saw fragmented pieces of Jude hiding there, it seemed not to upset her as much now.

"No, that's my Christian name. Why? Don't you know sugar is brown first? White folks couldn't stand the fact that something so sweet shared the same color as the people who cut the cane, slopped the hogs and picked the cotton. So they bleached it to resemble them, and now they done gone and fooled everybody. You included," Sugar said with a laugh. May Lacey was famous for telling that little story, and now here Sugar was repeating it.

"Oh," Pearl said, blushing at Sugar's chiding.

Another thick awkward silence hung between them.

"So uh, you family to Mrs. Wilks?" Pearl asked.

"Who's that?" Sugar asked, getting up from her chair. Sugar was quite familiar with the name but preferred to play dumb. This woman was asking too many questions and Sugar had no intention of giving up as many answers. The robe slid open a bit and revealed a corner of her thick, bushy triangle. Pearl saw this and turned her eyes toward the bright cross space on the wall. "The woman who used to live here, she been dead for some time now. You her granddaughter, maybe?"

Sugar pulled her robe close around her again and removed the towel from her head to reveal a short snatch of thick black hair. It held tight to her scalp and looked as if it would resist even the hottest straightening comb. "I don't think so," Sugar replied with no real interest in the subject.

Pearl was confused. Since there had never been a FOR SALE sign on the house, the only logical conclusion would be that it was willed to a family member, most likely her son. But here was this woman saying "she didn't think so," which made no kind of sense to Pearl. Either you know who your grandmother is or you don't know.

"Your daddy wasn't Clemon, Mrs. Wilks's son?" Pearl pressed.

"Miss Pearl, I don't know who my daddy is or was," Sugar said and walked out of the living room and to the front door. She swung it open and waited for Pearl to appear. Pearl pushed her head out from the living room into the hall and realized that her visit had come to an end.

Pearl cleared her throat and smoothed her dress; she lifted her head up a bit and started toward the door. She stepped over the threshold and turned to face Sugar. "I'm sorry 'bout everything and excuse me if I offended you with my questions. It's just that Bigelow is a small place and we all like to know who our neighbors are. You understand, don't you?" Sincerity was gleaming in Pearl's eyes.

"Sure do," Sugar said sarcastically and firmly closed the door in Pearl's face.

Pearl stood there looking at the closed door that was only inches from her face. She'd never experienced in her whole lifetime the humiliation she had encountered in this one day.

She looked down at the drying bits of pie and sure enough, the ants were hauling tiny loads of it away.

Chapter Five

"So you went in there . . . what it look like . . . what she look like. . . I only seen her once from afar . . . she look black, though, black like tar. What she sound like . . . she use all them big city words . . . what she got . . . more coming or just her one?"

Shirley was talking so fast it sounded like one long, bad soprano note. Shirley and the heat was not a good combination, not at all.

Shirley Brown was older than Pearl, probably by about a good twenty years. She wore a wig that seemed to defeat the purpose of wearing a wig. It was a stiff, bluish gray mass of horse hair that looked more like tangled piano string. It should have been discarded a long time ago, but Shirley loved it to death, preferring it to her head of soft gliding gray that resembled spun silk. Shirley wasn't frail, although she appeared that way. Time had bent her over a bit and life had kicked her in the behind on more than one occasion, so she walked tilted forward, looking as if she would tumble over at any moment. She was medium built and walnut colored. All in all, she was a comical-looking woman; her face was long and thin and she wore large black-framed glasses that magnified her eyes to ten times their normal size. You couldn't look dead at Shirley without wanting to laugh. So just to keep the peace, you didn't look dead at Shirley.

Shirley had been married three times, buried two husbands and was now alienating her third with her rumormongering ways.

Shirley Brown had been Shirley Brown twice in her life. At birth she was born into the name, and then she gave it up at twenty and became Shirley Jenkins. Twelve years after that she became Shirley Atkins. The name Brown was reinstalled when she married her third husband, Parker Brown.

Pearl and Shirley were friends by association. Shirley worked alongside Pearl's mother, Belle, in the McHenry house for more than thirty years, so Pearl had known her her whole life. Shirley moved to Bigelow with her second husband and had been there ever since.

And now there she sat spilling out word after word, sounding like a squealing pig going to slaughter.

"What were you doing 'round here anyways?" Pearl asked for the umpteenth time. Shirley was exemplary at picking and prying, but she was also the queen of evasion.

"Oh . . . I was coming over here to see you." Shirley was lying, Pearl could see it in her big magnified eyes. Shirley didn't have a car, and neither did Parker. They begged for rides to town. Pearl lived on the opposite side of Bigelow, a good twenty minutes' walk for a person still holding on to his youth; more than an hour for an old body with one foot slipping into the afterlife.

"Shirley Brown, you would not walk all this way to see me," Pearl said as she placed the kettle on the stove to heat.

"Sure I would, honey," Shirley said without looking at Pearl. Her eyes drifted to the open kitchen window. "So, her hair really blond?" Shirley asked, trying hard to keep the eagerness out of her voice.

Pearl gave a little laugh and shook her head in surrender. She sat down across from Shirley and folded her hands loosely on the table. "No. Her hair is short, black and nappy like the rest o' us."

"Uh-huh," Shirley grunted and dug deep into her oversized, overused black pocketbook, pulling out a bag of peanuts. Without being asked, Pearl got up and retrieved a plate from the cabinet. Shirley was a peanut fiend. She ate them the way people smoked cigarettes and she put them in her Pepsi and drank them. Pearl set the plate down in front of Shirley and turned to remove the kettle from the flame. At that moment a flutter of red and yellow moved quickly past Sugar's open window. They both saw it and each reacted in her own way. Pearl stood motionless, the kettle in hand, suspended in mid-air. Shirley stood up from her chair, so slowly it was comical. She moved as if at a baseball game, watching in amazement as the winning ball went sailing over the heads of onlookers and out of the stadium.

They stood there, frozen, holding their breaths, waiting for her to pass again. Waiting for the bright yellow and red to dance briefly in the window once more.

Nothing.

Shirley sat down. Pearl poured the hot water into the waiting teacups. They sipped in silence, both watching the window.

*T*he first thing Pearl heard after she saw the smooth dark chocolate skin was the shattering sound of bone china as it made quick and unexpected contact with the kitchen floor. The second sound was Shirley's quick intake of breath, and the last and final sound was her own voice whispering, "Sweet Jesus." It was said not in prayer, but in total and complete disbelief.

"Oh, my God, she's stark naked?"

Pearl was sure that Shirley wanted her words to form a statement, but it came out as gauche as the situation at hand.

Sugar had returned to the room and now she was sitting, as naked as the day she was born, in front of her window. One leg swung lazily over the arm of the chair and the other stretched out before her. A magazine rested on her lap and she flipped idly through the pages with one hand while the other languidly moved her cigarette to and from her mouth.

Curtains, white and transparent—nothing like the heavy drapes that graced the other homes of Bigelow—moved in and out like waves guided by a soft summer gale. They did not hide her, or Sugar's dark triangle of pubic hair.

Pearl stared at Sugar's pussy. But she did not see it as it was, she saw a memory of a day when a man came to her, head bowed, and unfolded a handkerchief that held her daughter's cootie-cat. That's what Pearl called it and her mother before her and so that's what she taught Jude to call her own. Cootie-cat.

Pearl had avoided looking at her own cootie-cat for fifteen years. And Joe, well, he wished he could say that he had touched it or caressed it within all those years.

He longed to be able to say it was so, but that would be a blatant untruth. If asked, Joe would say: No, I have not seen it since spring 1940. All I have is my memory of it.

John Lee Hooker's "Burnin' Hell" quickly filled the background and replaced the fog that shrouded her whenever she was forced to remember. She heard Shirley talking fast and she lifted her head above the fog, thankfully being able to tear her eyes away from Sugar.

"I ain't never seen no mess like this in my entire life! Who the hell sits 'round butt naked for all the world to see!? Lord have mercy, Pearl, what kinda trash you got living next door to you?"

Shirley was crouched down on the floor, her dress hiked up over her knees. Pearl could see her stockings, rolled up around her varicose-ridden thighs, choking them. She spoke in a conspiratorial whisper and her eyes were like globes behind her thick glasses. Pearl just looked down at her. She was horrified at what she'd just seen and at the memory it forced on her, but seeing Shirley crouched down below the windowpane, peeking up every three seconds to snatch a look at Sugar's privates, well it was just too humorous a scene and Pearl had to bite down hard on the inside of her cheeks to keep from laughing.

The guitar and harmonica were dying, the sound of John Lee Hooker's voice faded and Sugar was gone.

Shirley stood up and her knees creaked loudly. "Can you believe this?" she said, her hand extended out toward the window. Her mouth kept opening and closing in disbelief and sweat trickled down from around her temples. A sweet, sickening musty smell rose up from her body that was nearly as suffocating as her overpowering personality. Pearl stepped back, trying to escape it and Shirley.

"I gotta go . . . this ain't right and she ain't right, Pearl. You gotta husband, Pearl."

There is silence and Shirley need not say any more; her words carried heavy meaning. "That's all I'm gonna say on it."

She left, leaving peanut shells still on the plate, stepping over shattered pieces of china. The news would spread quick and fast now. Pearl considered pulling the phone from the wall.

Chapter Six

*T*HE morning came in raw. Smelling like a sea that was nowhere near Bigelow or Arkansas. The wind was blowing wrong, causing a backdraft to come off of the canning plant. It was mackerels then. It seemed every year the plant was canning something new. This year it's mackerels, and from time to time the smell of discarded fish parts traveled the few miles and settled thick as smoke in and around the towns that bordered Ashton. It didn't remind nobody of the sea. That smell reminded people of an unwashed woman.

That's all Pearl needed after what she saw yesterday. The smell of an unclean woman traveling around her nose and seeping in the cushions of her couch. Unwelcomed. That's what it was. The smell and the woman across the way.

Pearl was up early and was moving about the house doing nothing really, just waiting for the sun to come up full in the sky and then her job as wife would begin. The house was quiet except for the soft padding of her slippered feet against the wood and the linoleum-lined kitchen. There was the even breathing of her sleeping husband permeating the background. The kettle was on the stove and the water jumped and bubbled against the heat inside the tin structure. Pearl looked into her cabinet, and there were five teacups now instead of six. She reached for one and her feet carried her to the window. She hadn't meant to go there. Not right then. Not so soon in the morning. But she was there tugging once, twice and then the shade gave in suddenly and snapped up and out of her hand. Pearl jumped and dropped her teacup. There are four teacups now.

What she saw surprised her. Surprised him. The two of them; him on the outside passing between the houses, leaving his size twelve shoeprint in the wet earth, green jacket hanging over one arm and shirt half undone, revealing dark tight curls of hair on his chest. He glowed pale beneath the approaching dawn. He was smiling, thinking about what had just been done to him, over and over again. But the smile was frozen and unnatural when Pearl saw it. The crash of Pearl's teacup got him moving again, unfroze the stupid contented smile on his face. He stared hard at her, nodded his head and mouthed "Mornin'."

Pearl nodded back and pulled her thin, yellow robe around her. Looking into his eyes chilled her. A scream scrambled to the base of her throat. She threw her hand over her mouth and gagged instead.

She was at the front door before he rounded the front of the house, and she couldn't stop herself from grabbing hold of the cold metal doorknob and swinging the heavy door wide open. She stepped out on the porch and caught sight of him as he stepped into the green and white 1955 Bel Air Sports Coupe. Had Joe been witness to this, he would have whistled long and loud at the automobile. It was fine and slick.

The engine revved up just as the sky began to pale and then it was shooting past Pearl. She watched until the car blurred and then disappeared.

Something just wasn't right about a white man on Grove Street, in a fancy car, leaving a black woman's house in the early morning hours. Something just wasn't right. It was as foul as the raw air that was picking up potential with the morning sun.

*T*here was too much activity on the normally quiet Grove Street. Cars were coming and going, filled with men, a few with women—two, three, four times—up and down the street, people hanging out the windows and pointing at #10 Grove Street, wanting to catch a glimpse of the naked woman.

Joe nodded and waved at the people as they went by. Happy to see them at first and then confused as to why they were there at all, driving past his house over and over again. He waved one man over. "What ya'll doing?" he asked, scratching his head in bewilderment. He asked his question and then looked up at a truck filled with watermelon pulling up on the opposite side of the road. Customers were already lining up.

"You don't know?" the man said with a laugh.

"Nope," Joe replied and looked back at his wife, who had followed him out on the porch.

"Ya new neighbor like to walk 'round outside her house . . . naked." The man's voice thickened a bit when he said it. Joe recognized that sound and backed away from it.

"Is that right?" he said, and folded his arms across his massive chest.

The man was grinning, not paying Joe much mind now. He thought he saw movement in the front window.

Joe thanked him for the information and walked back to his porch. "You know anything 'bout all this?" he asked Pearl. Pearl did know about something, but these people couldn't possibly be here to witness what she had just yesterday. "Something 'bout the woman next door walking around outside naked?" Joe continued, looking at Pearl's forehead instead of her eyes.

"They here to see that?" Pearl said flatly. "That ain't right, Joe. She ain't no circus freak. And she wasn't outside, she was in the privacy of her own living room . . . the window just happened to be open, shifting the curtains a bit. Shirley was here when it happened, done blown it up to something it ain't. These people gotta go, Joe. Our home is here too. They can't be 'round here like this." She turned and walked back into the house. Her eyes never left the street when she spoke and her voice never rose.

Joe hitched his pants and lifted his head a bit higher, gathering his full six feet three inches and 250 pounds. Something was going to be done about this.

Pearl didn't know what he said, probably not much, and he only spoke to two people: the watermelon man and someone on a bike, didn't need to speak to more than that, the others would see and get the hint. The people respected Joe's words, not sure of what he was physically capable of, and not wanting to push him to test it, they moved along and away from Grove Street.

*S*he didn't tell him where she was going, wasn't necessary. He was asleep on the sofa, the television watching him, a half-empty glass of Coke sitting on the floor, the ice melting loudly within it, a half-eaten bologna sandwich on a plate next to the glass. Sunday afternoon found him snoring in his second favorite snoozing place, after the far side of the middle pew in Bigelow's First Baptist Church, the part that was hidden by a column.

She slipped quietly out the back door, pie in hand, and walked across the thick grass that separated her house from Sugar's. The screen door was open a bit, swinging back and forth on its hinges. "Hello," Pearl yelled twice before she walked in. She could hear a man's voice, happy and chipper, coming from the living room. A commercial for soap coming from a radio she couldn't see. "Hello?" once again and then she was on the stairs moving up to the second floor of the house one step at a time. Step. Listen. Step. Listen. Nothing.

The house echoed empty, yet she kept going.

The center hall was bright; dust particles danced in the fat slants of light that came in through the window at the far end. Pearl looked down at her black shoes, spit shined by her husband; they looked more expensive than their five dollars' worth against the worn, burgundy and gold swirled carpet. She stepped forward and found herself between two rooms, the bedroom and the bathroom. Both doors half open, revealing contents and details. She turned toward the bedroom intending to push the door open, but her attention was focused toward the hall window. She stepped forward and her hand missed the feel of the oak door, as it swung open before she could make contact.

Sugar stood before her, a towel wrapped around her body. A wasted effort, the towel was too small and like the half-open doors, revealed most everything and more than nothing at all.

"What you doing in my house!" Sugar yelled and stepped forward.

"I—" Pearl was flustered mute.

"What you doing in my house?!" Sugar demanded again. Her breath, heavy with cigarettes and pork and beans, invaded Pearl's nose and she coughed.

"I—I called out, but no one answered. I just wanted to try again . . . bring another pie for you since—"

Her speech was cut short. The pie was airborne and spinning above her head. Sugar's rage had overwhelmed her and triggered her hand to slap at the pie. When it landed, it landed on Pearl's head. Sweet potato and crust slid down the sides of her face and onto her dress, made a home in her hair and clung to her lashes.

Pearl didn't move, not even to wipe at the pie in order to remove it from her head and face. She just stared at Sugar. Sugar was stunned, stunned at her quick act of anger, and her face showed her surprise and growing regret.

"Sorry" tickled at her tongue but Sugar would not release it, so it moved into her eyes where Pearl interpreted it.

She laughed at the pie on her head and her stupidity. It was a full-bodied laugh, not at all as rich as a good bottle of wine, but it was a laugh nevertheless, and she had laughed so little in past years. Sugar laughed too, unsure at first and then more securely.

More than ten minutes passed before they got themselves under control. Sides aching and faces wet with tears, they knelt together to pick from the floor what had missed or left Pearl's head.

"Well, Miss Pearl, seems as if I'm never gonna actually get to taste your sweet potato pie," Sugar said as she scooped pie from the top of Pearl's head.

"Sweet potato pie your favorite?" Pearl asked.

"All-time," Sugar said.

"We'll make the next one together then," Pearl said, cementing her place in Sugar's life, using words she had used with Jude years before.

"I ain't much of a cook, no less a baker," Sugar responded.

"Don't matter, life's 'bout learning new things anyway," Pearl said.

Chapter Seven

"**I** DON'T need you!"

Sugar woke up and the words were spilling from her mouth. Loud and obnoxious. She believed she must have been screaming because the words still bounced off the walls of her bedroom.

They were bitter words, sour in her mouth where once upon a time they'd been familiar, tasteless things that were just a part of life.

I don't need you!

The words stayed with her, echoing in her mind. She closed her eyes and squeezed them shut, placing her hands over her ears to block the words out completely. That didn't help at all. They weren't outside of her, sitting in the chair across the room or even standing over her trying to poke her awake. They were inside her head, living in her soul, and now she was holding them in, trapping them there for good by holding her hands over her ears.

What had it been? A dream maybe, certainly not a memory of something that had actually happened. She'd never had to use those words in her real life. She never had to make a statement to anyone with regard to what she needed and didn't. No, she had been self-sufficient for most of her life—not counting time spent with the Laceys and Mary.

There had been no love to scrape away at her, leaving only

crumbled bits of flesh where there once was a whole person—
she didn't have to pretend that she didn't need him when she
knew she did. No, that was someone else's life.

Mother, maybe? No, she had never had one to rebel against.
Hmmm, strange.

Perhaps it was Pearl. She was quickly becoming a part of
Sugar's life. It had started slow. The baking of the pie was the
maiden voyage to their friendship, and then other things. Tending the garden that they both thought was dead. Turned out
that it was just dormant. "What it needed was a little love and
attention," Pearl said when the first pink blossom flowered.
Sugar wasn't sure if she was speaking about the garden or something else. She wasn't good at reading people without having
looked into their eyes. Pearl never held hers still enough to allow
that. They were always shifting here and there. Darting around
like a fly, resting only for short periods, and then on the move
again.

Joe was nice too, she felt an instant respect for him. Something she had never had for men. Something about his posture
and slow, careful talk.

They went to town together. What a pair. Pearl always in one
of her starched cotton dresses with the small, white, delicately
embroidered collar and Sugar in a glaring, red, hot pink or orange dress that sat dangerously above the knee, revealing a hefty
portion of thigh that was accentuated with spiked high-heeled
shoes. Red, black or blond wigs stretching down her back and
bouncing happily up and down on the rise of her backside. She
smiled at no one when she turned her heavily powdered, blue
eyelidded, crimson lipsticked face on them.

"Why do you hide yourself under all of that . . . makeup?"
Pearl often asked. Sugar never answered, just snorted air out her
nose, sucked her teeth or lit a cigarette.

People stared blatantly. Not caring if the two women saw.
They approached them from behind, making their presence
known with loud, stringent greetings that were directed at Pearl.
Small tiny words passed between them, dainty chitchat that was
weighed down with spitefulness. They ignored Sugar, pretended

that she was nothing more than air. Foul air. With noses held high and eyes boring in on Pearl, they really wanted to ask what would drive her to associate with trash?

Pearl would entertain them in conversation, uneasily, always aware of Sugar standing nearby. She tried once or twice to include her in the conversation, but the women as well as Sugar always seemed to walk away just as Pearl's words of introduction began to verge upon them.

"Don't you want to meet people?" Pearl, exasperated, would ask Sugar.

To the women, Pearl would say: "She's really very nice." The women didn't want to hear any more. They'd been hearing talk, seeing things that didn't sit right with them, things that should not be going on in Bigelow. Things that hadn't started happening until Sugar's arrival.

The men, however, were more accommodating, friendly even. They always spoke, went out of their way to do so. Came toward Sugar and Pearl with large, all-consuming grins. They tripped over themselves to get to Sugar—tipping their hats as they came, greetings rolling from their half-open mouths and a sparkle of desire in their eyes.

Very interesting.

Pearl wanted to ask Sugar where her money came from. She seemed to be available at any hour of the day. Most times. Maybe, Pearl contemplated, she was a wealthy heiress hiding out among simple folk for a spell or maybe she was a criminal doing the same.

A lot was absent from their conversations despite the friendship that was growing between them. Some things can't be broached so soon. Some things must be left unsaid for a while. Two months is not long enough to peel back the skin and reveal the truths that hide beneath it.

Sugar saw the curiosity in Pearl's eyes. It was growing more and more every day. Expanding, lengthening and maturing. Sugar was trying to avoid it. She did not want to reveal her life before Bigelow and she convinced herself that she wouldn't, no matter what. But something inside of her was weakening and she found the words of her life sitting on the tip of her tongue when she was close to Pearl and their hands brushed when planting or mixing dough for bread. Those words almost spilled out and she had to swallow quickly to keep them inside of her.

"Tell me 'bout up North. That's where you were before here, right?" Pearl asked one day as they sat at the kitchen table separating field peas. The morning was wet and by afternoon an uncomfortable gray heat had settled in Bigelow, pulling buckets of sweat from foreheads and underarms, sending the mosquitoes on a feeding frenzy. Sugar's hand slowed when the question was asked. "Oh, tell me about St. Louis. One of my childhood friends moved there," Pearl continued. Sugar rolled one lone, brown pea beneath her index finger and then she raised her eyes to meet the top of Pearl's head.

"Well?" Pearl said without raising her head. Her eyes remained focused on her chore. Her fingers moved quickly as she pushed the good peas to the left of the pile and the bad, bruised, discolored peas to the right.

"Ain't nothing much to say." Sugar's mouth moved to say more, but only breath came out.

"Nothing?" Pearl's head rose and her hand movements stopped. "C'mon, got to be something. What you do when you was up there?" Pearl's tone was light on top but there was a pull beneath the words that would surely suck Sugar in if she did not step carefully.

"I—I worked for a woman," Sugar said in a low voice.

"That true, doing what?" Pearl pushed. She leaned in.

"What?" Sugar asked stupidly, already tripping over the lie she was laying down.

"Yeah, what kinda work did you do for the woman?" Pearl's voice probed.

"I, uh . . . well she ran a house for uh . . ." Sugar was searching for the wrong words, the words that wouldn't tell the whole truth. The right words, the true ones, dangled before her and she had to shift her eyes and close her mouth lest they jump in and spill out.

"Well?" Pearl pushed again.

Sugar scratched at the heat rising around her neck. "She ran a house for—for women. I—I cleaned up around the place." The words were out as quick as Sugar was up and out of her chair. Pearl's eyes widened, but she said nothing else. She went back to pushing her peas. She let Sugar be, for now.

Sugar swallowed but it became harder to digest the truth about her time in St. Louis, Chicago and Detroit. She did not want to reveal her fifteenth year, the year she walked away from Short Junction. Small town ain't fit for a woman that ain't never had a mamma. It ain't fit for a woman that never had any friends. It ain't fit for a woman that dreamed beyond the confines and goings-on of the green and white Lacey home.

*S*he picked up and left with the next man that said, "Sugar, girl, you somethin' else! You something special! Oohh wee! Girl, I could really get use to this type of lovin' six days a week and twice on Sunday!"

They left Short Junction on a slow-moving train to St. Louis, surrounded by the sweet smells of fried chicken, sweet biscuits and by the steady buzzing of talk about the girl that was found dead in Bigelow, some twenty or so miles down the road. They said she was beaten so badly her own mamma didn't recognize her. Women covered their mouths and gasped in shock. A man called out over the sea of "I don't believe it!" and "Can you imagine?" and revealed the worst thing of all: " Her—her . . . privates were cut out and laid on the ground beside her."

Sugar didn't believe the whole story, small-town folk will stretch a story until it became a tale. But she did believe that that was a sign that her departure was right on time.

St. Louis was where life began picking away at her with the same slow, steady reverence of the train that brought her there.

She was awed by the buildings that stood taller than the pine trees in Arkansas, her eyes burned against the bright light of day that bounced off of the glimmering sidewalks. Sugar was completely unprepared for the fast-stepping, high-fashioned, quick-talking black people that moved around her like bees around a hive. She wanted to be one of them.

He dropped her off with a woman he called his sister. She lived in a brownstone house that looked like every other house on that street—the only distinguishable qualities about them were the variety of potted plants that graced the windowsills and the color of their doors. Mary Bedford's door was red.

Step behind the red door and you were accosted by the sweet smell of Midnight in Paris perfume. The perfume had been worn for so long by Mary and the women that worked there that it seemed to seep from the walls and move from room to room on the back of the air driven by the constantly whirling ceiling fans found in every room. Throughout the house the hardwood floors were so polished that you could look down and see what color drawers you wore.

The parlor had one small loveseat with a glass table in front of it. Other than those two items, the room was bare.

Farther down the hall was a small eggshell-colored kitchen. An ice box, stove and square white countertop table with two chairs filled the space to capacity, leaving little room for the sun's rays to settle. A bathroom, painted years before in pink and mauve, was adjacent to the kitchen. You could often find yourself sitting on the toilet and craving for the bacon that sizzled right on the other side of the wall.

The basement was for gambling. Plenty of men had nearly lost their lives over ill thrown dice or a slightly bent card, but Mary didn't play that shit, and would have you cut into unidentifiable pieces if you tried to pull a fast one.

He promised, without looking at Sugar, that he would be back in a while. Mary Bedford shoved some bills in his hand, closed the door behind him and told Sugar, "He ain't coming back, so don't look for him to do so. He's a liar, a cheat and a thief. But you've laid down with him so I suppose you know all that."

Mary Bedford was copper colored, short and stocky with breasts that resembled overripe melons. She wore a long black curly wig that touched her behind and often got caught in the spaces between chairs and sofas. Her laugh was loud and harsh and her teeth were yellow from smoking two packs of Luckys a day.

"You sure are black, gal" was the second set of words to her. And she reminded her of this fact every day after that.

"Your mamma black like you? Ah, it don't matter, they got a lot up here that like 'em like you. What's that they say? The blacker the berry the sweeter the juice?" She laughed.

Sugar was scared. Her heart beat a hundred miles an hour in her chest. The fear was plastered across her face and she fought to keep her tears from falling.

"Is your juice sweet, honey baby?" she asked her. Sugar could smell the left-behind scent of some man coming off her breath.

Sugar wanted to yell at her, hit her, but seeing she was standing in her house, she decided it was just better to leave and reached for the door.

"Gal, you don't know a soul in St. Louis, so make it easy on yourself. You. Not me. So go on up to the first room on the left and take off all your clothes."

All Sugar could think was: *This woman must be funny or something.* She'd heard tales about city women doing it with one another. Sugar had experienced quite a few things in her fifteen years, but laying with a woman wasn't one of them.

"For what?" Sugar said in her most vicious Lacey voice, placing her hands on her hips.

Mary just laughed. "So's I could check your hair for lice. Can't have lice, you know. A lot of you country bumpkins got 'em."

Sugar clucked her tongue and rolled her eyes. It was obvious to her where she'd been left. A whorehouse. Same shit, different state. "Shoot, I don't need to get butt naked for you to check my hair."

Mary just flipped a wisp of hair away from her brow and said, "You do for me to check them pussy hairs of yours."

Sugar spent five years with Mary. They weren't easy years— years done on your back never are—but they were years that could have been done harder somewhere else. Mary passed along forty years of know-how to Sugar and Sugar became second in charge of the house when Mary was away.

One Sunday as they sat together in the kitchen, absorbing the street sounds and smells of summer, Mary turned to Sugar and stared at her long and hard. "You leaving soon, ain't ya?" she said matter of factly. Mary never held her girls, they were free to go when they wanted to but hardly ever did.

"Thinking about it," Sugar replied without looking up from the magazine she was lazily flipping through. Mary sighed and scratched at her head. Her face was absent of the Monday through Saturday stage makeup she wore. Her salt and pepper hair was braided in a hundred pickney braids that stood straight up in the air. She looked older than her forty-five years.

"Hmm, figured that. Lemme ask you something, Sugar. Why you act like you hate everybody? Especially men. You talk to them like they dogs in a gutter somewhere." She continued, weary of waiting for her reply, "If you hate 'em as much as you act like you do, then baby, I'm sorry to say, you in the wrong business."

Sugar had had little episodes with a few of the men that came to visit the house. She'd cuss 'em and maybe even get in a slap or two. "She a little spitfire ain't she, Mary!" they'd say, wiping their lips on their way out through Mary's red door. Then to Sugar, "I'll see you next week, you little devil, you." They always came back.

"First of all I don't hate everybody. I don't even hate anybody. Men . . . well, really no need to talk to them any better than I do. 'Sides, this here is business, a business that involves very little conversation," Sugar replied.

Mary pondered that for a while.

"Still, I can't believe you get all the requests you do when you never even offer a smile or a kind word—"

"Well, it ain't hurting nothing, is it? It's obvious they like the way I talk to them. Shit, Mary, I could talk about their mammas and they'd still come back for more."

"Is it 'cause you didn't know who your daddy was? Is that why you talk to men like you do, treat them like you do? All men ain't like your daddy. All men don't walk out and leave their babies—"

Sugar viciously cut her off. "It ain't about me not having no daddy or no mamma, it ain't about nothing, I just . . . I just . . ." She slammed her hands down on the table in frustration, causing Mary to flinch with surprise. Something in her wanted to let go, but she didn't know how.

Mary was quiet for some time. They just sat and watched and listened to the children play and laugh below them.

"Sugar, ain't you ever had no good times?" she said with a bit of sadness in her voice.

"What you mean?" Sugar said, knowing all too well what she was talking about. Sugar had seen good times being had all around her, in the Lacey house, in Mary's house, but never had one that she could call her very own.

"It seems to me," Mary began, and then decided to get up and stretch, "Whew, seems to me that I ain't never see you look up from whatever you were doing and just smile."

"Just smile? Smile at what? At who?"

"Smile into the air, girl!" she said and waved her arm through the air.

"That's crazy . . . smiling into the air," Sugar said and turned her head away.

"Naw, chile, it ain't crazy, you smiling into the air 'cause a good long-time-ago thought caught you off guard. Not 'cause you crazy," Mary said, sat down and looked back out into the world.

"I guess you right, then. I ain't never had no good times."

Sugar saw the way Mary's eyes looked. Not hurt, but worried. Worried that she was sitting down with a twenty-year-old woman who had never had any good times.

"You better start, 'cause time is running and a life without good times ain't a life worth having."

Sugar left not too long after that conversation. There was something else she could do. Something that she'd been doing for years. First in the fields of Short Junction amongst the poppies and daisies and then later, alone in her bathroom, beneath the heavy sounds of the shower masking it away from the world. Or so she thought. Her voice had soothed Mary many nights as she listened to it filter through the walls of the house. Sugar could sing like an angel.

Mary hugged her tight at the bus stop. Sugar swore she saw tears swimming in her old eyes. Mary shoved a card in Sugar's hand. "He's an old friend of mine, lives in Detroit, owns a record company there. Tell him I sent you and he'll be sure to talk to you."

Al Schwartz – President

SAVOY RECORDS

Detroit, Michigan   Ph. #KL-2-5893

Sugar hugged her back hard and thanked her. For the first time she felt different. Special. Not just Sugar Lacey from Short Junction, Arkansas, but Sugar Lacey, ready for the world. Sugar daydreamed all the way to Detroit. She believed her days of working on her back were over and done with.

She arrived and called Al Schwartz as soon as she stepped off the Greyhound.

"Mr. Schwartz, Ms. Mary Bedford said I should call you to—"

"Who?" The whining, annoyed voice crackled back at her.

"Mary Bedford—"

"Mary Bedford," he repeated, "Mary Bedford? Listen sweetie, I don't know a Mary Be—"

"Mary Bedford of St. Louis," she said, cutting him off.

There was silence for a while.

"Yes," he said. The Hollywood had left his voice.

"Well, she said I should call on you while I'm here—"

"Oh really. Did she now?"

She felt it, the sleaze. She could detect sleaze a mile away.

"Yes, Mr. Schwartz. She said I should call on you and that you might be able to help me. You see, I'm a singer."

Silence.

"Okay, sweetie, if you're a friend of Mary's and she specifically asked you to look me up, well, then fine. Where are you now?"

"I'm at the bus station."

"Hop a cab and come on by."

Detroit was even bigger and busier than St. Louis.

"Say, listen," Sugar said to the cab driver as she ran her fingers over the business card. "What type of name is Schwartz?"

"Jewish," he said.

She had never met a real live Jew before. Well, not that she was aware of.

She walked into a building that had marble floors and marble walls. She walked into the elevator, a bent-over old black man mumbled a hello and then asked her which floor. "Fifteen," she replied and moved to the back. The elevator crept through each floor. Sugar smoothed down her tight red dress and fluffed at her short strawberry blond wig. The old man looked over his shoulder at her once.

A large desk sat no more than five feet from the elevator doors. Behind it was a woman whiter than the whitest white person Sugar had ever laid eyes on. Her skin was the color of talcum powder and you could see tiny river veins threading through her face, neck and hands. Her red hair was swept up into a beehive; her lips were so thin they disappeared when she frowned. She looked at Sugar with her baby blue cat's-eye-shaped glasses and asked her to have a seat.

Sugar sat for nearly an hour and a half. The woman behind the desk kept looking at her like she was a piece of rotting meat. Sugar knew that look. That look slowly stole away the special feeling she'd had with her all the way from St. Louis.

Wasn't that something, one look from a pale white girl with bad hair and glasses sent her reeling back to Short Junction and no good-time thoughts.

The box on the desk buzzed and some words came out.

" 'Scuse me," she said, snapping her fingers in Sugar's direction, "Mr. Schwartz will see you now."

She pointed toward a door at the end of the hall.

Al Schwartz was small, balding and white. He smiled and Sugar saw that his teeth were too big for his mouth.

"Well, hello, Miss. Uh . . . what was it again?"

"Sugar," she said as she shook his hand. It was clammy.

"Please sit."

Sugar looked around the large office. Fancy. White thick carpet, gold records hung on the wall. Pictures of Mr. Schwartz and a variety of singers Sugar knew and didn't know.

He sat behind his big shiny black desk, grinning at her with big teeth and rubbing his hands together like she was going to be his next meal.

"So, Sugar, how is ole Mary?"

"Oh, she fine," she said, trying to keep the pleasantness in her voice, trying to keep a smile on her face.

"That's good. I haven't seen her for quite some time, at least fifteen years or more," he said, kind of absently. "So, you sing, do you?"

"Yes."

"Where have you performed?" he asked, getting up and coming over to sit on the desk right in front of her. His legs were open a bit. Just a bit.

Sugar leaned back in her chair. She smelled his sweat, and it didn't smell good.

"Well . . . just church," she lied.

"Church? Really," he said, closing his legs. "You're a church woman, are you?"

"No," Sugar says and his legs open up again. Wider this time.

"Hmmm, interesting," he said. "So, how do you know *our* Mary?"

"Our Mary"? Mary always said she didn't belong to anyone. Maybe he hadn't heard that.

"I worked for her for a while," Sugar says. No need for her to lie about that. She hadn't realized that some lives were based on the lies people told to get by.

"Really . . . interesting," he said again. Sugar supposed he liked that word a lot.

"And Mary said you should call me?" He seemed a bit surprised.

Sugar's smile was beginning to waver and she thought, *We've been down this road before. How many times does he want me to answer that question?*

She did not answer him, not verbally, she just nodded her head because she felt that if she opened her mouth she might say something that might not be too nice. Mary begged her to be nice. This is Mary's friend and Sugar wanted to be nice, but she knew he wanted her to be nicer than she had intended on.

"Nice dress," he said and those teeth were showing again. He was closer now, so they were even bigger. She made a bet with herself that he was a biter. She didn't want to fuck him, she knew he'd leave marks.

"Thank you," she said. Quiet again.

"Yes, um, red suits you well," he said and his eyes traveled over her. She could feel them; sleazy, slimy little things that felt like fingers, moving down and over her breasts, across her stomach around her behind and then down between her legs.

They sat there in silence for a while. Him smiling. Her, not smiling.

His legs were wider and his hands were playing around the zipper of his pants. She didn't even look down at what was going on there. She just kept looking at those big teeth.

"Sugar . . . I want you to do one thing for me. Just one, before I hear your sweet voice." His voice was thick. She's familiar with that sound. She grew up hearing that sound.

"Just . . . just . . ."

He couldn't even finish. But still, she wouldn't look down. She heard the zipper of his pants come undone. She smelled his dick before she saw it.

"Just suck it?" Sugar innocently asked, still looking at his teeth. He couldn't talk, he just nodded yes, yes, yes.

"No, I don't do that anymore," Sugar said. "I'm a singer now." His eyes flew open; and his voice became clear.

"You don't do that anymore? You don't? Oh. I'm sorry . . . the rules are you suck, you fuck and anything else I want you to do, then you sing. Those are the rules."

Sugar looked at the pictures on the walls. Then down to his dick then back to the teeth.

"Did you tell Frank Sinatra that too?" Sugar said and got up to leave.

"You ain't no fucking Frank Sinatra . . . you ain't even no Bessie Smith! What you are is a colored whore!"

Sugar was out the door walking past the pale woman behind the desk and hoping she didn't see the tears in her eyes. But that man, Mr. Schwartz, he couldn't let her go just like that. He ran out of his big office, zipping up his pants, and he screamed:

"You ain't gonna get nowhere without me, now bring your black ass back in here and do what I tell you to do! Do what Mary sent you here to do! You don't really think I would just hear you sing just because you're—" He was stumped for a while, like he was trying to find a word that would insult her more than asking her to put his penis in her mouth.

"—you!" he finally screamed.

She wanted to turn around, to go back and slap him around for a while. He was so small it would have been easy to do. But she kept on walking and telling herself that he was a friend of Mary's and she had promised to be nice.

"I gotta tell Mary, he's a friend she don't need," she said aloud as she slammed out of the building and into the bright sunlight.

There she was, back to her beginning, but now it was worse. Now she was all alone. She traveled from city to city always trying to get someone to hear her sing, but all they wanted to do was fuck. So she gave up and gave in.

Chapter Eight

THE hammer that resided in her head was banging hard today, causing Sugar to squint her eyes in pain and massage her temples. The headaches had been with her since she was a teenager. The hammer . . . the bang, bang, bang just seemed to be the perpetual echo of a million headboards slamming hard against bedroom walls.

She rose from her bed and stiffly walked to the bathroom. Fragments of a dream fading in and out, trying to slip between the pain and the pounding. She couldn't bother with that now, she felt soiled, her body and hair were heavy with the left-behind smell of a john.

She sat on the toilet and let the urine fall from inside of her. She picked at the long dried rivers of cum that clung to her thighs; it flaked easily and fell weightless to the floor.

No different than the night, week, month or year before. Always the same, so why now did the sameness of her life bother her, cause her frustration and purple anger?

She wanted to slap at these men, the ones who came to find pleasure between her legs, she wanted to slap and claw at their faces when they used her roughly and wrongly, treating her as if she were a lavatory. These men who didn't stop to kiss the nape of her neck, or explore the lonely place beneath her breasts with their tongues.

She wiped herself and laughed at the comical indecency of it all, the business and the men that kept it prosperous. Who would know to look at them, Bigelow men; broad-backed, strong-chinned men that wore pride on their shoulders, spoke loving words to their wives and kissed the small foreheads of their children nightly. Who would know they laid with Sugar Monday through Saturday and asked God for forgiveness on Sunday. Same hands that cupped the soft cheek of a wife or held lightly to the elbow of an elderly grandparent, had also crossed Sugar's body and invaded her moist places. If only the Bigelow women knew, knew for sure. Right now all they heard were rumors that spelled something, but what that something was, they didn't yet know.

Sugar brushed her teeth, scouring her tongue with her toothbrush until it was pink with irritation. She worked feverishly at trying to rid her mouth of the lingering taste from the night before that otherwise found its way into every forkful of food she consumed.

She sighed and moved to the lower parts of the house, into the kitchen that held one table, two chairs, bare cupboards and a refrigerator that hummed empty. She would have to go out today, take a walk into town and shop at the small market underneath the quiet, hating eyes of the Bigelow women.

Maybe Pearl would need to go too; it would make her task so much easier. She could allow herself to be distracted by the constant sound of Pearl's voice.

Sugar moved to the living room and stretched out on the couch. She could hear the small laughter that sailed into her house from the Taylor home. Pearl. Sugar liked her, perhaps because Pearl did not question her outright. Although Sugar had caught the question in Pearl's eyes, saw it poised in the lift of her brow and slight purse of her lips. Never voiced, not yet anyway. Sugar knew it would not always be that way, the same way you knew night would not last forever and summer would follow spring.

*S*aturday. Bid whist night. Pearl, Shirley, Minnie and Clair Bell sat around the kitchen table, doing more talking than playing.

Bid whist was just the excuse to draw them together. Tall glasses filled with lemonade sat at the wrists of card-holding hands, water moved slowly down the outside of the glasses, forming tiny puddles around their bases. It was hot enough to have all of the windows open to welcome in any small breeze that chose to come, but what the other women were hoping for, praying and wishing for, was a glimpse of Sugar—preferably naked—to appear across the way.

Shirley and her sister Minnie had fought like children over a toy about who was going to sit in the chair facing the window, until Pearl threatened to lower the shade. Shirley gave up, conceding only because she had witnessed the maiden unveiling of Sugar's privates.

"I tell you, Pearl, somethin' ain't right about that woman. And now you and her spending time together . . . that don't look right at all," Shirley said, looking over her glasses at Pearl. "I say ya better keep a close eye on your belongings . . . and that means Joe too!"

"Believe it, Pearl, Shirley talkin' the truth, she may be crazy but she ain't stupid!" Minnie Grayson added in a laughing voice.

Pearl moved her gaze from her cards and planted it dead center on Minnie's thin face. Minnie was Shirley's baby sister. Nearly fifteen years separated them. She was the quintessential change-of-life baby. Although they were full-blood relatives, the two women looked nothing alike. Minnie was cobalt black, short and extremely thin. Her face resembled a vulture's, long, ragged and drawn—her life was written all over it.

The only similarities connecting the two were the large wide eyes and flair for minding other people's business. They were infamous for bickering amongst themselves and insulting each other was a way of life for them.

"The Lord don't like no slack mouth," Pearl said and turned back to studying her hand of cards.

"Sure don't . . . He must can't stand you at all, Shirley!" Minnie said and slapped her thigh hard with laughter.

"Hush up, woman . . . I done told you once already," Shirley said between clenched teeth. She was getting riled up and her head shook in anger and exasperation against her sister. "I ain't gonna tell you again!" She shook her finger at Minnie and adjusted her blue wig.

"Aw, cool it, Shirley, you know I'm just messin' with you." Minnie waved her hand at Shirley. Pearl caught the glint of mischief in her eyes and the short tail of the smile that moved swiftly across her lips.

"Alls I know is I heard Gibson down at Motley's talkin' 'bout her." Clair Bell spoke in her scratched voice. As a young woman, the thick coarseness of her voice had been seductive, but now, pushing seventy, it came out as if from vocal cords made of steel wool; hard, brash and unappealing.

Clair Bell, the great-granddaughter of the town's first reverend, was hardly outspoken. To share the same breathing space with Clair Bell was to be alone. She behaved the exact opposite of what her physical presence presented. A large woman, a full six feet, big boned and thick skinned, Clair Bell looked as if she could beat any man in four counties. In fact she was the exact opposite. She could chop her own wood and haul a twenty-pound bag of grain on her head from the general store to her front porch, but she couldn't snap the thin necks of chickens or handle the jelly-like liver of cows. She cried crocodile tears at the thin slicing pain of a splinter. Clair Bell was nothing that you would expect her to be.

And now she spoke in her small voice, the one that sounded lost in a cave deep inside her large body. Everyone was quiet, waiting for Clair Bell to tell what she'd heard. She seemed not to remember that she'd spoken at all, instead she moved her chair back from the table, raised one stockinged foot and placed it in her lap. She examined the off-color nude nylon that enclosed her foot and then began to massage her swollen protruding bunion.

The women quietly watched her for a while in disgust. All except Pearl were disgusted at the very fact that she would begin a statement of such magnitude and then forgo it to massage a bunion. Pearl, on the other hand, was disgusted that Clair was massaging her bunion right at her kitchen table.

"Well . . . what they say?" Minnie asked after the quiet and the lack of information began to take hold of her neck like a suffocating grip.

"Hmmm." Clair Bell looked up from her feet. Her face and eyes always retained somnolent characteristics, and she yawned, suggesting that it was more than a look.

"Gibson. What did he say?" Shirley pushed, leaning in closer.

"Say 'bout who?" Clair Bell was truly lost.

They all exhaled loudly. Shirley sat back and crossed her arms over her sagging breasts and rolled her eyes up in the air in disgust. Minnie shook her head in dismay and turned to look at Pearl.

"What did Gibson say about the woman Sugar," Minnie said slowly, making sure she left time and space between each word so that Clair Bell could fully grasp what she was trying to say.

"Oh . . ." Clair Bell stopped and tilted her head slightly upward, searching the air for the words she needed, and then very calmly she said: "He said she a whore."

There were just hearts. Hearts beating loud and excitedly, and finally they all remembered to breathe.

It was said; the damage was done. Clair Bell went back to her bunion untethered by the excitement her words caused.

"Oooh wee! Hot dang! I knew it! Right here in Bigelow . . . a whore! Lawdy, Lawdy!" Shirley's eyes sparkled behind her thick lenses.

Pearl's mouth was slightly open in disbelief and Minnie was holding her stomach and laughing loudly.

"You got the whore of Babylon right next door . . . and you call her friend." The word *friend* came out slick as blood. "Running 'round town with her like ya'll was cut from the same cloth. What you think about her now?" Shirley was pointing a crooked accusatory finger in Pearl's face.

"Take your finger outta my face." The words moved out of Pearl's mouth like steel pellets, her face turned to ice, her glare moved from Shirley and fell hard on Clair Bell. "That's a terrible thing to say 'bout someone. You spreading rumors, and that ain't right. How you fix your mouth to say such a thing? You don't even know her." Pearl's chest was rising and falling quickly as she struggled to take in and release air. Her heart was beating wild with anger. But her mind stepped back to a hot, heavy day when the sun refused to shine and field peas lay in waiting on the kitchen table between herself and Sugar. She remembered the questions she asked about Sugar's life and the answer she got: *"I cleaned up in a women's home."* The words echoed false in her mind, just as they did when Sugar first uttered them aloud. Pearl ignored the warning bells that went off in her soul.

Clair Bell raised her eyes to Pearl's and smiled a little. "I ain't sayin' it, I'm repeatin' it . . . there's a difference." She said this in the small childlike voice that was characteristic of Clair Bell, but the usual innocence it carried was gone. Challenge took its place.

Pearl lowered her eyes and then raised them again. She placed the cards face down on the table and got up curtly. Tears stung at her eyes as she turned her back to the women and peered out the window. "It ain't right no matter how you put it. You don't know that girl from Adam and here you are dragging her name through the mud based on hearsay. Ya oughta be ashamed!"

Who was she to protect Sugar and why should she? Didn't Jesus protect the whore by asking those who were without sin to throw the first stone? Pearl questioned herself and her actions. How much did she really know about Sugar? Not much, when you got right down to the nitty-gritty of things. Sugar hardly spoke and when she did it wasn't about anything that had to do with her directly. She spoke in circles. Pearl didn't want to prod and probe her, she could see that though Sugar had a menacing look about her, she was really very fragile. Pearl had come this far with her, had been in her home, sat with her on the porch quietly watching the sunset or listening to the sounds of life that surrounded them. Too far to let it go to waste. She was near to bringing her into the fold, presenting her to God as a saved member of the Bigelow First Baptist Church. And then there was her face. The face that reminded her so much of Jude. She couldn't turn her back and let all of that go. She wouldn't.

Confident, she turned to meet their gazes. She knew of their indiscretions. Their dirty little secrets, the ones they themselves had forgotten existed. She looked at them with eyes as black as coal.

"Maybe Gibson is confused . . . maybe he mean someone that look like her. Maybe someone told him about some *one time*, *long ago* thing that happened to her. Something she trying to forget that done caught up with her." The women listened to the excuses as they spilled one after the other from Pearl's mouth. Their eyes shifted between each other and then back to Pearl.

"Everybody gotta past, something they ashamed of." Pearl paused and looked directly at Shirley. They held each other's eyes for one long moment, Pearl revealing, with one look, what she'd known for years. Shirley's eyes were confused and then, as if a light went on, tears of comprehension, shame and then anger filled her eyes. She turned her head sharply away and lowered her eyes.

Pearl knew the story as did everyone else in Bigelow. But Pearl was the only woman bold enough to confront Shirley with it. And she would if Shirley pushed, she'd repeat what she'd heard from her own mother's mouth, if Shirley pushed her.

It was a story that was told amongst the colored kitchen help while they cleaned up after a birthday party or the field hands as they stole sweet relief from the sun beneath the shade of a magnolia tree. They would chew tobacco or drink heavily from tin cups filled with fresh well water and lean their backs against the bark of a tree or lay themselves down on the earth and speak of small things that had happened in their lives, or others they knew. Eventually, someone would start to speak of Crazy Ciel Brown.

"Her daddy was the white man from over in Ashton. He usta own the cannery and a few other things that ain't worth mentioning because they ain't no where 'round here. I believe his name was McHenry. Had lots of money, a wife and a pair of look-a-like girls. But I guess all that wasn't enough for him. He had to have himself a colored woman too."

"How you know so much?" a doubting Thomas would ask.

"I knows 'cause my cousin on my daddy side who usta cut cane down in Florida, knew the hairdresser by the name of Rebecca, who was acquainted with one of the maids that worked there who seen it all go down—her name be Belle. Belle Mason."

That explanation was usually good enough for any disbeliever.

"Anyways, like most low-down crackers that God seen fit to give abundance to, he felt like he should be able to have anything and anyone that happened to be under his roof. 'Sides, his wife wasn't no more good to him. She couldn't meet his needs. She was a drinker."

"I can't say that I blame a man for strayin' away from a wife who put away more liquor than him. I mean, a man's got needs, you know?" The same disbeliever would interrupt, yet again.

"Will you hush and let the man tell the story?" someone would say in an irritated voice.

"Like I was saying," the storyteller would continue, "the woman of the house be passed out somewhere, while her man just be a tipping on down to the maid's quarters, pick out the one he wanted and hop up on top of her like she was one of his horses."

"What the woman name be?"

And uncomfortable silence would rise like thick smoke.

"Man, if you don't shut your mouth and let the man tell the story!" someone would hiss.

"I believes her name was Shirley Brown. Don't know where she at now, or if she even still alive. But back then she was just a young thing, barely thirteen years old from what I hear," the storyteller would say in a voice filled with innuendo.

"When Shirley got big, they say McHenry known it was his because he was the only one she had been with and he had the bloody sheet to prove it!"

A gasp would emanate as they shook their heads in loathing.

"Now ya'll don't think that the missus of the house didn't know what was going on. She knew! And ain't say one single solitary word about it!"

"A colored woman would have bust him in his head!" someone would shout out and the crowd would fall out in uproarious laughter.

"That is the truth! But ya see, she was doing her own mid-

night tipping down to them stables. Now whether she was laying with man or beast, ain't for me to say, 'cause I wasn't there
and don't know one who was."

"Uhmph!"

"When Shirley got too big to ignore it any longer, McHenry
sent her away to have that baby. His wife said she wasn't going
to be shamed by what he'd done. She had to be able to go to
town and them functions white people are so fond of, and hold
her head up. Couldn't have people whispering behind her back.

I heard that that child, which is Ciel, was raised by an Injun
couple over in Shepardsville. Well, she don't look like she got an
ounce of white blood in her no how, so no one was the smarter."

"Yeah, git to the money part!"

"Well, once a month the couple would find money wrapped
in cheesecloth and nailed to their door. People say McHenry
was the one to send the money by way of his servants. The couple never knew where it was coming from and if they did, they
didn't say.

"That man provided for Ciel good and right! And after he
died, I heard that he left her a whole heap o' money!"

There would be an all consuming stillness, as the people digested the tale and drew their own conclusions from it.

No, Pearl wouldn't repeat it now, not if Shirley backed down
and found her place again in Pearl's home. She wouldn't speak
it but she would think it. Think it so caustically that the thoughts
themselves would burn from her mind and rest like flames on
Shirley's soul.

"How you all know it ain't just a downright lie," Pearl finished. Her tone challenged everyone in the room.

Clair Bell and Minnie stared mute. Shirley was afraid to raise
her eyes, lest she see her past looking back at her again. Then
Clair Bell spoke again.

"Well, he say he got a friend over in Hampton, who got a
friend . . . some high yella boy that happen to got a little
money." She rubbed her thumb and forefinger together. "Don't
know his name, though . . . well, he asked Gibson friend if he
knew one of them type of women." She tilted her head toward

the open window, indicating Sugar's house. Indicating Sugar. "And Gibson friend said, that he knew one of them type of women he was looking for. Told him her face wasn't much to look at, but she made up for that in the bed."

Silence.

"She, she, she! What that mean? Who is 'she,' she ain't Sugar! She could be anyone. Could be you. Could be me!" Pearl was near to yelling, her words came out in waves of trembling emotion.

"True. He ain't call her name directly. But he did say that she was over on Grove Street," Clair Bell said.

"Grove Street run near a mile long," Pearl said, running her open hands across her moist face.

"Uh-huh, that's what the man said when he told him, but then he made it clear that he should look for her at number ten."

Clair Bell's words echoed in Pearl's head. Shirley stood and placed her hands on her hips, a triumphant smile resting comfortably on her lips, her past sins forgotten for the moment. "Told you so, Pearl," she said.

Minnie saw the darkness suddenly cover Pearl's face like a widow's veil. "C'mon ya'll, I think it's time we get going." She could see they had pushed too far. She gathered the loose cards that had been forgotten on the table. "I think it's about to storm out there," she continued, feeling an appropriate excuse was needed. "Shirley, Clair Bell, let's go."

Clair Bell shot a questioning look at Minnie. The dark sky was speckled with brilliant stars and held no threat of rain. Minnie stretched her eyes wide and nodded her head a bit. "Let's go," she said again, stern this time.

"Shirley, you know you don't want that piece of wig to get wet. It'll smell like a dog when it do and take a whole week to dry." The humor camouflaged Minnie's growing nervousness. She was uncomfortable with what had been said there tonight. The look that blanketed Pearl's face was all too familiar to her, she'd seen it roosting there for years after Jude was killed.

"Why you messin' with me all the time—" Shirley started her attack on her sister, but Pearl cut her off.

"Out, now." Pearl spoke in a low hushed voice, one that carried despair, loss and loathing. "Get out now." Her anger and disappointment could not be repressed with politeness, not this time.

The women turned, open-mouthed, on Pearl and watched her as if watching a stranger. Shirley started to speak but Minnie pinched at the thick meat that was her waistline. Shirley sucked her teeth and slapped her sister's hand away. It was now obvious that they had pushed Pearl to the edge, she was ordering them to leave her home, to get out. Not feigning a headache or claiming that she had to rise early for church. No excuses this time, they had taken her way past courteous and dropped her off somewhere near I don't give a damn!

The women left, muttering under their breath and throwing cautionary looks over their shoulders at Pearl, who sat quietly at the table, her head resting in her hands. All uttered good-byes and the sound of clicking heels was replaced one hour later by an approaching Buick in need of a new engine. Joe walked in, his steps a bit unsure, his balance slightly off and the smell of beer swimming around him. He saw his wife, kissed her wetly on her cheek before heading upstairs. He only realized that she had not greeted him, verbally or otherwise, as his head hit the down-filled pillow and sleep claimed him.

Chapter Nine

*P*EARL sat still, barely realizing that Joe had entered the house and kissed her. Her mind was floating above her, concentrating on things she could not quite understand. She jumped at the sound of his boot hitting the floor above her head, the creaking springs of the bed as he lay down and the cutting snore as sleep took him over.

She heard a car's engine cut off, a door open and then close, the muffled sounds of knocking and then the quick clean closure of Sugar's screen door. Pearl squeezed her head between her hands; she would not get up and spy on her neighbor. Her friend. She would not.

Morning found Pearl still seated in the chair, in the kitchen. Her eyes were swollen from lack of sleep and weeping. She'd seen. Seen Sugar passing from window to window, naked and encased in the arms of a man Pearl knew to be Carlus Harden. The moon was high and illuminated the sky so brightly, it was as if heaven had lit a bonfire. Pure black nakedness that blended and united to form living breathing darkness.

Pearl wondered if Carlus held his wife Alberta that way. If he grabbed her head and pulled it back so far that another half inch would cause her neck to snap; all this to run his tongue across her chin and down the length of her throat. Pearl shivered, and wondered if she could ever eat at the Rib Shack again knowing those hands, his fingers that cleaned and seasoned the meat, skinned and cut the potatoes and shredded the cabbage and carrots for cole slaw also probed deep inside the womb of her neighbor and handled her breasts.

In the end though, Pearl did nothing but watch until the bodies tired of spinning past the windows and fell to the floor. She saw him leave, a full satisfied look on his face. He turned once to survey the house on his way out to his car. He put the automobile in neutral, released the hand brake and let it coast to the end of Grove Street. Only then did he turn on the ignition and the headlights.

Pearl couldn't sleep after that. It was near three in the morning when Carlus left. Another man showed up less than twenty minutes later. He came on foot and wore a large brimmed straw hat. The moon was bright but not so much so to glare or burn your brow. He came across the field, head low, hands shoved deep into the pockets of his overalls. He did not knock at the front door, but moved like a snake between the houses and entered quietly through the back door. Pearl watched for the spinning bodies to appear at the windows, like performers on stage, but no one showed. The man left twenty minutes later, head still hung low.

Pearl waited for another. Maybe one would approach by bicycle or mule, drop from the sky or crawl from the earth. She wouldn't be surprised or even gasp with astonishment.

*T*hat Sunday's service was less than uplifting. The strength Pearl usually claimed from the Reverend's words and the sweet sounds of Gospel singing was absent this day. Instead, her spirit had drained from her body, her faith had been torn from her soul. She sat there barely aware of the thumping feet and the hand clapping that filled the church before butting its melodic head on the rafters. Her Bible lay closed on her lap.

Joe sat stoically beside her, one hand resting gently on her knee. His eyes, dark with concern, darted from pulpit to Pearl and lingered there on her stricken face. He'd expressed his concern, more than once, in between the "Halle" and the "lujah." A squeeze of her knee or just a searching look into those vacant eyes. He did not know what had upset her so, and she would not tell. He'd found her still seated at the kitchen table, just as she was seven hours earlier when he stumbled in from his Saturday night poker game and planted a wet, sloppy kiss on her cheek. He noted she was still dressed in her sleeveless yellow and white summer dress, the one that reminded them both so much of Jude. "You been up all night, Bit?" he said through a yawn. "Yes." Her response was insipid. "You feeling okay?" Joe's question had a casual concern about it; he knew how much Pearl hated being fussed over.

Joe said church could lose them for one Sunday, but Pearl shook her head no and moved by him like a woman twenty years her senior.

Carlus Harden took Joe's hand in his, greeting him as he did every other Sunday morning after church. They were Mason buddies and before that, childhood friends. He tipped his hat to Pearl, who would have, on a normal day, smiled and placed her hand gently on his shoulder as a gesture of kindness and warmth. Instead, Pearl averted her eyes. She wanted to point her finger and call him a fornicator, but ignored his greeting instead, preferring not to lay her icy stare on him.

If Carlus was a fornicator, what would that make Sugar? Pearl wondered.

She bit her tongue and kept her mouth shut. Her eyes fell on Alberta Harden. She was big again. This was her fourth child in five years. A young thing, she was barely eighteen when she married Carlus. A beauty, that's what people said about Alberta. The color of honey with large brown eyes, thick, long dark hair that curled like a pig's tail at the end. A vision of loveliness, but as dumb as the day was long.

It seemed the only thing she was good for was making babies. Carlus cooked all the meals, cleaned the house and sent the wash out to be done. She could barely control the three boys she had. They treated her like a doormat, and she just smiled her doltish smile while they walked all over her.

Alberta leaned back against one of the eight trees that grew around the tiny church. She needed the shade, and the rest. Her three sons, Carlus Jr., Frederick and Edward, ran circles around the tree, beating their open hands against their mouths and whooping like Indians. Pearl walked toward her, intention bitter on her tongue. Alberta smiled and slipped her hand behind her to push her weight away from the tree and to meet Pearl halfway. She wiped at her brow, "Hello, Miss Pearl, how you this fine day?" She did not speak, but sang her words. Pearl nodded. At first she seemed to have forgotten how to smile, how to bend her lips to form a happy face. "You look like you due any day now," Pearl said. Her face was expressionless and her voice flat. Alberta's perpetual smile wavered. "Sure is. Overdue, in fact," she said and shooed at Edward, who was pulling at her pocketbook and whining "Want candy."

"Hmmm," Pearl said and looked over her shoulder to make sure that Carlus and Joe were still engaged in conversation. She stepped closer to Alberta, taking in her swollen belly and innocent smiling face. Her heart pained her. Did Alberta know she shared a bed with a man that shared himself with another?

Pearl's face twitched and her mouth opened to spill the baneful wisdom she had acquired overnight, but when she opened her mouth to speak, only silent words floated out, mingling with the bright morning sunshine and jasmine-kissed air.

She smiled at Alberta's waiting face posed before her, fixed with inquiry, waiting to absorb Pearl's words. "Hmmm," Pearl sounded again and laid her hand softly on Alberta's belly. "Somethin' fixing to give soon," Pearl said assuredly and turned to walk back toward her husband. Alberta fixed a quizzical look on the back of the old woman, not sure whether she referred to her impending labor or something else. "I sure hope so," she responded, not sure if her response was needed at all. She placed her hand over the moist imprint left behind by Pearl's own small hand. "Sure do."

*L*ater that afternoon, Pearl sat quietly sipping her Coke, watching Sugar move and glide in front of her. Ass slipping out like syrup from her hot pants. Breasts, loose and swaying beneath a T-shirt that said "Memphis." Chuck Berry was singing from the transistor radio that rested at Pearl's crossed feet. "Need more ice, Miss Pearl?" Sugar called to her over her shoulder. Pearl uttered a solitary no, even though the ice had melted long ago and the heat had claimed the sweet, dark liquid making it unbearable to drink. For now though, Pearl would bear it, the act of sipping kept her from speaking her mind.

Sugar tugged at the weeds that threatened the colorful life that Mrs. Wilks had worked so hard at cultivating, the fragrant spirits she'd died among. Pearl sat quietly in the backyard on one of the two chairs Sugar had removed from the kitchen table and placed in the yard.

Pearl was seething. She wanted to kick the transistor radio over, leap from the chair and pounce on Sugar. Instead she sat quietly stewing in her own fury waiting for Sugar to say a word, one word, that would prove or disprove what she saw and what was being said about her.

"You sure is quiet today, Miss Pearl," Sugar said, still not looking at her. She had a grip on a particularly tough weed. Her words came in jerks as she fought with the weed. "The sermon must have been something else, so good it took your breath away, huh?"

Pearl said nothing.

Sugar pulled the weed free and held it up like a trophy, waving it back and forth over her head. She came and flopped down beside Pearl's feet, stretching her long brown legs out before her; they glistened beneath the sun and seemed to illuminate the grass beneath them. Sugar bent her head back to smile at Pearl. She was feeling particularly good today, elated even. She couldn't put her finger on the reason, perhaps because she only turned two tricks the previous night instead of three or maybe because the last one just wanted to caress her breasts.

She looked into Pearl's face and saw misery there, but selfishly she refused to ask what the problem was, she refused to allow this rare feeling to be condensed by Pearl's foul mood. She arched her back and raised herself up on one arm while the other reached into her back pocket and pulled out a crumpled pack of Luckys. She examined the package for a while, not wanting to look back at Pearl's disapproving eyes. Pearl let out a sigh and Sugar lit the cigarette, grateful for the calming smoke that filled her lungs and encircled her head.

"What kinda work you do?" Pearl asked. Her voice was her own but embroidered with fierce hostility. Sugar refused to react and in fact said nothing.

"Where you get your money from?" Louder now. Sugar blew large smoke circles from her mouth. The heat was tearing at her scalp, making her head feel like an inferno beneath her wig.

"What you say?" she said, daring Pearl to repeat her forbidden questions.

"I said, I wanna know what kinda work you do?"

"What kinda work *you* do?" Sugar reversed the question.
Silence.

Pearl watched Sugar cock off the smoke.

"Why you gotta dress like that for?" Pearl continued, her tone becoming more spiteful.

"Why *you* dress like that?" Sugar was mocking her now.

Pearl let out a heavy sigh. She stared at Sugar's neck, at the thick scar that healed ugly and crooked like a dead tree branch. She stared at the false hair that adorned her head, at the skimpy T-shirt and tiny shorts that molded to her body like second skin instead of cloth. Who else other than a whore would dress this way?

Sugar stood and walked away from Pearl, cigarette smoke trailing behind her like a wedding veil. "I'm tired," she said and her voice carried a lifetime of weariness in its tone.

"You can't answer a simple question?" Pearl said, standing and taking two steps toward Sugar's back.

Sugar stopped, dropped her burning cigarette to the ground and placed her hands on her hips. She turned to face Pearl. She had had enough. "Why you so suddenly interested in what I do?" She spoke through clenched teeth.

"There's been talk, talk about what you do and who you doing it with. I just wanna know what's true and what ain't."

Sugar stepped close to Pearl. Pearl could smell her stale breath and heard the pounding of her heart. She held her eyes with her own. "I seen you walking 'round your house buck naked . . . windows open and all . . . I ain't the only person that seen you either, half the town done seen you too," Pearl continued, her voice shaking with the adrenaline that pumped through her body.

Sugar smiled, a half smile that made her look wicked. Pearl watched as Sugar transformed back into the woman that had walked into Bigelow three months ago. She leaned back on one leg and looked Pearl over from head to foot.

"What the hell gives you the right to question me about what I do, where I do it and who I do it with? Huh? I can walk around my house naked if I want to, upside down and naked if I choose to! You know why? Because it's my goddamn house, that's why! Do I ask you about your business? Do I ask you about your life? I didn't even invite your sorry ass into my life. You pushed yourself into it, you and your damn pies!

"Just 'cause we spend some time together don't mean it give you the right to question me about my habits of living or working. You done heard some talk? Fine, people gonna talk come hell or high water. Shit, even if there ain't nothing to talk about, they gonna make shit up. They'll make shit up about me and they'll make it up about you, that's just the way people is, Miss Pearl. Ain't nobody safe from small-time bullshit talk!"

Sugar turned and stormed into the house. Pearl was dizzy—the combination of her pulse, Sugar's swirling words and the bobbing and weaving of her head as she spoke had done a job on Pearl, but her question hadn't been answered, so she followed Sugar into the house.

"You answer my question. You answer my question, Jude!"

Pearl had referred to Sugar by her dead daughter's name before during light conversation. It would just tumble out, innocently, like cotton candy, sweet and light. Sugar never commented on it, she herself had called Pearl Mary on certain occasions. Hers was a slip of her tongue. Pearl's blunders went much deeper than that.

"Jude, people saying you allowing mens to have their way with you. Have their way with you for money!" Pearl's eyes were vacant, her face wet with perspiration and she shook uncontrollably. Sugar's heart skipped a beat. Was this old woman about to have a heart attack? She wanted to go to her, move her to the coolness of the living room and lay her to rest on the couch, but her feet were like stone and would not allow it.

"I ain't raise you like that, Jude. Me and your father ain't raise you to be loose! So you tell me now, tell me if it's true. Tell me!"

Sugar made a move toward her friend. "Miss Pearl?" She spoke softly, afraid that even the slightest lift of her voice would have a traumatic effect on the already bad situation. "Miss Pearl, you need to calm down. You need—"

"I need an answer!" Pearl pumped her fists up and down in the air, spit flew from her mouth. Sugar stepped back and clutched at her heart.

"S-some of us make our living breaking our backs and some of us in this world make our livings on our backs." Sugar didn't know why she put it that way. A simple yes would have been sufficient. She supposed she needed, in some small sick way, to sting Pearl, just as she had done to Sugar with her own words.

Pearl's arms dropped down to her sides. She stared at Sugar with eyes that held years of tears. "Why?" she uttered. Pearl was not seeing Sugar, but Jude. "Why," she said again as one small tear worked its way down her cheek.

Sugar shrugged her shoulders and hugged herself. She suddenly felt vulnerable, like a child.

"She lied to me, you know, lied to me about where she was going." Pearl's body went limp and her head hung heavy on her neck. "I didn't want her to leave 'cause I knew something was going to go wrong, you know." Pearl was quiet for a long time and then she lifted her head up to look at Sugar. Sugar had never seen so much pain and sorrow in a person's face, and was surprised that the sight of it caused her own heart to ache. "J-Joe had placed the shoes on the table, just for a second while he turned to put his hat on the hook. They was new, shiny black shoes, wing tipped and all. They had just come . . .

we ordered them from the Sears catalogue. You know, he just wasn't thinking."

She trailed off again and looked into the dusty realm of the house. Sugar knew she was seeing it all over again. "The tablecloth had a crease in it too. I forgot, don't know why but I forgot and placed it on the table anyway. I didn't even notice it until I saw the shoes." She shivered as if a cold wind had suddenly blown through. "Those were bad signs, the two of them resting against one another. Evil coming in twofold." She shook her head and a sob escaped her. "I told her maybe tomorrow she could go to her friend's house, but she insisted."

Pearl looked behind her quickly and then back at Sugar. Her eyes were wide with grief.

"They brought her to me . . . her womanhood cut from her . . . Jude."

She whispered the last eleven words. Sugar only caught the name, Jude.

"Who was she, Miss Pearl?" Sugar was afraid to ask, but propelled to.

"She was my daughter. She was my daughter," Pearl said and quickly covered her mouth. "She was my daughter," she said again in a whisper.

The words opened up old wounds in Pearl's heart and soul and she ran from Sugar's house, pain gripping her spirit like an old familiar enemy.

Sugar leaned against the wall and slid to the floor. Something had happened here, something that she knew she did not want to become a part of but found herself somehow already deeply rooted in. It was her past resurfacing all over again.

Before Sugar knew it, twelve years had passed, and it was becoming harder and harder to survive the streets and the men of Detroit and Chicago. She was tired of slopping toilets, wiping tables and slinging hash.

She was tired of her stomach turning from eating fish and chips fried in two-day-old grease. Tired of coming home to a rat- and roach-infested room in a three-story walkup that should have been condemned years ago.

One window, thin mattress, sink and hot plate: ten dollars a week.

Johns humping and pumping on top of her. Calling her all kinds of sweet things—ain't worried 'bout how she feeling or whether it was good to her or not. They ain't give a shit, just as long as they could and make *their* worries go away. Harder! Faster! They would ride her like a prized racehorse.

Thirty minutes of that shit was like living a whole lifetime in hell.

"You gotta pull it out sometime—it can't stay in there forever, honey baby!" she would coo into their sweaty necks.

See, these johns wanna keep it in there for as long as possible. It's warm and safe. They be smilin' and talkin' all kinds of shit hoping you let 'em go on just a little bit longer. It done got real good to them and they don't want out notime soon.

But then it's over. The cold air hits and reality kicks them in the ass all at the same time. The money is on the bed or the floor, and suddenly, Sugar ain't his sweet baby no more. She ain't his fine black thang. She ain't nobody, nothing but a whore.

His fantasy is over. But for her, the nightmare continues. You see, she ain't got no place or no person to go to to make her forget. Not even for a short time.

The circles under her eyes and the constant shaking of her hands were telling her she was near to falling apart. She needed to get out. She needed to get home. But where the hell was home?

She hadn't heard from the Laceys in years. She hadn't bothered to send a postcard or a telegram since she left Mary's house in St. Louis. For all Sugar knew they were dead, and if they weren't, they probably assumed she was.

A maniac john with a six-inch switchblade helped her make a quick decision as to when and where she would go. He sent her running for her life and straight to the next Greyhound bus bound for St. Louis. She left that city with a bleeding gash on her neck and the blood-stained clothes on her back.

St. Louis wasn't home, but it would have to do.

Sugar showed up at the stoop of what used to be the hottest colored whorehouse in town. The neighborhood had changed drastically. Twelve years ago, there were at least six different night spots in a four-block radius. Now those bars and clubs had been transformed into a butcher shop, Chinese laundry, store-front church and liquor store.

Twelve years ago you couldn't find a family on Sullivan Place, east of Macon Avenue or west of Joralemen Street. Well, not the mommy, daddy and baby kind of family. That area was comprised of hustlers, pimps and addicts. They of course called themselves singers and dancers. It was the place to live if you were colored and wanted to be thought of as somebody. Now there were children playing ball in the street and young mothers pushing carriages, smiling as they admired each other's babies.

The street still sparkled, just the way it did the first time Sugar arrived, and now she squinted her eyes against it, not needing to strain her neck to gawk at the tall buildings. She'd seen taller in the past twelve years.

A ROOMS FOR RENT sign hung pitifully in the first-floor, grime-laden window of the three-story brownstone. It replaced a sign that hung there twelve years earlier that proudly stated: PUSSY FOR SALE—INQUIRE WITHIN.

Sugar, her neck bandaged from the near-lethal cut she received in Detroit, sat down heavily on the steps that led up to the red door. Her sable-colored skin was ashen and chafed. Her once full figure was diminished by a good forty pounds, causing her clothing to hang and sag on her frame.

Never considered a beauty by anyone, she was now pitiful.

A round-faced little girl with large almond eyes, a small mouth wet and sticky with red Italian ice, stopped to stare intently at Sugar. Sugar hardly noticed the child, but when she did she asked her, "Mary Bedford still live here?"

The little girl was dressed in a red and white sunflower dress, her thick hair piled up on top of her head; the ends curled under. She gave Sugar a small queer sort of smile and slightly tilted her head to the right, examining the soiled rag that was wrapped around Sugar's neck. Satisfied, she plopped down on the stair step next to Sugar and began using her Popsicle stick as a shovel, digging out the dirt that lay between the cracks in the sidewalk.

Sugar looked at her, immediately reminded of the little girl from long ago who'd first asked her about her mother. The thought stirred deep emotions within her. Sugar looked around quickly and nervously, half expecting the little girl's mother to appear, snatch her up from the stair step and drag her away by the collar: We don't deal with the likes of them!

The little girl stopped her digging and looked up at Sugar. She shielded her eyes from the high noon sun and said in a distinctive Southern drawl, "Yeah, she live here. She be back soon, went down the road to the store." She considered Sugar a bit longer and then returned to her digging.

A heaviness consumed Sugar and she leaned into the hard stone stairs, allowing the heat to soothe her aching back. Her body, soul and mind were tired. She let out a loud sigh. Not one of relief but temporary contentment.

"You hurt?" the little girl's voice trailed up to her. She was pointing a tiny finger at the bloody rag that was tied around Sugar's neck. Her face was scrunched up like she was smelling something rotten.

"Yeah," was all Sugar managed to say and then sighed once again, looking off into the distance.

"Grandma, grandma!" The little girl shouted and bolted up and past Sugar. She ran into the waiting arms of a short, fat woman who looked like she'd seen better days. Sugar looked at them then turned away. Expressions of affection always made her feel uncomfortable.

The woman held the little girl tightly as she looked over at the bundled heap of a woman who sat on her stoop. She patted the girl's head and moved her behind her wide mass as she cautiously approached the woman. Mean was sparkling like diamonds in her eyes as she edged closer. Recognition quickly replaced the cold icy stare, and then pity.

"Sure nuff, if it ain't Sugar Lacey!" The short stout woman came toward her, the little girl behind her grinning and clinging to her skirts.

"She been waiting for you for a long time, Grandma," the little girl said and winked at Sugar.

It was Sugar's turn to shade her eyes with her hand. Was she seeing right? Was this Mary Bedford standing before her?

Grandma?

She looked up and into the aged face of Mary Lucille Bedford. It sure was Mary. Sugar had expected her to look older, but not as old as this. She certainly didn't expect to see her without one of her extravagant, flowing wigs. But there she stood, her thin silver strands pulled back into a tight bun. She wore a demure pink color on her lips and just a hint of blush on her cheeks. Gone was the heavy foundation, false eyelashes and light blue eye makeup that once graced her face.

Sugar thought Mary looked like life had slapped her around and then dumped her on the curbside to die. She looked horrible. The years of heavy smoking and drinking had taken their toll on Mary, but she was smiling.

"Mary Bedford, as the day I was born," Sugar finally managed to say. With difficulty she stood up, leaving her hands at her sides like limp weeds, staring at Mary and her grandchild. Mary's face gave away what she was thinking. It was a strange mixture of shock, pity and disappointment. "Come here, girl," she said, hugging Sugar. The faint smell of Evening in Paris filled Sugar's nostrils.

*T*hree months came and went. August faded swiftly into the past and Thanksgiving was upon them. The three of them sat holding hands around a beautiful golden brown turkey. The lights were turned off and Sugar looked around at the faces illuminated by soft candlelight. Mercy was looking so much like her grandmother—pecan-colored skin and thick rosy cheeks. She smiled at Sugar, winked and bowed her head.

Mary began: "Thank you, Lord, for the food that we are about to receive and thank you for the life you allow me to have every single day. Thank you for my beautiful granddaughter Mercy and for my beautiful friend Sugar."

Sugar bowed her head lower. Even after three months of living with Mary and Mercy, she still couldn't get used to the kind words, the hugs and the kisses. She felt she did not deserve any of this.

"Please continue to rain your blessings down on us, amen." Mary ended and Mercy echoed her amen. Sugar mouthed the words, feeling the soundlessness of it quake her soul.

They ate until their fattened bellies stuck out comically in front of them. Afterward they sat in the small parlor that now held a brown, somewhat battered tweed sofa and two ivory-colored wing chairs.

Boarders came and went through the day, wishing them Happy Thanksgiving. Mary did not allow one of them to leave empty handed. She sent them off with slices of sweet potato pie, bowls of cole slaw, slices of ham and turkey. "Ya'll just better make sure you bring my plates back clean!" she'd yell as they went through the door and up to their separate rooms.

"You are too nice," Sugar said as she stroked Mercy's lolling head.

"Girl, they ain't got shit. Look at them, young and living on their own. They should be home at they mamma's house where they could save some money and get good cooking all the time. But these children nowadays in a rush to get out and be independent."

Mary shifted in her chair and wiped at her chin. "I try to help them any way I can. I got so much and they have so little, what's wrong with giving a little away? It's better than letting it go to waste, ain't it?"

Sugar nodded her head and looked down into the sleeping face of Mercy.

"She is out like a light. I'ma take her up to bed," Sugar said, and lifted the six-year-old up from the couch. She moved slowly to the back of the house where she and Mercy shared a bedroom. "We'll play cards when you get back," Mary whispered to Sugar's back.

When she returned, Mary was stretched out on the couch. "Oh, what happened to the card game?" she said with a laugh. "You got niggeritis now!" she teased further. As she came closer to Mary she realized that her position was a bit awkward. Coming still closer, she saw that her face was locked with pain.

"Mary!" she screamed, "what is it, what's wrong?"

Mary stared at the ceiling; white foam oozed slowly from her mouth. Her body shook violently as each bolt of pain ripped through her like lightning.

"Oh shit, Oh shit, Oh God, Oh shit, *Mary*!" Sugar was screaming and shaking the old woman. "Help!"

The waiting room of Cook County Hospital was dimly lit and filthy. Cigarette butts spilled from the standing ashtrays and littered the floor. The thick smell of smoke and sickness hung heavy in the air. Beige-and-green-tiled walls added to the misery of the people who had to be there.

People wandered in and out of the area, moving around restlessly as they awaited word of a loved one's condition.

Sugar sat stone still. She was tense and wary of everyone and everything around her. She'd never been in a hospital and after tonight, didn't want to have to return to one. Mercy was in a fitful sleep on her lap; a blanket encircled the two of them like black butterflies emerging from a cocoon.

The ambulance had come quickly. Sugar cursed herself for not having thought of calling for one. A boarder named Jonah heard the screaming coming from his landlady's apartment and rushed down to see what was happening. He was the one to call for an ambulance. It would be him that Mary would have to thank for saving her life . . . if she lived.

"Is there someone here with Mary Bedford?" a tall, white, wiry-looking man asked in a gentle voice. He had a white jacket on and a clipboard in his hands. He peered patiently over the glasses that sat at the very tip of his thin straight nose.

"Yes," Sugar said in a voice so low, even she hardly heard it.

"Are you family?" the doctor asked, looking at his chart.

Sugar froze. She wasn't family. Would they tell her anything if she wasn't family?

"I want Grandma, Mommy," Mercy said in a sleepy voice. Sugar's heart stopped beating. The child must be dreaming. Mommy?

"Oh, so you're Mizz Bedford's daughter?" the doctor said, now peering at her with tiny black eyes.

Sugar's head nodded yes, as if some unseen force was guiding it.

"Well . . . Mizz. . . . uh . . . Mrs. . . ." The doctor stumbled and looked to Sugar for assistance. Sugar, still in shock by the turn of events, could not read the doctor's face.

"Well, Mizz Bedford has suffered a stroke and—"

"She comin' home now?" Sugar heard someone say and turned her head to see who it was. All the eyes peered back at her. She had spoken those words. And then suddenly, they were coming again, like water flowing from a faucet. She wanted it to stop but it wouldn't. "Shecominhomenowshecominhomenow-shecominhomenow."

Fear was thick in her throat like molasses, trapping the words.

The doctor was flustered. "Uh, no, she's suffered a stroke . . . not too severe, but she'll have to stay here for a few weeks until her condition improves," the doctor said carefully, aware that the woman he spoke to was on the verge of having a nervous breakdown.

"Can we see my grandma?" Mercy asked in a composed voice that stunned both Sugar and the doctor.

"Yes. Just for a minute, though," the doctor said and stepped back, pointing down a long corridor.

Mercy hopped off of Sugar's lap. She held her hand out to her. "C'mon Miss . . . uhm . . . Mamma. Let's go see Grandma," she said and winked.

How did this little girl get to be so strong? Sugar wondered.

Mary was in a ward with at least thirty other women. Some were moaning. Others were turned on their sides or stomachs, sleeping. Sugar was aware of the sound her shoes made as she walked down the long ward toward Mary, sounding like a large clock inside her head. *Clickclickclick.* She wanted to run screaming from there, but she looked at Mercy and found the strength she needed.

Mary lay before them, her pecan complexion almost white. Her silver, silky hair dry and brittle. Her face twisted to one side.

Sugar was overwhelmed with sorrow. There were tubes running out of Mary's nose, mouth and arms; her eyes were closed and to Sugar, she looked dead.

It's funny, Sugar thought as she washed up the last of the supper dishes, *how life repeats itself.* Here she was once again, taking charge of the Bedford house. Collecting money and making sure the boarders conducted themselves properly. No loud music after ten. No loitering on the stoop. She had handled it all quite well, just as she did twelve years ago.

Mercy was a tower of strength. She never complained, not even when Sugar overcooked the eggs or burned the bacon. Not even when her hair parts were crooked and her bangs drooped. She just smiled and went skipping off to school.

But Sugar knew the girl was torn up inside. She saw the tear-stained pillow cases when she did the laundry.

People in the neighborhood, the former hustlers, pimps and prostitutes (some gone straight, others still living the life), came and did what they could when they could. They brought casseroles filled with baked macaroni and cheese, sweet potato pie, smothered pork chops and fried chicken. They took away loads of dirty clothes and returned them clean, folded and smelling of Borax. They did all of this for Mary, because over the years, Mary had done so much for them.

Sugar went to visit Mary every day while Mercy was in school. She fed her soup with a shaky, unsure hand, while she tried to keep a smile on her face.

She made light conversation about Mercy and what was going on in and around the house. But none of it came out sounding natural, it was always strained with the fear Sugar had lodged in her mind.

Suppose she never comes home?

Mary's speech was slurred and so she chose, most of the time, not to talk at all. She would just nod her head and offer a crooked smile.

One day, as Sugar was gathering herself to leave, Mary started to speak. It was difficult and clearly took a lot of effort to get out the one word she wanted so badly to say: Christmas.

It came out as "Kissmmmmas," but Sugar understood it. She had been worrying about that herself. Usually it was just a day in a week for Sugar, but she knew that this was not just another week in her usual life. There was Mercy to think of now.

Sugar half hoped the holiday would come and go without the child noticing it, but the idea was shot down when Mercy came home from school with her scrawled pictures. Mercy had drawn a Christmas tree with tiny little gifts beneath it. She also had a wreath she'd drawn, colored brightly and cut out. Sugar saw the pride in her eyes as she presented her creation to her and asked her to take it to Mary. "This will make her happy and she'll get better soon. She won't want to miss Santa Claus," Mercy said, with a large smile and gleaming eyes.

The paper wreath now sat on Mary's nightstand propped up against the water container.

"Mary, won't you be home for Christmas?" Sugar asked, hoping her voice sounded cheerful. Mary shook her head slowly, painfully, from side to side.

Sugar was silent for some time, as she stared down at the large green and beige tile design on the floor. She eyed the Christmas wreath and could hear Mercy's excited babbling about the toys and dresses she hoped Santa would bring to her for Christmas. "Miss Shuga, I been a real good girl this year!"

Sugar squeezed her eyes shut and shook Mercy's voice from her mind. When she lifted her head to meet Mary's gaze, the eyes that looked back at her dropped responsibility heavy as stones on her shoulders.

"I'll try, Mary," she said solemnly, already convinced that her best effort wouldn't be good enough.

*S*ugar stood before the towering evergreen that practically swallowed the tiny parlor. There were ornaments of all colors, shapes and sizes hanging from its long, wide limbs. They gleamed and glimmered off the streetlamp light that filtered through the windows. The house was quiet except for the soft crooning of Nat King Cole's "White Christmas."

Sugar breathed in deeply, inhaling the sweet smell of the tree. It took her back to Arkansas, and she suddenly felt homesick, a feeling she'd never stumbled across before.

She turned to face Mary. "It's beautiful, ain't it," Mary said. It was still difficult for her to talk, but she was improving quickly. She'd come home by taxi just two days earlier, surprising both Mercy and Sugar.

"I just had to be here with my babies. I couldn't be in no damn hospital on Christmas, no siree!" she said as Sugar helped her up the front steps.

"I'm sure glad you're home. I didn't think I could have done it without you being here," Sugar said as she sat down in the wing chair across from Mary. She sipped her eggnog and allowed the whiskey it was spiked with to move through her, numbing the emotion she felt rising within her.

"Girl, what you talkin' about? Without me? You did it. *You* got the tree, the gifts. You did it all, girl, without my help," she said, and raised her own glass of eggnog in salute. "You didn't need me here, but I'm sure glad to be here. Thank the Lord," she added and bowed her head in a silent, quick prayer.

"I did use your money, though," Sugar said with a wry smile.

"My money is your money. You know that. 'Sides, it was all for my grandbaby."

Sugar looked back at the tree and for the first time noticed the ornament of the mother and child embracing. "Ahhh," Sugar uttered and moved closer to examine it. "I remember this," she said almost to herself as she touched it gently with the tip of her finger. "Do you remember this?" she asked, looking back at Mary, light dancing in her eyes, her finger still resting lightly on the gold and silver ornament.

Mary nodded slowly. She was the one who'd placed it there. It'd always been her favorite. It was special to her, given to her by her mother. She kept it wrapped in paper, in her hope chest at the foot of her bed.

"You tried to get me to hang it on that tree you had . . ." She trailed off, recalling a long-ago Christmas. The thought of it brought a wisp of a smile to her face.

"Oh, look!" Mary shouted and sat straight up in her chair. Sugar jumped and nearly fell into the tree.

"What?" she yelped and ran toward Mary.

Mary was pointing a crooked finger toward her. "You having one. You having one I seen it don't try and deny it!" Mary was cackling and coughing like an old hen.

"I'm having what?" Sugar was confused, a puzzled look shadowed her eyes.

"You just looked up and smiled. You had one, thank the Lord, you done finally had yourself one!" Mary was laughing and slapping her thigh with glee.

Sugar smiled, finally understanding what Mary was excited about. It was true, the thought of that Christmas did make her smile. Yep, she'd had one. Christmas brings on all sorts of things. It was a magical season.

Sugar figured she'd be doing it quite often. She'd stored up plenty of good-time memories during the time she spent in the Bedford household.

"Sugar." The voice was hesitant. "Will you sing for me?" Mary's eyes were hopeful and pleading.

"Mary, I . . . I told you, I don't sing no more . . ." Sugar got up and walked back over to the tree. How could she deny this woman such a small request. She felt low down for doing it.

"Please, Sugar, it's Christmas. And as much as I need to hear it, I believe you need to do it," Mary said in a quiet voice.

They were silent. Sugar standing in front of the tree, Mary sitting staring at her back.

The song started small and muted with emotion, and then it rose like a wave coming out of the Atlantic. With every word, Sugar's voice stretched and grew until it was higher than the tree and overpowered the room. Mary had never heard "Silent Night" sung like that before. So much soul, so much sadness.

When she was done, both of their faces were wet with tears.

Spring came early that year. The streets came alive again with the sounds of squealing children and crying newborn babies. Sugar decided it was time. Mary was up and about. She moved a bit slower, but Sugar told herself it was age, not sickness, that slowed her movements.

By then, she was considering going west, where she heard the weather was always like a warm spring day.

"California? Who the hell you know out in California?" Mary asked, when Sugar announced her plans. "This time you won't just come back with your neck slashed, you'll come back in a damn box!"

Mary was yelling now, and Sugar tried to shut her mind to her words. She told herself—and for the most part it was true—that Mary just flat did not want her to go. Sugar didn't want to go either, but she needed to move on.

Mary ranted and raved for nearly two hours. Walking from room to room, slamming doors and cussing as she went.

"Them crackers out there don't like no kinda colored peoples. I hear they worse than the ones in the South. A soot-black girl like you don't stand a chance in hell in California!" she said before she slammed the bedroom door in Sugar's face.

That was bad, but the worst was yet to come. Sugar turned to see Mercy slipping silently into the kitchen, tears sparkling in her eyes. Up until then, Sugar had never mentioned to Mercy the fact that she would be leaving soon. The child had formed an impenetrable bond with Sugar. Sugar knew by the way she curled into her at night, matching her breath as they lay sleeping in the bed they shared.

Sugar felt like a low down snake.

Lower than she did when she lifted a can of beans from a store in Detroit owned by a gentle old man who had only the day before extended her credit.

Evening came in with a chill, and Sugar supposed this helped in cooling Mary down. She came into the parlor where Sugar was sitting and staring out of the window. Her eyes were heavy with apology.

She stood before her, leaning heavily on her cane, and reached into her bosom, pulling out a piece of paper that was aged yellow. "Here," she said and handed it to her with a shaking hand.

Sugar took it and her fingers began to tingle. "What's this?" she said as she rose from the chair.

Mary clucked her teeth and then began to ramble like a small child. "It came 'bout four years ago. I had all but forgotten it. Well, I ain't hear nothing from you in all them years. Didn't have a clue as to where you could be and I just now run across it again. Well, go on and read it."

Sugar tried to read Mary's eyes, but they held nothing but excitement. Sugar slowly unfolded the piece of paper that Mary must have folded and unfolded hundreds of times. Maybe hoping that the sheer ritual of it would someday draw Sugar back.

It was a telegram that read:

OCTOBER 1ST, 1951 *STOP* YOUR
MAMMA IS HERE *STOP* COME
HOME *STOP* LACEY *STOP*

Sugar read the words over and over again until they were no more than a black blur of nothing before her.

Mamma. Home.

Those two words seemed to burn into her mind.

Sugar looked from the telegram to Mary and then back again.

Mary stood in front of her, her breast heaving up and down with excitement. Sugar didn't speak. Couldn't speak.

"I almost forgot 'bout it, but like I said it's been quite a while." Mary stopped. She sat down because her legs were shaking. She breathlessly began again. "I sent word back sayin' you weren't here. I told them that you'd gone off to Detroit when you left here, but no telling where you could be by now."

Sugar blinked and reread the words again.

"Oh, Sugar, ain't it wonderful. Your mamma done come back for you. I know you grown and all, 'course it don't matter how old you are, you always need your mama. Lord knows I wish mine was still around. Lord have mercy, Sugar. It's like getting a second chance." Mary was grinning from ear to ear.

Second chance? I never had a first chance. I suppose this should be considered as my only chance, she thought to herself.

Sugar didn't know what she was feeling. Something was whirling inside of her, causing her to swoon. Was it happiness? Anger? Sadness? Did this woman who abandoned her, now after thirty years, deserve to have her?

She grabbed for the table to steady herself. Mary moved in close and took her face in her hands. "It's time," Mary said in a tender voice. Mary's face was so close to Sugar's that she could smell the Juicy Fruit gum Mary chewed by the pack. She could see the stained yellow teeth and the scar that was barely visible on the tip of her nose. But what she concentrated on were her eyes. Mary's eyes were calm and all knowing. "You got to go. Not to California, but Arkansas. Home," she said with such quiet strength it shook Sugar to the bone.

"Baby, everybody got their own reasons for doing things they do in life. It don't matter what her reason was at the time, what matters is she come back for you, and even though you might think it's too late, it ain't never too late where a mother and her child is concerned."

Chapter Ten

WEEKS later, the banging was becoming irritating enough to drag Sugar kicking and screaming from the precious little sleep she could manage to steal. Sugar sat straight up and waited for the sound to come again, not sure if it was inside her head or outside her front door. It came again, a demanding knocking at her front door that caused her to jump, knocking over the nearby ashtray filled with butts and roaches.

Reefer was a new soothing friend in her life. A joint and a drink made everything okay. Veiled her vision and made the tricks she turned bearable. Yes, it was a magic plant and it was helping Sugar to play the greatest trick of them all on herself.

Lappy Clayton introduced it to her the first time they fucked. She liked the way it made her feel, how it lifted her out of herself while at the same time allowed her to go deeper into herself. It made her laugh uncontrollably until her sides ached and tears fell in floods down her cheeks.

He had taken to bringing her at least two joints every time he paid Sugar a visit, which was as much as twice a week now. "Consider it a tip," he said one early morning as he dressed, the morning sun rays dancing across his cream-colored back.

There was a part of Lappy that Sugar was comfortable with. The part that reminded her of herself, the part she wouldn't admit existed inside of her, the innocent side that at thirty years old still remained untouched by the type of life she lived. The side that came out and took in the sun and skipped rope on a St. Louis sidewalk. She liked that side of herself and she saw it in Lappy Clayton too. Behind the slicked-back hair, fine suits, hip talk and gold tooth of the man Lappy, was the boy Lappy.

Sugar caught a glimpse of that boy, white on top, all black beneath. She saw it when he booked her for the whole night and showed up with fried chicken dinners and Coca Cola. The nights they laughed away. On those nights he didn't want to fuck, he just wanted to talk shit and laugh. He brought a record player over one night and a few seventy-eights. They kicked back and listened to T-Bone Walker and B.B. King. Lappy bragged that he had met both men. "They always be down at my man's place, the Memphis Roll. You can't come through Arkansas and not play the Roll."

Sugar found herself there too, among the hand clapping and loud laughter of sharecroppers, house mammies and uncles celebrating their blackness, full of their sires' spirits, getting down but not laying down for no one, not even the almighty whitey. Sugar was swept up in the raw, pulsating madness the people and the music produced. Liberated by drink and smoke, she found herself on stage next to a blind man that sang the blues so slow and sweet, people spoke on it for days afterward.

The blind man had other one-night gigs to do, the chitlin circuit was sixty-five nights of giving yourself over to segregated toilets and drinking fountains, and scared white people that suspected your lyrics carried something other than sadness or happiness. Suspected that maybe those words carried seeds of contention.

So they couldn't have him, but Sugar was just a forty-minute ride away, and her voice rocked the men like an over-heated lover and made the women fan beneath their dresses and decide against denial that night. The Memphis Roll claimed her for their own, and Sugar found extra income and a brief release for her troubled soul.

Then there were the other times, times when Lappy came in and said nothing, just walked past her and up to the bedroom.

She could put it off on the tracks that ran up and down his arms—if it wasn't for his eyes, wild and raging with madness. During those times he did not seem to know her, and treated her like a whore, forgetting that they had broken wish bones together. During those times he rode her until she begged him to stop. When he could not find release and ordered her to take it into her mouth, he'd ram away, cussing her if her teeth got in the way. She'd have to swallow his seed; he would not allow her to waste it in the piss pan she kept beneath the bed, she had to digest it. He paid her to do it, he enjoyed watching her do it. And then he would leave, car screeching into the night, leaving Sugar shaking and bleeding.

$\mathcal{S}$ugar swung the door open and was knocked back by the brilliant August sunlight.

"I been thinking that maybe we could try this here thing one more time," Pearl said, stepping in, sweet potato pie in hand, and closing the door behind her.

It'd been weeks since Pearl and Sugar spoke to each other. Each went about her life as if the other didn't exist, both miserable without the other. Pearl confided in Joe, leaving out the real reason she and Sugar had fought.

"You call her friend, Bit?" Joe asked when she mentioned that Sugar and her had had words.

Pearl nodded yes.

"Friends forgive," was all he said and the matter was solved as far as he was concerned.

Pearl made it clear to Sugar that coming to her home did not for one moment mean she approved of how Sugar made her money. She was there because she believed all of God's people could change their ways, save their souls.

Sugar stifled a laugh and lit a cigarette. *I ain't got no soul to save,* she thought to herself. "So I hear, Miss Pearl, so I hear," she said and exhaled enough smoke to cloak the doubt that she was sure was evident in her eyes.

"Miss Pearl, tell me about Jude," Sugar asked delicately, realizing that this was the cause of great pain for Pearl, and most recently Sugar. Sugar had felt uneasy after she and Pearl fought. Since Pearl had called her Jude, Sugar could not sleep without waking in a cold sweat and Jude's name on her lips.

"They never found the killer?" Sugar asked again, unable to believe that a person responsible for a crime so abominable would be allowed, by God himself, to walk this earth unpunished.

Pearl shook her head. Her hands were shaking and her voice was barely a whisper, but she assured Sugar she was fine. "It's still hard to talk about it even after all this time," Pearl said and wiped at the mist in her eyes. "Now you. Tell me about you. How you came to doing what you do."

Sugar's mouth opened and then closed. She got up to get her cigarettes. This wasn't going to be easy. She wouldn't start at the beginning but in the middle where the pain was numbing.

*S*ugar arrived back in Short Junction by bus. Fifteen years hadn't really changed Short Junction. It was still made up of clapboard houses and barnyard dogs, except now the dogs were older, their bark less threatening, and the houses slouched a little more.

People still moved like molasses and greeted each other with Mornin' or Evenin' whenever they passed you in town or along a quiet patch of dirt road. No, not much had changed.

Sugar paid a young, broad-necked boy to fetch her bags and to bring them on to the Lacey place. She wanted to walk. She needed to walk. Walk Chicago, Detroit and St. Louis out of her soul.

She made her way down Route 4. The rain had come during the night and left the road muddy in some parts. Sugar's heels sank deep into the earth, holding her hostage for short periods of time. She removed them, allowing the cool earth to seep through her nylons and kiss the soles of her feet.

She stopped to admire a field of wildflowers, resting her head against the damp wooden post and plucking at the barbed wire that entwined it. She recalled her childhood and the easy joy she'd experienced among those brilliant flowers.

She stopped two or three times to ask for directions to the Lacey home. Not because she was lost, but because she wanted to exchange words with the people of Short Junction. She needed to re-connect with what she was before she'd become Sugar the whore.

They never answered immediately; they'd have to take her in first, allowing their eyes to travel down the blue silk dress with the Chinese collar. The one with the tiny red embroidery around the neck and hemline. The one that held Sugar like a calfskin glove, one size too small. They had to take in the six-foot woman with the jet black skin, heavily shadowed eyes and blood red lips. Only after they had traveled the world that was Sugar would they point or nod (in that way country people do) in the direction she needed to go. She'd thank them and begin walking again, leaving an overall-clad old man staring after her, watching her behind roll and wiggle beneath the dress.

As she traveled farther down Route 4, moving closer to the outskirts of Short Junction, Sugar noticed that where sprawling fields of cotton once grew, now stood large homes. Great white structures with windows that traveled from the floor to the ceiling.

Her mouth fell open with astonishment. "When the hell did this all happen?" she said aloud as she stopped to marvel.

A colored woman opened the front door and stepped out, waving at Sugar as she did. Two small dogs, barely taller than her ankle, rushed out behind her and started to jump and yelp happily about her legs. The woman waved at Sugar again, smiling broadly.

Sugar stood staring. The thought of a colored woman living in a house this fine in Short Junction, Arkansas, was overwhelming.

The woman was walking quickly down the long walkway that led up to the house, trying not to step on the small dogs that encircled her feet. As she came closer, Sugar could see that the baby blue dress the woman wore was not a dress at all, but a uniform. Sugar understood now.

"How you?" the woman said breathlessly, a genuine smile resting on her lips. The dogs stopped their yapping and sat obediently at her feet, watching Sugar with their small black eyes.

"Lord have mercy, it's gonna be a hot one today and only April," the woman in the blue uniform exclaimed and pulled a handkerchief from her bosom, dabbing quickly at the perspiration forming above her lip. She gave Sugar a sweet smile.

"You the new girl?" she asked and snatched a quick look at Sugar from the neck down. The smile remained, but not as sweet.

"New girl?" Sugar repeated stupidly.

"Yeah, new girl. This here is the Floyd house, we expecting a new gi—maid today. You her?" The woman's smile was visibly crumbling. "If you ain't the new girl then what you doing 'round here?" The smile was completely gone and the voice was turning rancid like week-old milk.

Sugar leaned back hard on her heels. "I ain't nobody's girl or maid. I was just admiring the house, is all," Sugar said, falling back into the Southern twang she'd so easily let slip away.

"Well, we don't need the likes of you sniffin' 'round here, so off with you," the woman said and waved her hand at Sugar as if she was a bothersome fly.

The likes of you.

There was that phrase again.

"You live too far South to be so damn uppity. You and me, we the same. The likes of me is the likes of you!" Sugar said, her voice gutted with anger. She threw her bare arm out before the woman's face so that she could see that their skin color was nearly identical.

The woman folded her arms across her bosom, rolled her eyes and clucked her tongue in disgust. Sugar's words had left her agitated and speechless. She swung around and started back up the long walkway to the house. The dogs, startled by her sudden retreat, began yelping and jumping about her feet again.

As the woman turned, Sugar was struck by her sharp features

and small slanted eyes. Like a brick, it hit her. This was the same little girl who'd questioned her so many years earlier outside Short Junction's general store: *Ain't you got a mamma?*

The words stirred like a whirlwind in her head, preventing her from walking away. "Yeah I got's a mamma!" she yelled to the back of the woman and waved the aged telegram like a victorious flag.

The woman turned, giving Sugar a brief puzzled look.

Later, Sugar found herself standing on the porch of the Lacey home. The once-white paint was now graying with age and peeling in large thin slices. The porch, in desperate need of repair, slouched heavily to one side.

The yard was absent of the roaming, clucking chickens that once filled the front and back yards. Sugar bent her head slightly to the left and could see that the pen that once held Shelby the hog was now empty and overgrown with weeds.

The windows were open, allowing the light spring breeze to flutter the old lace curtains. Soft music sailed out and for a fleeting moment hung in the air over Sugar's head.

Pots and pans banged and clanged nosily inside as they were placed, moved and filled. This caused a slight smile to tickle at the ends of Sugar's mouth. It was a familiar and expected sound for a Friday—fish fry day.

Sugar rested her hand lightly on the door and then pulled quickly away when she realized, as if coming out of a trance, why she'd come in the first place.

She wanted to run. Run back to the bus and board it, begging the bus driver not to stop until they reached St. Louis.

She wasn't ready. She wasn't ready to meet her mother. Coming had been a big mistake.

The broad-necked boy came up behind her, pulling a makeshift wagon filled with her belongings. He smiled, not at her, but at her legs and hips. He moved slowly and placed each case down carefully on the porch. All the while not raising his eyes past her neck.

"Ma'am," he said, his tone curious and strangely sexual at the same time.

Sugar nodded and dug into her pocketbook, pulled out a quarter and tossed it to him. The boy thanked her and took one last look at her long fish net–clad legs before he started down the stairs.

"Boy," Sugar said, not turning to face him.

"Ma'am?" The voice came from behind her.

"You got a mamma?" she said, her legs quivering now.

There was a long pause.

"Yessum," the boy said.

"You live with your mamma?" Sugar asked.

"Yessum."

"She expecting you soon?" Sugar said, just wanting to keep him there with her, until strength came and moved her forward.

"Yessum, but if you needs me to . . . uh . . . do something else I'll be right able to do it," he said. His voice closer now. Hopeful.

Sugar said nothing.

"No. Don't keep your mamma waiting," she said more to herself than to the boy. He stood there for a while, bewildered by her strange questions. City women were funny that way, he thought to himself as he trudged away, his cart squeaking noisily behind him.

Sara Lacey, still small and fragile, but now wrinkled and gray, came to the door and swung it wide open. The sound of the retreating wagon had brought her to investigate who was on her property. Or perhaps it was the deafening sound of Sugar's heart beating hard inside her chest.

"Who you?" Sara asked, wincing her milky eyes.

Sugar just stood there, unable to utter a word.

"Who you, I said. Are ya deaf, dumb or both?" Sara demanded, taking a bold step forward.

Sugar parted her lips to speak and still nothing came.

"Gal, we don't like no strangers hangin' 'round this here house. Now, if you lost, say so. If you hungry, I'll be glad to feed ya and send ya on ya way." Sara paused, tilting her head slightly, trying to get her eyes to focus on the person in front of her. "If you selling somethin, I probably already got it, can't afford it or don't need it at all."

"Sara, it's me, Sugar," Sugar said in a small voice.

Sara winced again as if stung, and then took a few steps closer. At her tallest, Sara had only reached Sugar's chest; now, old and slumped, she stood up on her tiptoes until she was nearly face to face with her.

"Sugar? Well, lookee here . . . it sure nuff is you, ain't it! Good God almighty, come on in this here house." She snatched at Sugar's hand and led her into the large foyer.

The dilapidated exterior masked the beauty and order that remained within the Lacey home. It was just as Sugar had left it. High-polished dark wooden floors. Massive mahogany furniture. Nothing had changed, and Sugar felt like she'd stepped right back into 1940.

As they made their way past the dining area and on to the kitchen, Sugar saw that the large oak cabinet that sat in the wide hallway still held the stolen pieces of china.

The smell of frying catfish and simmering turnip greens accosted her senses and she was overcome with nostalgia.

When she was a child these food smells were always accompanied by hard-drinking, heavy-smoking men and women. Clinking glasses filled with white lightning, clay ashtrays overflowing with lipstick-stained cigarettes. The sound of a palm coming down hard on a thigh intertwined with glorious laughter.

The bedrooms may have made most of the money in the Lacey house, but the kitchen was its lifeline.

That was 1940, when Sugar walked away from Short Junction. That was 1940, when Joe Taylor had mistakenly placed his new shoes on the dining room table and sweet Jude lost her life. That was then and this was now.

Sugar did not find loud-laughing, good-time people in the kitchen. Instead what she found were two old women crouched over the large wooden table, peeling potatoes and fussing about something that only carried meaning to them.

When Sara and Sugar entered the kitchen, they stopped bickering and briefly observed the two women. After a short moment they went back to what they were doing, as if the two women were merely a passing wisp of air.

Sara left Sugar standing in the kitchen's entrance and joined her sisters in their potato peeling and bickering.

They don't even know who I am, Sugar thought to herself, as she watched them ignore her.

Sugar composed her thoughts and prepared to speak. But May, the eldest sister, beat her to it.

"Sugar, 'bout time your black ass got here," she said without looking up from her work. "I sent that telegram four whole years ago. Had I known that Western Union moved like a turtle I would have sent it regular mail," she said sarcastically, looking up to meet Sugar's gaze.

May spoke quick and emphasized each word by jabbing the air with the small pointed knife she held.

Like Sara, May's face was weathered and her hair gray. She now wore thick, black-framed glasses. From what Sugar could see, Ruby, who'd said nothing so far, was the only one who still had perfect use of her eyes.

"Go on and wash your hands and git with these here potatoes," May demanded, as she stared over the rims of her glasses. "It's Friday, gal, or have you forgotten what Friday is in this house?" she said and smirked.

Sugar hadn't forgotten. But she wasn't there to peel potatoes or fry fish. She was there to see her mother. There were no signs that another person was living there but she hadn't been upstairs yet. Her mother could be resting, Sugar told herself as she went to the sink to wash her hands clean of the road dust and perspiration.

She decided to humor the Lacey women and sat down to do what she had been told to do.

The Lacey women spoke amongst themselves, each sister picking up where the other left off. They were completely immersed in a world that Sugar had long ago lost her place in. She peeled potatoes and sat quietly, glancing up every once in a while to watch at their gray bobbing heads.

Sugar thought that the steady activity of potato peeling would keep her calm and focused until her mother came in, but it wasn't working. Distress clung to her like syrup, causing her, at times, to become short of breath.

Sugar stood up abruptly and the table rocked a bit as her knee hit into the side.

The other women gave her a quick look.

Sugar half walked and half ran into the parlor. The air seemed lighter there. She gulped it down like fresh well water and leaned, panting, against the wall.

There were beautiful crystal decanters, filled with rich dark brandies and whiskeys, set along the mantel above the fireplace. Sugar snatched one up, removed its bulb-shaped lid, held her head back and allowed the liquor to flow freely into her open mouth.

The liquid hit her stomach like acid and she staggered at the fire it lit there. Tears welled up in her eyes as she broke out in a sweat.

She sat down heavily on the velvet chaise, her legs wide open, decanter, half empty now, still in her grip. She leaned back and closed her eyes against the day.

May's calls from the kitchen for her to return pulled her back and she half walked, half stumbled out of the parlor, taking up a cheap tin ashtray from the table. At the center there were brightly colored letters written as palm trees screaming CALIFORNIA.

Sugar placed the decanter and the ashtray down on the table and moved to the cabinet to retrieve a glass. The women kept their heads bowed as they worked feverishly. Two large bowls were already filled with skinless potatoes.

She sat down and reached into her pocketbook that hung lazily on the back of her chair to pull out a wilted pack of Lucky Strikes. One stick remained and she breathed heavily at the thought of spending the coming hours without cigarettes.

She lit it and pulled deeply. Cigarette dangling from the side of her mouth, she tilted her head slightly as she poured a tall glass of whiskey. She was calming down now. The even flow of the brown liquid and the cigarette smoke that curled above and around her head helped her move into her old self. The Sugar that wasn't scared of much of anything or anyone. The Sugar who had worked the streets of Chicago and Detroit with just a switchblade and her own hard-hitting hands.

The women stopped to look at Sugar and then at one another. Disapproval coated their faces as they watched Sugar knock off three quarters of the whiskey she had just poured into her glass.

Sugar slowly licked her lips, savoring the warmth that spread over her entire body. She took a few more drags of the cigarette and then began peeling potatoes again.

The sound of the sharp blade removing the thick brown skins of the potatoes was the only sound to be heard for some time.

The day stretched into a smoky purple evening. The crickets started up a chorus that would last until dawn. The Lacey women had finally broken their wall of silence. A conversation erupted, filled with low tones and clucking tongues, as the Laceys spoke of Short Junction, past and present.

Sugar realized that their lives had settled into a grandmotherly pace. Friday and Saturday nights no longer found their home filled with loud music, men, women and sex.

They too, like Mary Bedford, had aged and changed. Their famous fried fish and potato salad was now served at church functions and sold at Friday night bingo games.

Sugar, who had finished the decanter of whiskey and who should have been stone drunk, experienced instead a type of relaxed hysteria. She said very little, attempting to keep her composure.

The back door swung open and an aged woman walked in shouting her "Good evening"s and "Howdy do"s.

Sugar stood bolt upright, toppling the decanter and sending the last drops of whiskey sailing the length of the table. The woman gave her a quizzical smile and handed May the town newspaper, exchanged a few pleasantries and left. They hadn't even bothered to introduce her.

Sugar felt like an idiot and told herself to stop watching the door. Stop waiting. You've been without her this long, a few more minutes won't kill you.

The Lacey women were nowhere near to giving an explanation about Sugar's mother. No, they wanted to know about Sugar's life away from Short Junction. They wanted to know why she never took the time to write. They wanted to know how she got a chipped front tooth and what about that split earlobe?

But they especially wanted an explanation for the long crooked scar that ran from beneath her chin and disappeared behind the small collar of her dress.

There was concern in their voices when they asked, but their eyes revealed other thoughts.

Sugar was ashamed to share her ordeal with them. Stories filled with abusive men, broken limbs and nights when her belly burned empty with hunger, her soul with loneliness.

She spoke quickly and briefly about her time in St. Louis, Detroit and Chicago. She avoided the true stories that would explain her scars and made up tales that construed them as light mishaps instead.

The Lacey women eyeballed her and shook their heads as she spoke. They did not give birth to her, but she was their child just the same. They had raised her from a babe, and although she did not suckle at the breast of any of the three women, they knew her well and knew she was lying.

In the end, when Sugar was done talking, she looked up at them and tried to decipher what she saw in their eyes and what she saw frightened her.

Ruby was the first to speak. She started off slowly and softly.

"Sugar, I believes we've kept you waiting long enough. We know why you here and what you come for. But this was our way of letting you feel the way we done, when you ain't come four years ago. Now, we know that you weren't there in St. Louis when the telegram come. But we raised you, and your whereabouts should have been known by us. You should have kept in touch.

"Now, before we go on and tell you 'bout your mamma, let me just say this: We did the best we knew how to raise you. We saw that you ain't go hungry, cold or unclothed. We treated you like you came out from inside of us."

She stopped for a minute. Looked Sugar from head to toe and shook her head, unable to continue. Sara placed a comforting hand on her shoulder and squeezed it tightly. Sara picked up where Ruby left off.

"Can't say we did everything perfect while you was here. We know that now. But we can't go back and change it now. The past is the past, and that's where it belongs—behind you."

Ruby leaped up from the table, suddenly remembering the fish, which was beginning to smoke. Her sudden movement startled Sara, and she lost her chain of thought.

"Uhm, oh yes. See, we feel we did our best where you were concerned. We gave you our name and our love."

Sugar's skin crawled at the word "love." What did the Laceys know of love? Whatever it was they gave her, it wasn't love. She'd seen what love was at Mary Bedford's house. She saw the hugs and kisses that were shared between Mercy and Mary. None of that went on at the Lacey house. Not without a price tag attached to it.

Sara looked down at her hands, away from the frigid expression that had settled on Sugar's face. May nudged her to continue.

"We know you been waiting to hear 'bout your mamma and we know that your feelings for her ain't what it should be. But we want you to understand that it ain't fair for you to judge her by what she done, 'cause she did what she had to do. She had her reasons for running off and leaving you with us like she did. But we glad she chose us, 'cause you brought a lot of joy to this here house."

Sara's voice thickened with emotion and she took the hem of her apron and dabbed at the corners of her eyes.

"When she showed up here four years ago, we was shocked to see her. We ain't heard nothing from her since the day she come and leave you with us. She look real bad. You see, she had the cancer, and that thing had ate her down to near nothing. She was no more than a bag of bones, and almost completely blind," Sara said, and her voice trailed off.

Sugar's heart felt like it had stopped beating a while ago. They were talking about her mother in the past tense. Like she wasn't around. Like she wasn't napping upstairs in one of the rooms or in town shopping for vegetables.

May was the first to see the turmoil in Sugar's face. The rage and despair was blending together and rising quickly to the surface.

"Baby, we are so sorry. So sor—" was all she was able to get out before Sugar exploded. Her fists were clenched so tight you could see the veins straining against the skin. She raised them and shook them in fury at the women.

"You're sorry? You're sorry! Sorry for what? Sorry that she ain't here? Sorry that you made me wait all day long before you told me she ain't here! Or are you sorry for the love you didn't give me the whole time I lived here? Exactly what in the hell are you sorry for? I'll tell you all something . . . you're a bunch of sorry asses, that's what you are!"

The women sat quiet while each word rocked them like a blow.

"Ya'll love me? Really? When I left here ya'll didn't even have the time to look over your shoulders to say good-bye. Ya'll just acted like I was heading down the road somewhere. Didn't even ask me to stay. Love would make you want me to stay." Sugar slumped back down into her chair. She picked up the empty cigarette pack and dug a shaking finger into it, hoping one would be there. There wasn't and she slammed it down hard on the table. "Just tell me where my mama is," she said in a voice that was low and tired.

May, who had been relatively quiet for the most part, stood up slowly. Anger was etched into her face. "Sugar, you don't forget whose house you in. We don't deserve that trash talk. Like we said, we done the best we knew how where you was concerned." She slammed both hands down hard on the table and sent potato peelings flying in all directions.

She walked around to Sugar's side of the table, and for the first time, Sugar realized the woman had acquired a limp. She walked past Sugar and retrieved her cane, which was set in the corner of the room next to the large black cast iron stove. She leaned heavily on the cane and walked out of the kitchen.

No one said a word. No one looked at the others.

When May returned, she carried an envelope, which she flung onto the table. It landed dead in front of Sugar.

"That there is what your mamma leave here for you. You know, the one you always thought ain't give a damn about you," May said sarcastically.

"What she do, write me a letter?" Sugar said in disgust. She would not look at the envelope. "What, she was too afraid to stay around and wait to tell me what she had to say?" Sugar didn't want to hear what she already knew to be true.

May sucked her teeth and said, "You telling me you expected your mamma to wait around for four years? Lord, child, she wasn't able to wait for four days! Weren't you even listening? Your mamma was sick. She was dying. Your mamma come here to try to set things right between the two of you. Your mamma came home to die!" May said and grabbed her hip in pain. She sat down next to Sugar. "She died right here. Right here in this house, waiting on you to come." The words dripped from May's mouth like poison.

There was a long quiet that was broken now and again by a passing car along the outer road. The guilt May's words inflicted welled up inside of Sugar and gushed forth in waves of sorrow. "Why . . . why did she leave me?" Sugar asked between sobs and tears. Ruby shook her head in ignorance. The real story, the truth, would be too hard to repeat and just make it worse for Sugar. Ruby turned her eyes up to the ceiling and quietly asked the Lord for strength. Did she want to tell Sugar of the madness her mama, Bertie Mae, endured under the roof of Ciel Brown? The emotional and physical battering she lived with up until the day she left Short Junction with Ciel's man, Clemon Wilks?

No, she didn't want to tell it, but she did tell Sugar that the day she was born everyone in the Low came out to bear witness to her life. Sugar's wet eyes looked up at her. "True," Ruby said, and embraced her.

The truth be told, Bertie Mae ran scared. Scared that she would go mad and abuse her child like her mother abused her. She'd rather abandon her child than put her through that hell. But Ruby, May and Sara would keep that truth to themselves. Better that truth stay in the ground. Better for all of them.

That evening, when the house was quiet and the only sound

to be heard was the muted sound of music traveling from the small radio in Sara's room, Sugar sat propped up on the bed in her childhood room staring at her mother's envelope.

The unmarked envelope stared back at her from its place on her lap. She traced its sharp borders with her fingers, and turned it over and over in her hands. Long after the music had stopped, she finally peeled it open and removed its contents.

There was a deed to a house and property in Bigelow. There was a will, that clearly stated Sugar as the owner of the house.

A small black and white photograph showed a woman leaning against a tree. Her hands were not visible, they were hidden behind her back, her long hair hung loose and wild about her face. The woman would have looked provocative, had it not been for the sad eyes. Sugar knew those eyes well. She had the same ones.

She flipped the picture over.

Bertie—Waco, Texas, 1928.

The scrawled writing told Sugar this was her mother.

She stood up and went to the large, square mirror that hung on the wall above the dresser. She held the picture up to her face and stared intensely at the vision before her. She wanted so desperately to see something of that woman inside her. Something other than the sad eyes.

Sugar lay back down in the bed, placing the picture gently down on her pillow. She looked down at her hands, and thought how much she wanted to see the hands of her mother. A tear escaped and slid quickly down her cheek.

The envelope also held a newspaper clipping from the Junction *Gazette*. It was an obituary:

Mrs. Ciel Venita Brown

SHORT JUNCTION, ARKANSAS. (January 3rd, 1932)
A colored woman was buried during the night in a casket furnished by the county. Wrapped in a shroud that had once been used as a tablecloth, the emaciated remains of Mrs. Ciel Brown, who died Saturday morning, were taken to a private

cemetery on the edge of town and buried Sunday
night. No friends assisted in preparing the body
for burial and no preacher spoke over the body or
to the grief-stricken sons of the deceased, who
stood by silently.

Mrs. Brown died while in the confines of the
Arkansas State Home for the Insane (Colored
Section). She was taken ill while her son, Abel,
visited with her. There she breathed her last
breath.

She leaves to mourn three sons, Abel, Finis and
Wylam. One daughter, Bertie Mae.

Sugar read the obituary twice. This was her grandmother.
Sugar had uncles. Where would they be? The Lacey women
didn't mention anything about family. Perhaps they didn't know
anything about Bertie's family.

Sugar thought some things were better left as is.

She replaced everything except the picture in the envelope.
She was disappointed that there was no letter. Some comforting
words from her mother to her. She looked at the woman in the
picture and the only word that came to her mind was: Why?

The following morning, as the jay birds perched themselves
on the limbs of the great pine trees and oaks to sing the world
awake, but not before slop jars were emptied or breakfast made
and coffee brewed, the Lacey women pulled their robes tight
against the early morning spring air and led Sugar across the
dewy grass to the edge of the property where her mother was
buried alongside the Lacey ancestors.

Fresh wildflowers, pink, yellow and vibrant purples, covered
the grave like a colorful blanket. The Laceys stepped back a bit
to give Sugar grieving space.

Didn't they know she'd been grieving her entire life?

She thought of the little picture of her mother with the sad
eyes, now wrapped inside the Mary Bedford handkerchief and
pinned safely inside her bra. She touched it gently as she stood
over her grave.

A sudden breeze swept by and shook the weeping willow

limbs that hung heavy above her mother's final resting place. Ruby looked up and pointed toward the branches that still quivered in the aftermath of the breeze.

"That's yo' mamma saying hello," she said, her eyes sparkling with wonder. Sugar smiled up at the sky and mouthed, "Hello mamma."

Knowing each other's past helped both Pearl and Sugar. Secret pains, now told, bonded the women together tighter than anything else in this world.

They held each other and assured each other that better days were coming. Sugar wanted to believe it, but life had taught her otherwise.

Chapter Eleven

"*B*IT, you sure you won't come with me?" Joe asked again as he and Pearl stood watching the train pull into the station. The rush of air it brought in teased at the hem of Pearl's dress, causing it to flutter about her ankles and threaten to rise to meet her knee.

"We done been through this already, honey . . . we go through this every year."

Joe shrugged his massive shoulders in defeat. Pearl had not set foot out of Arkansas in fifteen years. The annual trip they took together each year to visit his family in Florida had come to an end when Jude died, but Pearl had insisted that he continue to go. "Joe, you acting like you gonna miss me or something," Pearl said and slapped playfully at the hand he rested lovingly on her shoulder.

The whistle sounded three times, signaling the departure of train #2438 to all points south. Young and old scrambled around them saying their good-byes. Redcaps moved swiftly through the crowd of people, expertly guiding dollies heavy with large black steamer trunks and beaten luggage to be loaded aboard the train. Children clung to the skirts of their mothers, crying to stay or begging to go along. Lovers pressed lips and bodies together as if it was the last time they would ever touch in that way again.

Joe and Pearl stood in the midst of tears, kisses and smiles and said their own good-byes. Joe kissed her gently on the cheek and Pearl squeezed his hand and smiled lovingly into his eyes. "I'll be back and blacker than ever before you know it." He tweaked her nose and winked and then he was gone on #2438 down the same tracks he helped lay so many years earlier.

Pearl found Sugar sitting on her porch and humming softly to herself. One leg folded beneath her, the other swinging back and forth like a long, brown pendulum trying to keep time with the rest of the world.

"Hey, Miss Pearl," Sugar called to her and waved her over. Pearl sighed heavily, not sure she was in a congenial mood. The heat had drained the little bit of energy it took her to see her husband off. She felt lonely and depressed. At the last minute she wanted to pull Joe back to her and beg him to stay, but she had fought that impulse and had waved instead, offering her biggest and brightest smile. Now she was hot and tired and wanting nothing more than to retire to her empty house.

"Miss Pearl!" Sugar called to her again. She was standing now, hands on her hips, annoyance in her voice. "C'mon!"

"*J*oe get off okay?" Sugar asked as she sipped slowly from a chilled glass.

"Uh-huh," Pearl answered in awe. "How you do that?" she asked, pointing at the frozen glass.

Sugar laughed. "Just put it in the freezer, Miss Pearl!" she said in lazy exasperation. She got up and walked into the house to retrieve another glass for Pearl. Moments later she returned. "Here you go, something to cool you off." She handed Pearl a frozen glass filled with yellowish liquid. Sugar sat down on the steps, giving her chair to Pearl.

They sat quietly for a while watching the day recede and the night stroll in on the back of the cool September evening. "What is this?" Pearl asked after draining the glass dry. The liquid, which went down cold, did not seem to cool her body; instead it ignited a small warm fire in her belly.

"Oh . . . Pike aid," Sugar answered. "You drank it too fast to really appreciate it, though," she said, laughing loosely.

"Pike aid?" Pearl said stupidly and pulled at her collar, allowing a space for the heat to ease out from beneath her dress.

"Uh-huh. Lemonade and corn liquor—"

"What!" Pearl shouted and jumped to her feet. "Corn liquor! Have you lost your mind, child? I don't drink!" She spat on the ground.

"Oh calm down, Miss Pearl, it's just a little dab of it in there, not enough to take any effect on you at all," Sugar said, trying hard to control her laughter. "It's just there to give the taste a little pick me up, is all."

Pearl calmed down a bit. "Well, even so, you should have told me." She looked at the glass. All of the frost had melted away, leaving behind the worn rose pattern that clung to its sides for dear life. "Want another?" Sugar asked innocently.

"I don't suppose I should," Pearl responded, but licked her lips in memory of the first glass.

Sugar smiled and disappeared back into the house to retrieve the pitcher of pike aid. Pearl leaned back in her chair, shaking her head at her own foolishness. "Here you go." Sugar was looming over her, refilling the glass Pearl still held in her hand. "Just a little bit, right?" Pearl's eyes questioned.

"Aw, go on, Miss Pearl, it ain't gonna kill you," Sugar said and stretched her body across the top step.

Pearl took her time with the second glass, enjoying the slight giddiness that was gradually taking over her mind. Her fingertips tingled and she felt a strange quivering in the lower regions of her body. She shot a glance at Sugar to make sure she wasn't watching her, then she squirmed in her chair, trying to quell the sensation between her legs. She patted the damp space between her chin and her chest and searched the sky for clouds.

"Ain't it beautiful, Miss Pearl," Sugar suddenly said in a breathless voice. "Just sky and land for miles, umph!"

Yes it certainly was beautiful. September days were unique in Arkansas. The sky was an enormous, pale blue pallet with white streaks and puffs. In September the horizon lowered itself and it seemed like you could reach up and touch it. The soil turned a deeper, richer brown and the trees, plants and flowers gave their all, knowing that in a matter of weeks fall would claim their brilliancy and tuck it safely away in winter's pocket, keeping it safe till spring.

"I didn't know you noticed those type of things," Pearl said.

Sugar didn't respond. She was beginning to notice quite a few things. Not only notice but appreciate them in a way she never dreamed possible. She smiled at the joy her small observation seemed to bring to Pearl's face.

Pearl sipped quietly and thought of the only other times she had ever digested alcohol. The first was as a servant in the McHenry home, during one of their infamous parties. It was the first party of the summer and rich white folks came from all over Arkansas and neighboring states to take part in the festivities.

Men in starched white and blue seersucker suits and women in long flowing silk dresses that captured every color of the season glided here and there hiding their smiles behind gloved hands or tilting their heads back in polite laughter. Clinking glasses resounded around the property and added to the comically composed festivities. Tennis, lawn bowling and croquet filled the daylight hours before dinner was served. At the drop of the sun, massive quantities of food were laid out beneath huge canopies. Whole pigs lay staring with dead eyes, their mouths stuffed with huge apples. Cornish hens, one for each of the two hundred or more guests, goose liver patés, English crackers, chilled cantaloupe soup, wild rice, pheasant and duck—Pearl saw that the white people certainly did have everything and so much of some things she never thought existed.

The mood would change after the meal. The band, brought in from Mississippi, would play ragtime and Dixieland music for the guests to kick their feet up to. Women would lift their legs to reveal seamed stockings. The liquor would flow like water, ice clinking against glasses; liquid falling out and over onto white patent leather shoes. Oh, a high time was being had.

Laughter became raucous, stories became full-fledged lies and Pearl watched as wives ran their long painted fingernails down the napes of other husbands' necks, while husbands whispered deep into the ears of their partners' wives—or their wives' best friends.

When it was all done, guests gone that could, others that couldn't retired to the many guest rooms, Pearl was left alone on the great lawn, gathering the delicate crystal that still held the liquids that made the guests talk louder and laugh longer. Cigar, cigarette and pipe smoke still clung to dew-wet eaves and the crying branches of the weeping willow trees. She didn't know why she suddenly tilted the glass up to her mouth. It was a quick and jerky motion, as if her hand was guided by something other than her mind. The drink traveled down her throat tickling as it went until it finally reached her stomach and settled there like glowing embers. Oh, the feeling was unique, and the only thing that came close to it was the feeling she got when she thought of her Joe and the way he kissed the under part of her arm.

She could think of the two at once and get a sharp pleasurable stabbing sensation in her womb, one that would keep her feeling silly for hours.

Even now as she sat and reminisced, her stomach contracted and she hid her smile behind a mock cough and her hand.

The second time had not been pleasurable at all. Her wedding night. She and Joe lay together in her own childhood bed, in her room that shared a wall with her parents' room. They spoke in whispers and giggled in the moonlit darkness of her room. She could tell the urgency he had for her. His sex organ pressed against her hip and throbbed there like a second heart. She would not, could not, remove her starched new cotton nightgown given to her by her mother as a wedding gift. She did allow his hands to travel beneath it and explore her virginal body. She was embarrassed by the moans that escaped her, heavier and even more sexual than the ones that emanated from Joe. When his mouth clasped hold of one of her erect nipples, she thought for one split second that her mind would snap.

He could not enter her, even though she was slick. The pain was too much to bear. He placed his hand between her legs and massaged her opening with his finger, he glided it effortlessly in and out until she thought her whole body would fall apart with pleasant convulsions. But when he mounted her again for the third time, she still squirmed against him, pushing him away instead of pulling him forward. He became desperate. "Take a little of this," he said. His voice was thick with want as he guided the small flask of whiskey to her lips. The smell alone intoxicated her, but to please her new husband she drank the whiskey. Moments later her head was spinning and her stomach turning. She spent an hour in the outhouse, puking up her wedding cake. Joe spent some time there afterward too, pleasing himself.

Pearl was consuming her third glass of pike aid, and wondering why the name began to sound familiar to her. She thought hard and long about it, but could not remember. She forced her attention on Sugar, who was smoking a cigarette. For the first time she realized that Sugar did not have on one of her many wigs. Her head was tied with a rag. Her face was absent of makeup, which was a rare occurrence. She looked normal for once, even fresh. Her scantily clad body seemed less threatening without all of the fixtures. In this chaste state, Sugar looked more like Jude than ever before. Pearl looked away and tried to consider something else, but again her vision was drawn back to Sugar. The cigarette smoke sailed over to her and invaded her nose. She coughed a little and fanned it away with her free hand.

"You need to stop that," she said, her voice lagging a bit.

"Stop what?" Sugar said.

"That smoking. You smoke too much and you don't wear enough clothes, either." Pearl was speaking matter of factly, her tone was less than accusing, just tottering on the verge of drunkenness.

Sugar, realizing this, just rolled her eyes and looked back toward the fields.

"Gimmesomemore to drink." Pearl's words spilled out like poor man's pearls, strung together and worthless.

Sugar looked over at her, and realized by the way Pearl was shoving the glass in her direction that she'd probably had too much already.

"I think that might be it for you, Miss Pearl. How about a Coke?" Sugar said, not moving.

Pearl set the glass down between her legs and leaned her head back against the house. "Sugar, don't it make you feel ashamed when you take off your clothes for everyone and anyone?" Pearl asked, curiosity lacing her voice.

"No," Sugar said quickly and shifted her body. She was uncomfortable, knowing what the questioning was leading up to.

"Umph," Pearl grunted and shook her head.

"It ain't no big deal. You take your clothes off in front of Joe all the time. That don't make you feel shame, do it?" Sugar said, a bit sarcastically.

Pearl had never disrobed in front of Joe, in fact when they made love, it was in the thick darkness of their bedroom and her gown was simply lifted above her waist. But that was so long ago; she had not been able to perform that wifely duty since Jude's death. It had been fifteen long years of nothing more than caresses and quick kisses, sleeping with even breath against a neck and a hand settled into the curve of a waist. Joe and Pearl simply shared a bed now and not each other.

Pearl did not respond.

"I feel free when I ain't got no clothes on," Sugar continued.

"How does being naked make you feel free?" Pearl sat up now, wanting to understand Sugar's words.

"I can't explain it, Miss Pearl, it just do."

"I think it's downright disgusting," Pearl said, frustrated because Sugar could offer no valid explanation.

"Well . . . don't knock it until you've tried it."

Pearl huffed. "I don't know nothing about you, Sugar. You live next door and we spend time together, but you still a stranger to me."

Sugar laughed. "Miss Pearl, I see you one of those soupy drunks."

Pearl scratched at her nose. "I ain't drunk." Her words were slurred and she squirmed again against the warm feeling between her legs. "Tell me something, what you think your mamma woulda said 'bout what you do?"

Sugar stiffened at the words. They hit her like pellets. "Okay, Miss Pearl, I think it's time for you to go now." She stood and stretched her long brown frame. Any high she had was quickly seeping from her.

"Y-you think she woulda approved of you being a whore?" Pearl continued, oblivious to the anger that was building up in Sugar.

Sugar flinched at the questions and swallowed hard. She did not want to discuss a mother she never knew.

"She dead. How am I suppose to know what she think?" she said and bent down to snatch up Pearl's empty glass.

"I don't think she wouldalikeditverymuch." Pearl's bottom lip was stuck out and her head began to look too heavy for her neck.

Sugar just smirked.

"You think maybe she was a whore too?" The words fell effortlessly from Pearl's mouth and luckily Sugar had sense enough to realize that Pearl's words were only alcohol induced.

"Miss Pearl, if my mamma was a whore then she did what she felt she had to do. I ain't gonna judge her, cause I don't want to be judged. Anyway, we whores ain't all that different from the rest of you."

Pearl's eyebrows went up. "How you figure that?"

"Well we all got working pussies. We all whores in one way or another—"

"I ain't no whore. I know that for sure!" Pearl exclaimed.

"Yes, you is, Pearl, you and your mamma before you—"

"I ain't no whore!" Pearl was standing now.

"You lay down with your husband and in return he clothe and feed you—keep a roof up over your head. You stop laying with him, all those things disappear." Sugar snapped her fingers for emphasis.

That was not true. And Pearl shook her head insistently no, but she would not tell of what didn't go on in her bedroom. She would not.

"Look here, I do what I have to to put food on my table and clothes on my back and will keep on doing it same as you."

Pearl raised her hands in defeat. She did not want to argue again, but she had Sugar angry now. Sugar's tongue flicked words at Pearl like a whip.

"The only difference between you and me, Miss Pearl, is you began your whoring life in front of a congregation, dressed in white and with God's blessing!"

She slammed into the house, leaving Pearl sorry for speaking at all. Pearl heard the glasses crash into the sink. The refrigerator door opened and slammed closed three times and by the time Pearl's foot landed on the last step Sugar was back on the porch, huffing and puffing like a wild, angry boar.

"You right, Miss Pearl, you don't know me at all. I been on my own since I was fifteen fucking years old. Fifteen! And did you forget how I told you I survived? Have you forgotten!" Sugar's anger had the best of her now. Pearl turned to meet Sugar's enraged eyes but she did not utter a word.

"With my pussy, that's how! Men pay to fuck, eat or smell *my* pussy!"

Pearl blushed at Sugar's use of language; she wanted to throw her hands up to her ears.

Sugar was spent, the anger was mellowing down to simple annoyance now. Her breathing slowed and she sat down heavily on the steps.

"I ain't bad, Miss Pearl, I just ain't had no crossroads in my life is all."

Pearl traced Sugar's jawline with her hand. "Yes you have, child, you just wasn't able to recognize them when you came across them."

Chapter Twelve

*H*ER headache was finally withdrawing. Just to be sure, she took another aspirin and kept the ice pack on her head. Her first hangover at sixty. She laughed out loud in the five o'clock darkness of her bedroom. She thought of Joe and her stomach trembled. She moved her hand across the empty space his absent body left in their bed. Not one full day had passed and she was already missing him as if he had been gone for twenty.

Her body was weak from the pike aid and lack of food. Cooking was something she did not want to consider after the heat and angry words from Sugar; the cans of tuna fish stacked in the cupboard would remain stacked until another day. Her mouth craved barbecue, but her feet would not carry her to town to get it. Perhaps buttered bread and a cup of tea, she thought.

Shortly before seven Pearl found herself eating exactly what she craved. Sugar appeared at her front door with two barbecue rib dinners, complete with corn bread and potato salad and Coca-Cola.

Sugar seldom visited Pearl's home, and when she did, she never left the confines of the kitchen; her visit was always short. Pearl felt they both preferred it that way. Pearl was uncomfortable having her around Joe; Sugar was uncomfortable with Pearl's apparent uneasiness having her there. But today they sat and listened to the radio.

Sugar bore another bag, a large heavy brown paper sack, its top rolled tightly closed. Pearl eyed it on and off, wanting to know exactly what it contained, but Sugar made no effort to disclose its contents to her.

"Miss Pearl, I got something I wanna do to you," Sugar said as they cleared the table of the dinner remnants.

"What?" Pearl was surprised at her statement. "What you want to do to me?" she said suspiciously.

"C'mon," Sugar said and grabbed the brown sack and headed up the stairs.

"W-wait a minute," Pearl said and rushed to follow her.

Sugar found herself standing in the upstairs hall of Pearl and Joe's house. The differences were few. Pearl's floors were bare, the unfinished floors dull against the old beige wallpaper with the tiny light blue flowers. Sugar turned into the bathroom. Unlike her own bathroom, Pearl's walls were painted white, and butterscotch towels, washcloths and hand towels added brightness to the room, even though it was dead darkness outside the window. "Sit down," Sugar said as she dropped the toilet seat down.

"What are you up to?" Pearl asked and sat down after a slight moment of hesitation.

"You need a new look, Miss Pearl. Not that there is anything wrong with the look you have now, it's just that it's too Bigelow," Sugar said, her hands fiddling with Pearl's tight bun trying to find the pins and release it from its present confined state.

"Stop it," Pearl said and tried to slap Sugar's hands away. "Ain't nothing wrong with my look." And then curious now, "What you plan on doing?"

Sugar stood back and placed her hands on her perfectly curved hips. She still wore the denim shorts and bright orange tank top she'd lounged in on the porch earlier that day.

"I plans on making you look forty instead of . . . fifty?"

Sugar questioned and leaned forward, hoping Pearl would reveal her age.

Pearl blushed, joyful that Sugar had missed her true age by ten years. "I believe I look just fine," Pearl said and turned her bashful smile away from Sugar.

"I ain't say you don't, all I'm saying is that you could look better, better than fine."

They laughed together, and Pearl did not resist when Sugar went at the bun again. "Lord, Miss Pearl, you've got a whole head full of hair, pretty too," Sugar said as her fingers played in Pearl's long, thick mane. "Why you always wear it up? You hiding it from someone?" Pearl shook her head no and placed her hands over her mouth, hiding the smile that was plastered to her lips.

"First off, the gray has got to go." Sugar reached into the bag and pulled out a dark bottle of liquid.

"What's that?" Pearl said, looking around Sugar to eye the bottle.

"Dye. Dye for your hair."

"Oh no!" Pearl said, trying to stand. Sugar pushed her back down on the toilet.

"Just be still, Miss Pearl. Trust me, I know what I'm doing."

Pearl sat shaking as Sugar parted her hair into sections and squeezed the dark liquid onto it. She listened to Sugar talk about her time in St. Louis, the time when Sullivan Place was hot and Mary Bedford's house was the place to be. She did not explain in full exactly why it was so, but Pearl got the gist that it was a whorehouse, and she held her tongue still from speaking against it. "I usta dye a lot of heads then. No one ever wanted to have their own hair color. Always red or blond. Ha, me, I never went in for all that, I was happy with my wigs."

Pearl listened and prayed that her hair would not simply slip off her head and drop to her tiled floor. The only person she had allowed on her head for years was Fayline. Every other Thursday at two, a wash and press and then back into the bun. She herself barely dislodged her bun, except to take it down to give her head a good scratching and greasing.

By nine o'clock Pearl came face to face with a woman that she'd known so many years earlier. She stood and stared open-mouthed at herself in the mirror, unable to believe that the woman who grinned back at her was indeed her.

"Oh my Lord," were the only words she could repeat over and over again.

Her hair hung limp and wet, shining blacker than night around her face. She stood that way for a while, running her fingers through her hair, and pulling at the curls that had begun to take hold of it as it dried in the humid house air.

"You look beautiful, Miss Pearl," Sugar said. She, too, was amazed. A bottle of dye had weeded out the age that had grown there.

"You miss her, she sure look like she been missing you, Miss Pearl," Sugar said as she coiled Pearl's hair into a French roll, leaving ringlets of curls to hang loose around her face.

"I ain't never seen her before," Pearl said in profound awe. She touched her face lightly, afraid that any contact with her fingers would cause the vision before her to waver and then distort, like a disturbed reflection in a pool of water.

"Joe is gonna love you, Miss Pearl!" Sugar yelled in delight and clapped her hands together like a gleeful child.

Joe's name brought Pearl back to reality. "Oh no," she whispered. Her face took on a fretful look. She turned to Sugar, wringing her hands, tears formed in her eyes. "Oh Lord . . . Joe?" How could she have forgotten that she had a husband? She'd made a decision, a drastic decision without consulting her husband. Suppose he hated it? Suppose he hated her for having done it?

"Oh Sugar, what have you done?" Pearl shrieked and dragged her hands down the length of her face, as if the very action would somehow change her black hair back to the ravaged gray it'd been just minutes ago.

Sugar looked on, bewildered at Pearl's sudden reaction. She was hurt.

"Miss Pearl," she started slowly, "what do you mean, what have I done? What I've done was make you look younger, beautiful. What's wrong with that?"

Pearl did not respond, she just stood staring at herself and shaking her head in dismay.

"What you want me to do, turn you back? Make you look old again?"

"I am old!" Pearl screamed and pushed past Sugar.

Sugar followed her into the bedroom. "You're older, not old, Miss Pearl," Sugar said. Pearl sat down on the bed and placed her head in her hands. Sugar leaned against the wall and examined the tight neatness of the room. The room lacked life. By instinct, Sugar knew nothing close to sexual passion had occurred there in a long time.

"You know what you need? You need to go out. Get away from this house, this town," Sugar said. She walked over to Pearl and knelt down beside her. "Miss Pearl, why you acting like your life is over? It's just a dye job. In time the gray will come back."

"Before Joe gets back?" Pearl asked hopefully.

"No, not by then," Sugar said with a wisp of a smile. "C'mon, we going out and show you off."

Pearl looked at Sugar as if she'd gone mad. "Out? Out where?" Pearl's eyes sparkled in spite of herself.

Sugar just smiled. "Just get dressed," she said. "I'll be back." And then she was gone. Pearl heard the front door close and quick footsteps move the few feet down the pavement to #10 Grove Street.

Pearl sat on her bed staring at the floor. Periodically she would look over at the worn Bible that sat conspicuously on the nightstand beside the bed. Its black cracked cover seemed to fill the whole room and dwarf her. There was nothing in the Bible that said you shouldn't dye your hair. There were no words that said, Thou shalt not befriend a whore. No, Pearl knew the Bible from cover to cover, and those shalt not's did not exist.

Pearl got up and went to the full-length mirror that stood in the corner of her room. She stood before it and looked at herself, the new her. She fingered her hair, soft, silky and black. She touched her face, ran her fingers over the face that was absent of wrinkles. Her eyes held her age, not the skin on her face. Slowly, methodically, without being totally conscious of her movements, she began to disrobe. She slipped her dress over her head. The slip followed, as did the brassiere and stockings and panties. She stood before herself, her naked self, and began to re-familiarize herself with her body.

The once flat stomach was rounded and protruded forward; it was scarred with motherhood marks three times over. If she could, she would not even sell those long, black marks that crisscrossed her abdomen, no, they made up who she was—a mother.

The breasts that once sat high and curved now sloped, but did not sag. Her hips were thicker, rounder, and so were her legs. She turned to examine her behind. It was large, expanded by time and good eating. All in all, Pearl did not have a body unworthy of wanting. She released the French roll and let her hair cascade down onto her shoulders. Wild, black waves of hair. She giggled to herself and hurriedly covered her mouth with her hands.

The night was dawning dark blue as the full moon took its place high above Bigelow, giving light to dark back roads and lost souls. A breeze kicked up, late-night September air that prepared you for October and beyond moved through the open window, provoking the curtains into shrill and frenzied movements. Without thinking, Pearl moved to close the window, and in doing so, exposed herself to the night. She stopped, but did not draw back. The night air moved seductively across her naked body. It was tantalizing and invigorating. Slowly, the night caressed her, transforming her nipples into resistant pebbles and teasing the small, pointed, pink flesh between her legs. Pearl parted the curtains and leaned the top part of her body out of the window, allowing her breasts to sway slowly in the night air. The night welcomed her nakedness. It felt so good, so right, so free. Suddenly, she understood.

This sudden empathy she felt for Sugar sent her reeling back from the open window. She snatched her clothes up from the floor and wrapped them, best she could, around her nakedness. What was she if she was able to take part in, understand and even enjoy an act that was clearly amoral? Had her acceptance of Sugar made her susceptible to her low-down traits? Was being a whore like having a flu—could you catch it like the diseases that hid and floated invisible in the air?

A shaken, unsure laugh bounced off the walls. "I'm being so stupid," Pearl said aloud and dropped her clothes back down to the floor. She started toward the closet door to retrieve her gown from the hook it hung on during the day. As she went, she caught, once again, the naked sight of herself in the mirror and something in her smiled.

"What you gone and done?" Sugar stood before Pearl, dressed in a dress so tight, it was as if her body was smeared with red paint and dusted with white gardenias. The tops of her breasts sat recklessly at the edge of the low curved neckline and jiggled like currant jelly with each draw of breath she took. "Why ain't you dressed, and why is your hair all undone?"

" 'Cause it's bedtime, that's why," Pearl said solemnly and looked back at the open Bible in her lap. Sugar shifted her feet and swung her tiny red handbag onto the bed.

"It ain't, either, Miss Pearl. You ain't gonna sleep on my hard work and time. We going out to show you off. I don't give a shit what you say!" She grabbed Pearl by the shoulders and pulled her into a standing position.

Pearl raised tired eyes to Sugar's face. A glint of newfound knowledge lingered in her dark eyes. Sugar recognized it, she'd seen it in her own eyes some time ago. She walked over to Pearl's closet and began rummaging through the frugal, dreary-colored dresses that hung there. Dress after dress she pulled from the closet, examined and then tossed to the bed. "Ain't you got nothing a little spicy?" Sugar asked in frustration.

Pearl was sitting again, flipping through her Bible. Every once in a while she would throw a look over her shoulder to see Sugar's progress. Her mouth was tired of saying no, she could not remember having to use the word so often in her whole life, except of course when she was raising her children.

"I guess this will have to do." Sugar held out a long pale pink dress. It was sleeveless, and had a large white collared neckline that came together as a huge bow in the front. The bottom was a million tiny pleats. Pearl turned to see what Sugar had found mildly approving. It was a dress her son Seth had given her for her birthday. It was a beautiful dress, but Pearl never wore it. She always imagined a younger woman wrapped in its silky cloth, but she could not bring herself to part with it, and so it hung at the back of the closet waiting for Pearl to remove it, admire its print and the sweeping sound of its material, only to place it back in the closet until she was moved to do it again.

"I ain't wearing that," Pearl said. She saw Sugar smile a little. "And I ain't going," she quickly injected and shook her finger at Sugar.

"I said you are."

"Ain't."

"Are too!"

"Ain't." Pearl was unmovable.

"Okay, Miss Pearl, what can I say or do that will convince you to go?"

"Nothing."

Sugar looked down at the old woman. Pearl's lips moved silently as she read her Bible. Sugar sighed and began surveying the room again. A small cross sat on the wall over the bed, and another, fashioned out of palm leaves, rested atop a jar of Vaseline on the dresser. Sugar suddenly realized how she could persuade her.

"If you go . . . I'll come to church with you."

Pearl's lips stopped moving and she raised her eyes to meet Sugar's.

"You can have me for a month of Sundays," Sugar continued. She was grieving inside. Church wasn't the place she wanted to spend her free time, but she knew that was probably the only way Pearl would agree to go. What she didn't know, was why it was so important to her that Pearl actually went.

Pearl closed her Bible and considered Sugar's offer. Sugar craved a cigarette, but instead bit her thumbnail in anticipation.

"Two months of Sundays," Pearl said, holding up a pair of fingers.

Sugar bit her lip, and then in surrender she said, "Okay, two months."

The dress hugged Pearl's hips a little too snugly, and embraced her bosom like an old familiar friend. She kept tugging at the material, hoping that she could stretch it loose.

"Stop it," Sugar said and slapped Pearl's hands away from the material. "You look just fine." She was applying a light dusting of baby powder to Pearl's face.

"That lipstick is too bright," Pearl said and shrunk back as Sugar tried to apply the flaming red lipstick to Pearl's lips.

"It ain't. That stuff you got there is too boring and too damn old," Sugar said, referring to the fifty-cent, doughy pink lipstick Pearl had tried to give to her. It *was* old, and was already in the beginning stages of decay.

"I ain't putting that loud color on my lips." Pearl turned her lips inside her mouth and folded her arms across her chest like a stubborn child.

"Okay, okay. Have it your way, then," Sugar said and threw the lipstick back in her bag.

Pearl looked like a doll. Her hair was back in the French roll, her eyelids lightly dusted with blue shadow. The color wasn't completely flattering to Pearl's skin color, or Sugar's for that fact, it was just a wild ocean that raged on your face and called attention to your eyes. Pearl put on her Sunday fake pearls, but Sugar made her take them off.

"You ain't going to church, Miss Pearl."

Pearl kept examining herself in the mirror, still unsure that it was her that looked back at her.

"So where are we going and how are we getting there?" Pearl asked. She was beginning to sweat and would need to move out to the front porch soon to try and catch a breeze.

"I gotta friend coming by to get us," Sugar said as they walked down the stairs.

"What kinda friend?" Pearl asked suspiciously.

"The kind that drives a brand new car and pays for everything," Sugar said, finally giving in to her craving and pulling her pack of cigarettes from her bag. They were on the front porch now, Sugar leaning over the railing and peering down the dark road. Pearl went into her own pocketbook, a hard black leather bag that she'd had for years, and pulled out a stick of Doublemint. "Umph," she said to Sugar's back as she popped the stick of gum in her mouth. She pulled at her dress again, and wiped at the blush on her cheeks.

"Will you stop that," Sugar screeched.

"Maybe this ain't a good idea." Pearl was having second thoughts. The night air had cleared her mind. She finally realized the extent of her commitment and the approaching headlights made her mindful of the possible consequences involved.

"Oh, Miss Pearl, you only gotta worry about one thing."

"What's that?" Pearl said, concern in her voice.

"You just gotta remember you is a married woman and tell all them men that's gonna be sniffin' around you that you already got a man!" Sugar laughed out loud, her laughter competing with the approaching car's motor. "Here he is."

Sugar walked slowly down the stairs, her body swaying in time with Pearl's quickening heartbeat. Pearl could see that with every step, Sugar was transforming into the Sugar that worked the night, the Sugar that appeared in the dreams of men and whose name, usually during heightened passion, suddenly rested on the tips of their tongues.

"C'mon, Miss Pearl." After a brief exchange with the man behind the wheel, Sugar called to her. Pearl looked up and down the dark street and half walked, half ran to the car, hoping to get safely inside before she was spotted.

The driver's door opened and out stepped a white man. Well, what Pearl thought was a white man. The same white man she saw passing between their houses that early morning not so long ago. She took in too much air and began coughing.

"You okay, Miss Pearl?" Sugar was next to her now, patting hard on her back.

Pearl blinked the tears away and looked again at the man before her.

"This here is Lappy. Lappy Clayton. Lappy, this here is Miss Pearl Taylor."

Lappy smiled and his gold tooth sparkled under the moon-light. He took Pearl's hand, bent his head and tried to kiss it, but before his lips could brush against her hand, she snatched it away. Terror, then confusion, glistened in her eyes.

"Nice to meet you," he said, mildly annoyed at her reaction.

"Same here," Pearl muttered and looked down at the ground. What she'd seen in his face, or thought she'd seen, would not allow her to look directly at him.

"Well, ya'll ready to have a good time?" he said as he opened the driver's side door, pushed his seat forward and stood back so Pearl could climb in. She hesitated, but Sugar was already in, beckoning her to hurry.

Pearl sat quietly in the backseat trying to avoid looking at the sneaky eyes that watched her in the rearview mirror. She shifted her body, said the Lord's Prayer and looked out into the darkness.

*F*orty minutes later they came to a stop. Pearl was shaking; she looked out the window and saw a large wooden shack that was supported on slate-colored mason stones. Christmas lights—red and green—were hung around the doorway and carelessly from the sloping roof. It stood in the center of a wide open field. Large trees bordered the land and Pearl could hear the sound of water moving restlessly behind it.

The shack vibrated and shook under the weight of five dozen stamping feet, as the people kept time with the soprano and the piano that wailed away inside.

"It's okay, Miss Pearl," Sugar assured her for the hundredth time that night as they stepped over the threshold and into the smoky abyss called the Memphis Roll.

They sat down at a tiny round table that was covered with a purple-and-black-checked tablecloth. One lone candle sat in its center, the flame threatening to give in to the night wind that slipped in through the aging rafters.

Pearl kept her head bowed. She felt nothing but pure shame

for being there; it pulsed through her body, contaminating her arteries, threatening to extinguish the remnants of her moral character.

"Drink?" Lappy was leaning over her, the candlelight illuminating his gold tooth. Pearl could smell his cologne and the stink of his breath. "Uh, no—no thank you." She responded without raising her eyes to meet his.

"Bring her a beer, and you know what I like," Sugar said as she lit a cigarette.

Pearl looked at her over the dancing flame. Sugar avoided her and turned her attention to the large mass of people swirling around them. Too much skin and loud let-go laughter clothed in hot tangerines, blood reds and hot pinks made up the women. Quiet, slanted-eyed Negroes that moved like serpents through the crowd and sported slick suits made up the men.

Lappy, dressed in a saffron-colored suit, pushed through the crowd, making his way toward the bar, stopping every few feet to shake an outstretched hand, slap a back or pinch a curved tight ass. Pearl watched him disappear into the crowd and wished that it would swallow and digest him, finally discharging him as the shit she knew he was. She tried to convince herself that Joe's leaving and the heat of the day were to blame for the departure she'd obviously taken from her senses. But now, she felt something else had a hand in things. It would have to be the case—either there was a greater force at work, or she was going mad, because what she saw, or what she thought she saw when Lappy took her hand in front of her house, was unsteadying enough to make her want to have the drink that Sugar had requested he bring back for her.

Men circled the table like vultures; their eyes caressed Sugar's body, their hands took brief liberties on her knee. They knelt down beside her and spoke into her bosom, or had a conversation with her leg. Her face and who she was were of no concern to them, and they made no attempt to pretend that it was.

Upon Lappy's return, the men scattered. He set a bottle of beer in front of Pearl and a glass of whiskey before Sugar and took his seat.

"This your first time, Miss Pearl?" Lappy asked. He spoke to her in a loud, slack voice usually reserved for friends.

"Yes," Pearl said. She did not want to talk to this man and absolutely did not want to look at him again, especially his hands—those pale long things, adorned with gold and glass. No, to look at his hands again would send her screaming from the Memphis Roll and down the dark road that brought them there. Because when she looked at his hands, she saw fresh, dripping blood.

"*T*hank you all for being here at the Memphis Roll. For all of you who ain't never been here before, welcome. And for the rest of you—ain't you got noplace else to be?"

The short, dark, round-faced man had a booming voice; it rolled like thunder over the lofty levels of laughter and conversation. People waved their hands at him in amusement and begged him to bring on the band. He told a few more jokes, none that even brought a wisp of a smile to Pearl's face.

A group of men entered through a side door and took their place on the small makeshift stage that was directly in front of Sugar and Pearl's table. A piano, guitar and drum set awaited them. The shack was quiet, except for the sound of people ordering drinks and chicken frying in a room behind the bar area. The band struck up and played tune after tune that ignited the shack, causing men and women to grab at each other and then send each other in wide, wild circles. They separated and came together again in a slow steady grind.

The temperature rose as the music became more feverish. The band members were soaked with sweat, but did not seem to tire beneath the music they put forth. The floor was alive beneath Pearl's feet and more than once she caught herself bopping her head or tapping her feet to the music, before she quickly composed herself.

Sugar yelled obscene praises to the band while slapping her thighs and keeping time with their frantic harmony. "Ya'll is too damn hot tonight!"

The music had hold of the people, compelling them to dig deeper into the rent, bill or mortgage money they foolishly carried with them. "Shiiiit! Pour me another!" reverberated throughout the shack as people slammed dollar after hard-labored dollar on the bar, pushing further and further back the consequences of their pleasure. Eviction, screaming wives, hostile husbands and hungry babies. They would deal with that when the sun fulfilled the promise of another day. For now there were good times to be had, and good times cost.

The band took a break, and people retired breathlessly to their tables, dark corners and the comfort and support of a wall.

"Ain't they hot, Miss Pearl?" Sugar's voice was filled with excitement and she continued to snap her fingers to the memory of the music that lingered in her mind. Pearl nodded in agreement. During the chaos, Lappy had disappeared. Pearl searched the crowd and spotted him pushed up against another woman. Pearl looked quickly away. Her watch told her it was almost three a.m.

"You think we could get going?" she said above the noise.

Sugar couldn't answer, the round-faced man was back.

"Right about now we gonna have our girl belt out a couple of tunes for you." His eyes fell on Sugar. Pearl blinked, and was sure she misunderstood his meaning.

"C'mon people, and give the lovely Miss Sugar Lacey a nice Memphis Roll welcome!"

Hands came together at a quick and deafening rate. Sugar turned, faced the crowd and did a little curtsey. Pearl's mouth dropped wide open.

Three songs later the crowd begged for more. The fifth and final song brought down the house and Sugar had to fight her way off the stage. "Let's go," she said and grabbed at the hand of a dumbfounded Pearl. "Miss Pearl, you better close your mouth, you likely to catch something other than flies in here."

They fought their way out of the Memphis Roll, the exit continually interrupted by someone who wanted to commend Sugar on her performance. Once outside, beneath the flushed dawn, Pearl finally found her voice.

"Why ain't you never said you can sing?" she asked in awe.
Sugar shrugged her shoulders.

"You got a voice worthy of angels and you choose to do . . .
what you do?"

"Let's not start." Sugar's voice was stern.

Pearl shook her head in utter bewilderment. They walked
across the field that was wet with morning dew. The car was
gone, and Pearl found solace in that. She'd rather walk back to
Bigelow than get back in that car with Lappy Clayton.

"Shit," Sugar said under her breath. They turned and started
back toward the shack. People were spilling out now. Some
stumbled and fell flat to the ground, while others linked arms
with friends, shoes in hand, and started down the road home.

Isaac, the round-faced emcee who was also the owner of the
Memphis Roll, took them home in his beat-up pickup. The ride
was bumpy and the truck slow. Discarded soda bottles and candy
wrappers littered the floor and the seats.

"I been trying to get Sugar to let me manage her. She could
make a lotta money with her voice," Isaac confided in Pearl. "I
got's a lot of connections in the music business and everyone
that work the chitlin circuit gotta play at the Memphis Roll!"

The truck groaned as Isaac shifted into third gear.

Sugar sat sleeping between them, her head resting on Pearl's
shoulder. In her sleep she was the image of innocence—not a
whore or flashy juke joint singer—just Sugar.

"I dunno, I'm all talked out . . . maybe you can talk some
sense into her hard head," Isaac said in exasperation.

"I'm gonna try," Pearl said as the sun followed them into
Bigelow.

Chapter Thirteen

*T*HE shop was filled with searing sounds as hot combs killed kinks in the Bigelow women's hair. The radio brought sounds from the world that mixed in among the Saturday conversation. Women complained about the dryers being too hot, flinched at the sting of the relaxer placed on an over-scratched head, but most of all, they talked about the happenings in and around Bigelow, especially Grove Street.

"Fayline, you say that woman been in here?"

"Naw, ain't come in, just walked by. Sometimes stopping to look, but ain't never step in."

"You wouldn't let her in, would you?"

"Hell no!"

"Good thing."

"Sure 'nuff."

"She been spending a lot of time with Pearl."

"Pearl Lawrence?"

"No, girl, Pearl Taylor!"

"Is that right?"

"Right as rain."

"Hmmm, ain't Pearl heard 'bout that woman?"

"Ain't you heard? Of course she has . . . probably just don't believe it though."

"What's there not to believe?"

"You know how Pearl is. Naive 'bout lots of things. Life things. Anyways, she got Pearl doing all sorts of strange things."

"Really, like what?"

"Well you should know . . ."

"Me? Know what?"

"Well didn't you dye her hair? Fayline? Fayline, honey, I think that curl is done now, you can take the curling iron out. Fayline!"

"Oh, s-sorry."

"Jeez . . . damn Fayline."

"Don't mess with it, just let it cool off. It'll be okay. So you say she dyed her hair?"

"Black as night."

"Well, shit on me."

"Shit on that woman."

Ring—Ring—Ring

"Hey girl."

"Anna Lee."

"Josephine. Fayline."

"You got a wait ahead of you."

"I ain't here to get my hair done. I'm here to tell you something about someone."

"Oh, who?"

The women looked cautiously at Josephine. "Aw, you don't have to worry about Josephine."

"Yeah, well, when the shit hits the fan, and it will, I don't want nobody bringing it back to me."

"Talk, girl."

"I seen Pearl and that woman last night."

"We was just talkin' 'bout them. Audrey! Go get Miss Mable from under that dryer, she about done. Go on girl, tell it."

"I seen them at the Memphis Roll last night."

"Pearl?"

"Uh-huh, her and that whore."

"Pearl at a juke joint? You sure your eyes seeing right?"

"I ain't blind, Fayline, I know what I saw. She was dressed all loose and drinking up a storm."

"See?"

"See what, Josephine?"

"I was just telling Fayline about Pearl's strange behavior since that woman moved here. Her hair was dyed, wasn't it?"

"Now that you mention it, there was something different about her hair. She had a lot of makeup on too."

"Get out of here, Anna Lee! Pearl Taylor?"

"She was dancing around and hiking up her dress. It was a shame."

"What were you doing there?"

"W-what . . . We ain't talking 'bout *me*, are we?"

"Where Joe at?"

"He outta town, Red told me he went down to Florida to visit with his people."

"And he ain't take Pearl?"

"You know she don't go nowhere since Jude."

Silence.

"Well, he better hurry on back here and set his wife straight."

"Well, shoot, he ain't gotta if'n he don't wanna. Plenty of women be ready to take her place."

"Like you, Anna Lee?"

"Humph."

"I hear you wouldn't mind being Mrs. Taylor, Fayline."

"Go on with that bullshit!"

"What ya'll talking 'bout over there?"

"Shoot."

"Ain't nothing, Shirley."

"It's something all right, ya'll been huddled whispering and cackling like a bunch of hens over something, not nothing, and I wanna know what it is, so tell me."

"She ought to know, she know Pearl better than the rest of us."

"That's true."

"What you say about Pearl?"

"She was at a juke joint last night."

Shirley stumbled forward as if the words themselves shoved her. "Shirley, you all right? Sit down, sit down and breathe. You need some water, Miss Shirley?"

"What you say?"

"She said Pearl was at a juke joint. Her and her *new friend*!"

"Anna Lee, please."

"Well she ain't heard you the first time."

"The devil is at work."

"Sure is."

"Shirley, she done dyed her hair, too!"

"Stop it, Anna Lee."

"She should know."

"Lord have mercy. Lemme use your phone, Fayline, I gotta call my sister. We gotta go on over there and reintroduce the Lord back into Pearl's life."

"Sure, Shirley, you know where it is."

"She was wearing makeup and drinking too."

"Enough already, Anna Lee!"

"Uh, Shirley, you want me to doll up your wig a little before you go?"

*P*earl's character was stretched, tugged and pulled until her name only left grainy particles of soil on the tongue of anyone who spoke it. She had become, in the eyes of the most influential women of Bigelow, nothing more than dirt.

"You sick? You look terrible." Shirley was peering through the screen door at Pearl, patiently waiting for her to open it. "I came right over when—" She stopped herself, she really had no good reason for being there except to pry. "You sick?" she said again.

"No, just a little tired." Pearl's voice floated through the gray that surrounded and concealed her from Shirley's bulging eyes. It was nearly two in the afternoon and she had not parted the curtains or opened the windows to let in the sunshine and warm fall air. Sleep had not taken her until late in the morning, when her body and mind were finally able to put aside the events of the evening.

She reluctantly opened the door; her better sense told her to send Shirley away.

"Jesus, Mary and Joseph, what have you done to yourself!" Shirley shrieked as she stepped through the doorway, Minnie following close behind. Pearl sighed; she had not noticed Minnie. Now she would have to contend with the two of them.

Shirley and Minnie scrutinized the woman that stood before them, her eyes red and swollen from lack of sleep and from watching wide-eyed at a world she'd never known. Pearl's hair was wild about her head and its newfound blackness almost sparkled against the rays of the sun. They followed her to the kitchen, looking over their shoulders to see the dress thrown over the banister and amber brown stockings lying like driftwood on the staircase. The women exchanged glances and wondered what awaited Pearl at the top of the stairs, in the bed. Thoughts of infidelity ran wild through their minds and their mouths watered at the illicit image.

"Why your clothes thrown all over the stairs, Pearl?" Shirley was the first to ask. She questioned her in a wary voice.

Pearl breathed in again, and turned the flame on under the teapot.

"Is Joe back yet?" Minnie had not ventured completely into the kitchen, she stood in the doorway staring up the stairway, trying to hear the heartbeat of the man she knew for sure lay in waiting.

"He ain't due back till next week sometime." Pearl's response was sober. She didn't want to play the game with them. She was all too familiar with how they handled things, asked questions, heard the answers they wanted to hear and then went out into the small world of Bigelow and told the story they wanted to tell.

"I—I called you last night and you wasn't here. Where were you?" Shirley adjusted her glasses and folded her arms across her breasts, waiting for Pearl to lie.

" 'Round what time?"

"What?" Shirley hadn't expected a question to her question. She was thrown off. "I believe it was about eight or eight-thirty." Her voice was unsure and she looked back at Minnie, who'd taken a step closer to the stairway.

"Oh, I was here." Pearl began clearing the table.

"Maybe it was later then." Shirley pulled out a chair and sat down.

"Hmmm, how late?"

Another question. Shirley scratched at her wig.

"Listen, Pearl, I heard you was in some juke joint. Is that true?" Shirley's voice came out as a controlled scream. Veins stood out on her chicken-thin neck in frustration.

"Do you think it is?" Pearl looked directly at her. The look alone was persuasion enough to get Shirley moving. She stood quickly, upsetting the chair and sending it toppling to the floor. "That girl done put some roots on you! You ain't use to be like this. You done changed, Pearl, and it ain't for the better either! I can't believe Joe would approve of what been going on here in his absence—"

"What you know about what *my* husband approves of?"

Pearl's words were hot. Shirley backed away from her. She would not turn her back on Pearl and so she walked backward to the front door. Minnie, who'd made it to the third step, quickly moved in behind her sister.

"So nice of ya'll to come by. See you in church tomorrow," Pearl said smiling and softly closed the door.

$\mathcal{B}$efore visiting Pearl the women had made a decision. Shirley, Minnie, Clair Bell and a few others, each for their own reasons, decided to confront the evil spirit that had entered their town. They discussed their plan of action amidst the shampoo, hair grease and plastic curlers of Fayline's Beauty Shop. Words of discord, unlike any that had been spoken in Bigelow since slavery times, flew between them like cat-o'-nine-tails.

Anna Lee had only seen Sugar in town, buying vegetables or picking up packages. She'd thought nothing more of her than as a brightly clad woman, cursed black. To Anna Lee's dismay Sugar did not seem to mind this at all. Anna Lee's suitors, men that once lined up at her door just because she was half of something they could never own outright, now ignored her, choosing instead to pay Sugar for whatever it was they needed, rather than come to Anna Lee.

She had not had a long-stemmed rose left on her porch since Sugar's arrival. No small wrapped surprises left between the letters in her mailbox, or midnight telephone calls from men who professed their love in hushed tones, while their wives slept beside them. Sugar had taken all of that away from her. Anna Lee felt it was her birthright to have all of the attention of the Bigelow men. She was the half-breed of the town, the illegitimate child of Abraham the white storekeeper, the silky-haired girl with the dove gray eyes, tight high ass and abundant bosom. She should be the pinnacle of Bigelow's black male desires, so she felt, not Sugar. Anna Lee wanted her gone.

Fayline wanted Sugar gone. At least six of her customers had started wearing wigs they'd ordered from the back of a movie star magazine. Sugar was taking food out of her mouth. Those women no longer needed to come in every other week for a wash and press.

To make it worse, Sugar had also taken a man out of her bed. Or she assumed as much. Cyrus Green wasn't a man of substance or good looks, but he had shared her bed twice a week for the past ten years. She was barren and would not bear him children, which meant he could do anything he wanted to Fayline and the only thing she would produce for him would be groans of pleasure and squeals of delight. Groans and squeals did not require feeding or clothing.

Over the years, Fayline had grown used to seeing his overalls hanging on her bedpost, his large straw hat resting on her bureau. She was accustomed to kissing his fingers, the nails dense with dirt, and the way his tongue tickled her thick belly. She boiled over at the thought of Cyrus smiling down on the ass of Sugar Lacey.

Yes, Fayline wanted her gone.

Shirley, Minnie and Clair Bell wanted her gone because Sugar represented all that was wrong with Bigelow, and nothing had seemed wrong with Bigelow until right before Sugar Lacey had waltzed into town. They still consoled the women who'd lost their children during the spring. The Bigelow five. And now those same women and quite a few more confided to them amidst tears and wringing hands the fact that their men were often absent from their beds, paid little attention to their living children and always seemed too tired to slop the hogs or clean the barn.

Shirley, Minnie, Clair Bell and the rest of the Bigelow women all wanted Sugar gone.

*T*hings had not gone well at Pearl's house. Shirley and Minnie returned to Fayline's and it was decided. The four of them: Fayline, Clair Bell, Minnie and Shirley, climbed into Fayline's old Ford and were off to Grove Street. Faces set in hot contempt, adrenaline pumping, they did sixty from one side of town to the other and arrived on Sugar's front step just minutes later.

Sugar opened her door and came face to face with Shirley. She had her arms folded across her sagging bosom and her foot thumped impatiently on the wooden porch. Sugar was surprised, and her face gave it away, but then she saw the rest of the women milling around the porch, looking at her, through her and behind her into the house.

"Yeah?" Sugar said. Her voice was pure St. Louis street. "What ya'll want?"

"We wanna talk to you," Shirley said and pushed her head forward until her forehead was near to touching Sugar's.

" 'Bout what?" Sugar said and stood back on one leg.

"About Pearl. You and Pearl and where you all was last night," Minnie chimed in from behind Shirley. The women moved in closer.

"Pearl know ya'll here?" Sugar asked and nodded her head toward Pearl's house.

"No, it ain't for her to know," Fayline said and flicked grit from under her nails in Sugar's direction.

"Can we come in?" Shirley asked and took a step forward.

Sugar put her hand up. "No. Anything you gotta say can be said right here on this porch."

"This here is private talk, not for anybody and everybody who pass up and down Grove Street. Just you and us." Shirley looked over her shoulder at the women for support. They all nodded their heads in agreement.

"Don't nobody hardly come down Grove Street, ain't but seven houses between the corner and the field, so I don't think we have to worry about people passing by and hearing what you got to say. But if it's so important for you all to be on the inside, why don't I come over to one of ya'll houses, we can talk and you can serve me lemonade and sweet cookies. How's about we do that?" Sugar's eyes challenged them.

If the look of horror that swept across the women's faces also made a sound, then all of Bigelow would have been on Grove Street.

"I wouldn't 'low nothing like you on my porch no less in my house!" Minnie yelled out. Shirley turned around and threw Minnie a warning look. "Hush up, Minnie," she whispered to her and then turned her attention back to Sugar.

"We all Christian women here—"

"Not all," Sugar corrected her. Shirley cleared her throat, nodded her head in agreement and continued.

"We don't want no trouble, we just concerned about what you done gone and done to Pearl, is all. She ain't use to nobody of your sort. You know what I mean, don't you? She a Christian woman like us and ain't never been exposed to your kind of people—"

"My kind of people? What kind is that, black people? Nah, can't be black people, 'cause all that live around here is black people, so what kinda people you talkin' about?" Sugar stepped out onto the porch, forcing Shirley to take a step backward.

"Girl please, you know what kinda people we talkin' about." Fayline stepped up, moving Shirley to one side. "You a whore and worse of all you a whore with bad luck as your pimp. Now we come over here to ask you to leave Bigelow, just pack your shit and be on the next train outta here."

"A whore? How you know I'm a whore, somebody done told you so or you been with me to know so?"

Again the sweeping silent look of horror.

"Uh-huh, thought so." She stared at them, those faces that could no longer look directly at her. "Ya'll need to go on back home now. Go on." She waved them away.

"You're influencing Pearl to be with other mens, just like you do. It ain't right."

Sugar was puzzled. "What you talkin' about, what other mens you talking about?"

"Don't act like you don't know, you She-Devil, you! I seen it with my own eyes. Clothes all over the floor, a shadow at the top of the stairs, hiding. I seen it! And she done gone and colored her hair too!" Shirley was yelling and spewing saliva as she spoke. Her wig vibrated on her head as she shook uncontrollably.

"You old and crazy, ain't no man over there." Sugar waved her hand at them again.

"Who told her she should go and dye her hair?" Fayline asked. She had a sly look on her face.

"I did, but that don't mean she's fucking for money now too!" Sugar's patience was running out.

"You a devil!" Shirley said and shook her two balled fists at Sugar.

"Yeah, well, so are you," Sugar replied, her voice rising.

"God's gonna damn you to hell!" Shirley was screaming now. Minnie was tugging at her, trying to get her to follow her back to the car where Clair Bell was already waiting.

"Shirley, I been in hell all my life."

"C'mon, Shirley, let's go." Fayline turned and descended the stairs. The fight was over. It didn't go at all the way they'd envisioned it. For some reason they thought the sheer number of them against Sugar would be enough to send her packing. They were wrong. Shirley gave Sugar one last long look and then she turned her back on her. Before she could get her foot firmly rooted on the last step, Sugar called to her.

"Shirley, are you jealous of me? Hmmm, jealous that ain't nobody been sniffin' around your skirts for a while? Even that man you got don't come sniffin' anymore. Well, I guess maybe you ain't pay no mind to it. Maybe you thought you and him was past that stage in your lives. You and, oh, what is his name again?" Sugar raised her head and scratched her chin. "What is his name?" She searched her mind or pretended to. Shirley turned around, his name escaped her mouth as soon as she thought it.

"Herbert."

"Oh yes, ole Herbert! He okay? I ain't seen him for a while." Sugar smiled smugly and was more than satisfied with the look of despair and hurt on Shirley's face.

"Tell 'em I miss him," Sugar added gleefully.

"Y-you ain't never had my man. You ain't never had my man," Shirley chanted. She was moving back up the stairs toward Sugar.

"Sure I have, he a nice old man. And you know what, I don't even mind that his dick don't stand up no more. Shoot, there are a hundred other things I can do to get his juices flowing." Sugar's head tilted back with laughter.

"You lying. You lying," Shirley whispered as she edged dangerously closer to Sugar.

"Am I now? You sure about that? Think now. Think about them nights when he claimed he was hangin' out down at the Rib Shack with the rest of them old men, think now. Could he have been with me? Could he have?"

"He wouldn't," Shirley said. Even as the words left her mouth she was unsure about them.

"How would you know? You too busy minding everyone else's business except your own. Counseling people on how to take care of their men and here you ain't even taking care of your own man."

"Shut up, you whore!"

"Oh yes, you fucking in everyone's life except your own!"

It was sudden and quick. Shirley's handprint seared scarlet on Sugar's jet black cheek. The echo of the slap reverberated through the fields that surrounded them.

Sugar wasn't sure what had happened. She saw Shirley's hand

rise and then hang suspended before her, she heard the sound and saw Shirley's mouth form a large circle and then she felt the sting and knew she'd been assaulted. She stumbled backward, tears clouding her eyes, her anger increased.

"Did you smell me on him, Shirley? Did you smell my pussy all over Herbert? Think! Think hard now!" Sugar's voice was loud and hysterical. "Ya'll better think about it!" She pointed at each woman and shook her head knowingly at them.

"Fuck you," Shirley said as she turned to walk away. She had never used that word aloud. Did not even find it suitable to use on the worst of God's two-legged creatures. Never thought she would be saying it to another woman. Would never know she had said it to her own great grandchild. Nevertheless, those words felt comfortable and familiar as they flowed from her mouth. "Fuck you," she said again.

Chapter Fourteen

*P*EARL squeezed Sugar's hand as they ascended the three steps that would lead them into Bigelow's First Baptist Church. They were late, and the place where she and Joe usually sat was already taken. The minute Pearl and Sugar walked in heads turned and stayed turned. The men slid down low into their pews and the women followed Sugar's hips with hot contempt. Sugar had dressed in the most demure dress she owned, a midnight blue sleeveless sheath that clung to her body, the neckline a flurry of sheer silk that cascaded like a waterfall down the front. The dress was supposed to sit open revealing the side curves of her breast, but Pearl had taken the time to pin it closed.

Pearl and Sugar had an argument about the wig earlier. "Why can't you wear your own hair sometimes? You got a good head of hair. Healthy and shiny," Pearl asked as Sugar donned her short red wig. "You don't need so much of that paint on your face, either. Why can't you just be yourself, Sugar?"

"I guess I don't know who that is, Miss Pearl."

Eyes, both male and female, burned into them. Pearl avoided the stares and opened her Bible instead. Sugar leaned back, crossing her legs, allowing one arm to rest on the back of the pew while she fanned herself lazily with her handkerchief.

Even the Reverend stumbled through his sermon. Reverend Foster, whose words always flowed smooth as buttermilk, was having a noticeably hard time; it was clear his attention was somewhere else. Sugar smiled and shook her head. What would his dedicated flock think if she stood up and told them that their beloved Reverend Foster liked to rub his nose in between the soft mounds of her breasts and paid weekly visits to her house, without his Bible, hours before he stood in front of the good people of Bigelow?

The idea tickled her to death and she laughed again. Pearl nudged her in the ribs and gave her a quizzical look.

Sugar amused herself by counting the men who'd visited her. Almost all of them had been in her house at one time or another; socks on, boxers curled around their knees, drooling and wanting Sugar so badly they said it hurt. And now they didn't even look at her. They kept their heads forward or lowered in shame.

Sugar saw Shirley. She sat almost directly across from her, and had not moved her eyes from Sugar's form in the hour they'd been there. Sugar smiled at her, winked and blew her a kiss and even then, Shirley's death stare did not waver. She saw that Clair Bell, who sat two rows ahead of them, and Minnie, who sat beside her, were doing the same. The heat and their perpetual staring eyes were taking their toll on Sugar, making her uncomfortable and causing her to shift restlessly in her seat.

"When's the choir going to sing?" Sugar whispered to Pearl. Her behind was going numb against the hard wood.

"Soon," Pearl whispered back, and dropped her eyes back down to her Bible.

The choir was made up of six women, three men and ten young girls and boys. And when they sang their voices climbed up into the rafters and spread out like blue flames. Sugar perked up and the heat that pulled at her skin was gone. She felt an autumn breeze sneak in through the windows and embrace her.

It started with one tapping foot and built up to the hand-clapping, foot-stomping, screaming frenzy that could only be found in small-town Baptist churches. Sugar was swept up in the music, and had forgotten about the staring, hateful eyes of the Bigelow women. And they had momentarily forgotten about her. People jumped up and danced down the aisles, calling out to the Lord. Some fainted while others bent over and wept.

When service was over, the congregation, emotionally drained and spiritually fulfilled, walked out into the September sunshine, still humming. Smiles stretched wide across a rainbow of black faces, and hands that shook in greeting, gripped longer, harder. It was Sunday and it was a feel-good day.

"Now that wasn't so bad, was it, Sugar?" Pearl said as she adjusted her hat and stepped back to let a running child pass.

"Not at all, Miss Pearl," Sugar responded.

People dressed in their Sunday best positioned themselves in front of the church, exchanging small talk, waiting for the Reverend to appear so they could compliment him on his strong sermon. Children ran around adult legs, laughing and forgetting that a torn stocking or soiled pants leg could mean the switch.

"Oh, hello, Fayline," Pearl said when she saw Fayline pushing through the crowd of people toward her. Guilty, her hand went directly to her hair and then dropped back down again.

"Pearl," Fayline said coldly as her eyes expertly traveled around her head like it was a familiar road. "So I see you've dyed it black." Her words were clipped and she threw Sugar a dirty look. Sugar just crossed her arms and smiled.

"Oh, um, yes. Do you like it?" Pearl asked hopefully.

"Not really, Pearl. A woman your age don't need to have no jet black hair. A rinse would have done you just fine. But then it ain't my hair, so to each her own." Fayline turned, exchanged one last nasty look with Sugar and walked away.

"Well," Pearl huffed. "That's Fayline, you know. She owns the beauty shop in town. Have you met her?" Pearl spoke to Sugar but her attention focused on the crowd and the three women who stood huddled just beyond its border.

Sugar had chosen not to tell Pearl about the words that were exchanged with her friends earlier. Some things were better left unsaid, and that was one of those things. "I—I've seen her in town, but we have not been formally introduced," Sugar responded, following Pearl's eyes to the huddled mass of women just a glance away. Shirley, Clair Bell and Minnie stood, shoulders touching, mouths moving, looking directly at them. It was obvious that Pearl and Sugar were the topic of their conversation. Pearl shaded her eyes with one hand. "Good Lord, what are they up to now?"

"Morning, Sister Pearl." Reverend Foster's voice was moving past them, but Pearl caught him by the arm and gently pulled him back. Her smile said, "See, Reverend, I did what you asked me to." She nodded in Sugar's direction.

"Reverend, I'd like to introduce you to Miss Sugar Lacey. Sugar, this here is Reverend Foster."

Sugar stepped in and extended her hand. All eyes were on them. The Reverend took her hand in his cold, shaking palm. He did not look her full in the face.

"So nice to meet you, Su—Miss Lacey." His voice was uneven, swiftly changing from adult to adolescent in pitch.

"So nice to meet you, Reverend. What a beautiful service, just wonderful. You certainly are a *powerful* man."

Reverend Foster pulled at his collar and cleared his throat. "Thank you, Sister." He wanted his hand back, but Sugar wasn't letting go. She wanted everyone to see, see their beloved Reverend holding the hand of Sugar Lacey.

"Will you be attending next Sunday?" he said in mock optimism. He did not want to ever see Sugar sitting in his church again, and he would be sure to make that clear to her during his next visit.

"I sure will, Reverend. Miss Pearl got me for two months of Sundays, but I'm sure I'll extend it beyond that." She released his hand, and he fought the urge to wipe it against his robe. One final nervous smile, a nod of his head and then he was gone.

Sugar's smile was mischievous as she turned to face all of those who'd been watching her. She looped her arm through Pearl's and they began the walk home. Women turned their noses up at them, grabbed at their children and moved back, giving them plenty of space to pass. Men watched sideways, risking a slap on the back of their heads from the heavy hand of a watchful wife.

*T*he air was dancing by the time they pulled up to the house. A storm was coming for sure. Black clouds fragmented the beauty of the pink slashes that could usually be seen right before pale yellow painted the sky.

They laughed together in Pearl's kitchen and put an extra cup of sugar in the last batch of lemon pound cake. "This gonna ruin that figure you got, girl!" Pearl said and snapped the dish towel off of Sugar's behind. "Sure will," Sugar responded and then laughed, not caring if she spread twenty sizes bigger. Life suddenly meant more to her than a small waist and perfectly shaped hips.

The two women had spent every waking moment together. Talking, cooking or just sitting quiet together and marveling at the world that lay out before them. Sugar had never in her life taken the time to adore a tree or dote on a splendid blade of grass, but her growing friendship with Pearl was changing that.

Mornings found a trick from the previous night dressing in the background of her room and Sugar eager to get him gone so she could watch the dawn break alone.

"Joe coming back today or tomorrow." Pearl smiled it more than she said it.

"You miss him, huh?" Sugar questioned, looking up from the chicken she was cleaning.

"Sure do," Pearl said, looking into the bright light the sun lent to the kitchen.

Sugar was happy that Joe was coming home. Happy for Pearl. She tried to push her selfish feelings aside, knowing that what they had now would change or maybe disappear altogether once he was home.

That afternoon Sugar continued to bare her soul to Pearl in painful slivers. From her time growing up in Short Junction, to her migration to St. Louis, Detroit, Chicago and then back to St. Louis. She spent a long time speaking about Mary and Mercy. The scare that almost took Mary from her, the comforting feeling she got from Mercy's tiny arms encircling her neck at night and the pain that plagued her still for leaving them. Once or twice Sugar turned away while she spoke and Pearl was sure she saw tears in her eyes.

Over the past week Pearl had taught Sugar how to bake, and

Sugar showed Pearl, with the help of a large ripe cucumber, the technique of giving hand and giving head. Pearl wriggled her nose in disgust and shook her finger at her in reproach, but her eyes never left the cucumber. Sugar saw that Pearl had finally allowed curiosity and possibility to couple.

Pearl told Sugar about her happy childhood, meeting and falling in love with Joe. The birth of her three children and the hideous, aching loss of one.

"Jude," Pearl said and her voice quivered. To Sugar, that name and the way Pearl breathed it out sounded like a great work of fiction. Pearl straightened her back, pulled back the years and finally began to tell Sugar about Jude.

"You know, you remind me so much of her." Pearl's eyes were gleaming and they seemed to smile and cry all at once. "You got her color, you know. Like Joe, strong, black skin. The old ones call it pure African skin. They say when you the color of darkness, your lineage is pure, never been touched by a white man." She laughed and waved her hand. "That's what they say anyway."

"You always calling me by her name," Sugar said, wanting to keep Pearl talking about her daughter. She still woke from wild dreams with Jude's name pressed to her lips like a lover's kiss.

"Do I." Pearl's reply carried no surprise. "I suppose that happens when someone is always on your mind."

"Tell me more about her." Sugar wanted to hear about the daughter that took so much of Pearl with her when she died.

"I done told you about her already," Pearl snapped. She did not want to dwell on it now, not when her life was beginning to take on some joy again.

"You told me about what happened to her, not about her." Sugar touched Pearl's face with a gentleness she did not know she possessed. "Please." She turned soft, soothing brown eyes on Pearl's own.

"She—Jude was my only girl, my last child. I didn't mean for her to be the last, God made that decision for me." Pearl wrung her hands and spoke in quick bursts. "We all doted on her. Me, her daddy, Joe Jr. and Seth. She was a sweet dark thing. Joe usta call her his sweet licorice stick. Hmmm, she was sweet, but don't be fooled, she was a tough thing. Jude ran before she walked, you know? Humph, always trying to keep up with her older brothers. I tried to keep her feminine, but Jude was a hard one. Always tearing her dress, losing her ribbons, ripping and running like a new colt all over the place.

"But we loved her anyway. Can't help but love a child that lived inside of you for nine months. She was smart as a whip, could out-spell both of her brothers and add up big ole numbers without using paper or pencil. Joe and I told her she was gonna make a fine teacher or doctor. We were saving to send her to college after she finished her schooling here. One of them fine Negro colleges. I was gonna go back to work to bring in a little extra." Pearl sighed and looked at her hands.

"The boys ain't have no interest in schooling," she continued, "Joe Jr. was talking about going in the army; and Seth, well he had big dreams, was going to start his own business. He said 'Mamma, I ain't going in no white man's army to get killed for a country that don't want me to piss in the same toilet they do. Me, I'm gonna start me my own business, one that the white man gonna find a need for and when they come into my place of business they gonna have to call me Sir!'

"That Seth was always talking big. Still talking big. Always got ideas that go beyond normal colored people's dreams."

Pearl showed Sugar a picture of Joe Jr. and Seth. Handsome men. Joe Jr. in his service uniform and Seth, all teeth, hand-painted sign in hand that said SETH'S FIX IT SHOP.

"Another dream that never made it." Pearl traced a finger over the letters and grimaced.

"Where's Jude's picture, Miss Pearl?" Sugar flipped through countless photo album pages that held black and white pictures of picnics and birthday parties, hoping to find Jude.

"I—I took them out. I couldn't bear to look at them, at her. It was just too painful, so I took them out and put them in here." Pearl went to the closet and retrieved a large white jewelry box from the top shelf. The age-old paint was yellowed and chipped at the corners, revealing the pale pine wood. A smiling ballerina stood gracefully on its top, her painted lips pursed in perfection. "This use to be mine when I was a little girl and I gave it to Jude on her eighth birthday. She loved it so, would lift the top and let the music play for hours. It don't play music no more, it stopped the day . . ." Pearl trailed off.

"It's okay, Miss Pearl." Sugar gently took the box from Pearl and went back over to the bed.

"I only look at them when I feel I need to have her near me. When I miss her the most."

Sugar lifted the lid and saw herself staring back at her. She jerked as if struck. Her hands were shaking as she lifted the first of many pictures from the box. Jude rolling in the grass, Jude swimming in the lake, Jude sleeping, Jude laughing. Sugar's head was swimming. If someone had brought these pictures to her and said, "Here you are in the life you can't recall," she would have believed every word of it and ignored the slight differences that remained between Jude and herself. Jude's smaller nose and thinner lips, her rounder eyes and fuller brow. But the smile was the same; sure and solid. Sugar knew that smile, it was her own.

"You see," Pearl said, standing over her. Sugar shook her head yes. She did see and it scared her to death. "They say everyone got a twin, you hers, I guess," Pearl said and sat down beside her. "God done sent you here to soothe my hurting heart. I see that now. He could have sent you anyplace else, but he chose Bigelow. He sent you here to put a smile back on my face and laughter back in my mouth. He knew I had turned my back on him after Jude, I told him I would continue to serve him, but I couldn't trust him no more. That was, until you showed up." Pearl placed her hand over Sugar's. "I love you for helping me trust again."

Pearl's words melted over Sugar, coating her in warmth and sweet affection, but simple acceptance was hard for Sugar after so many years of rough callused hands handling her body.

"You think you love me because I remind you of Jude," Sugar said quietly.

"That may have been so in the beginning, but now I love you for you, not who you remind me of."

Chapter Fifteen

*J*OE stepped into his home just as the long hand on his watch skipped past the two, dawdled a while and then landed squarely on the short hand, which comfortably kissed the three. Welcomed by an empty home, Joe was immediately aware of the untidiness of his house. Thick dust covered the coffee table and the plastic lampshades. There were dishes in the sink, an unwashed bowl, batter still clinging to its inside walls. Clothes were strewn across the unmade bed and globs of blue Pepsodent littered the bathroom basin.

He unpacked, and carefully placed his clothes in the closet. All the while he wondered where his wife could be.

He moved to the lower parts of the house, discovering the warm smell of lemon pound cake. Joe scratched at his chin and walked to the living room. He thought about calling Shirley to see if Pearl was there, but as his hand made contact with the phone, large yellow headlights traveled quickly across the room, blinding him for a moment and then disappearing. An engine hummed contentedly outside his door and he heard loud, loose laughter that for some reason reminded him of the French brothels he visited during the war.

He opened the door slowly, not realizing he had moved to do so, and what he saw made him catch his breath. A woman he thought to be his wife, but was quite sure she wasn't, was ascending the porch stairs; her smile, painted burgundy, was fading quickly until it was just a line. "Joe?" She must know me, he thought, she's called me by name. The first drops of rain began to fall, within moments it was driving, drenching the stranger before him. Pearl was thankful for the rain, for it hid the tears of sudden shame that sprung as if on cue when Joe opened the door.

Blue and black ran down her face and washed over the painted burgundy lips. "Joe?" Why wasn't he saying anything? He was tormenting her with silence. She was misreading his eyes, and for the first time Pearl felt fearful of her husband.

Sugar was standing in the background, her off-white dress soaked through revealing her naked breasts and bright red French cut underwear. Darkness had swallowed up Bigelow, thunder clapped loudly behind its curtain, but Sugar remained. Isaac was gone before the first drop fell, barreling his beat-up pickup down the road, one hand hanging out the window waving good-bye. Sugar looked around to see if there was something she could use to protect Pearl, should Joe strike her. Nothing. She clenched her fists and summoned up every bit of strength she had. She would take him with her bare hands if she had to. She waited.

"Joe, I got's a lot to tell you. Uhm, something's done happened since you been gone." Pearl was yelling over the driving rain and booming thunder. Bolts of lightning sliced through the damp darkness, lighting up her frightened face, reflecting the terror that was eating its way out.

"Bit?" Joe leaned forward and Pearl flinched. "Jesus Christ, that you, Bit?" His voice was pure amazement. "Bit, w-what, where you been? Come inside before you catch cold, woman!" Joe stepped forward and grabbed Pearl's hand, pulling her to him in a quick, wet embrace.

Sugar's racing heart began to slow. Her fists relaxed and then laughter, nervous at first, bubbled out until it poured like the rain that soaked her.

*P*earl sat in the warmth of the kitchen, her grandmother's quilt wrapped around her damp body, her feet soaking in a warm tub of water. Blue and yellow flames danced below the kettle encouraging the long, high scream that pierced the quiet calm of the house.

Joe was moving about; mixing eggs for scrambling, bending over and looking in the refrigerator to check for slab bacon; shaking his head in dismay when he found none. Searching cupboards and finding a half-empty box of grits and flour for biscuits. "We got buttermilk?" he questioned and looked over his shoulder.

"Some left," Pearl responded. She had insisted that he sit while she made breakfast, but Joe would not have it. He'd pause every once in a while and fold his arms, shaking his head, marveling at the beauty that reclaimed Pearl's face. "You sure do look different, Bit."

Slowly, as the grits cooked and her tea cooled, she unfolded for him the two weeks spent with Sugar. The helpless connection she felt toward her, the affection that grew beneath it. Her face moved in angry waves as she told of her so-called friends' disdain for Sugar and their relationship; the threats and warnings that would certainly befall her should she continue on the path she'd chosen to take.

Joe listened intently as he scooped the grits onto two plates and stirred the eggs. She used her words carefully, side-stepping exactly what Sugar was and always had been. But Joe knew, he'd heard talk from the men in town. She described in detail Sugar's time in Short Junction, growing up at the Lacey home. Joe's mind cringed at her words and he stood quickly, attempting to avoid the question he knew would come.

"You know about that place, the Lacey place over in Short Junction?"

"Yep, heard about it when I was there." Joe knew he'd answered too quickly. They both heard the false composure in his tone and fell silent. Over the years he'd tried to expel the memory of the beautiful brown woman with hair that touched her shoulders and a smile that seemed to warm the air. Her name had passed his lips once since he married. And that was while he slept beside Pearl and dreamed of the time he spent with the woman beneath the sycamore trees.

Bertie Mae.

Even now as he sat remembering what he'd tried so hard to forget, he could taste the sweet dew that was her lips.

He'd met her while laying railroad tracks just on the outskirts of Short Junction only days after he'd decided to marry Pearl. His days in Short Junction were long hard ones. Lifting steel and laying steel was not an easy task for any man, but the black man seemed to complain less and accomplish more. Those long hard days laboring beneath a relentless sun were made bearable knowing that the sun would set, the heat recede and evening would find him at the Lacey home.

His path crossed daily with the beautiful Bertie Mae, since she'd taken to sitting up on a grassy incline beneath a sycamore tree. She said that was her place of solitude. Later it would become their place of passion.

Joe was not a man who took advantage of women. It wasn't in his character to do so, but Bertie Mae did something to him that tested his morals and caused his stomach to quiver. When she touched his cheek, her hand hot with desire, he knew that he would not, could not deny her.

Evening fell and she slowly undid her blouse. He had all intentions of saying no. He saw the first button slip and disappear from its opening and then the second. He'd found his voice by the third. "No, Bertie, please don't." He reached his hand up quickly to still her movements and found his palm pressed against the swell of her breast. She shuddered and covered his hand with her own, pushing it down hard.

Joe was still. He felt her nipples harden and strain against the thin worn fabric of her dress. He reached up and undid the remaining two buttons of the blouse. The material fell away to reveal two full, round, brown breasts. Bertie's breathing quickened and her chest seemed to beckon him.

He leaned forward and kissed each jutting nipple gently. Flicking them with his tongue, causing Bertie to moan aloud, grabbing his head, anchoring his mouth on her hot breasts. Joe sucked like a hungry newborn, and pushed Bertie down to the ground.

He ran his tongue lightly up and down her neck. He came to her chin and nibbled at it. He moved to one ear and then the other, exploring it with his tongue and teeth. He kissed each eyelid and her nose. Joe paused when he came to her mouth. It was open, wet and ready. "You are so beautiful," he said as his mouth came down on her own burning lips. Their tongues danced together for what seemed like forever.

Quickly and awkwardly, Joe removed his boots, overalls and thin white T-shirt. He stood before her, nude, his body as strong and dark as the trunks of the century-old trees that surrounded them. Bertie ogled at his penis. It stood long and erect, throbbing before her like his second heart. He removed her skirt and slip. She wore no panties, as she had only two pair and both were drying on the line in her yard.

Her stomach was flat, smooth and as unblemished as a river stone. He bent and kissed her navel, inhaling the sweet musky scent of her. Bertie gasped.

His tongue made circles on her thigh and then found itself between her legs, relentlessly toying with her womanhood. Bertie moaned and called his name over and over again. The grass beneath her was slick with her liquid. He pulled himself up and straddled her, placing her legs over his shoulders. As he entered her he kissed her, softly at first, and then with more urgency. Bertie winced in pain, pulled him closer, deeper until the pain was replaced with pleasure.

He slid in and out of her and breathed her name heavily in her ear and neck until they both cried out to the heavens.

They lay there beneath the sycamore tree, its branches whispering above them in the receding twilight.

They parted, no promises between them, not knowing their union had spawned a new life.

Pearl watched her husband remember some long ago indiscretion and as she was about to question him about the look in his eyes she heard her mother's voice in the back of her mind: "What you don't know won't hurt you." Pearl obeyed those words and went on with her story.

"... and Joe, she sing like you wouldn't believe! Her voice

just lifts you up and takes you where it wants to. It's powerful, you know?" Pearl's eyes danced when she spoke of Sugar's singing. Joe smiled and touched a small damp curl that clung to the side of Pearl's cheek.

"That's how she make you feel?" he asked, realizing now how much Sugar had played in his wife's transformation.

"Me and a whole lot of other people. Joe, I been to a juke joint. Twice." Pearl's eyes were lowered, avoiding the disapproving look she was sure Joe was casting on her.

"Is that right," he said between bites of food. Pearl heard the surprise in his voice and replayed his words in her mind to locate the anger that she expected to be there.

"You heard me?" she said and raised her eyes.

"You been to a juke joint. Yes, Bit, I heard you," Joe replied, stuffing another biscuit in his mouth.

"Well, ain't you got nothing to say about that?" She was looking full in his face now.

"Uhm, no I don't. You went 'cause that's what you wanted to do, right?"

"You think it's all right for a Christian woman to be keeping time in a juke joint?"

"Well, I never thought about it before, but I do know there are worse places than a juke joint a Christian woman could be spending her time at."

"Like where?"

"Like Shirley Brown's!"

They laughed together over Joe's little joke and finished the remainder of their meal by discussing his trip to Florida. In between Joe's words and her questions, Pearl thanked God that she had picked correctly, and had been picked correctly. There weren't many men who could come home to an unkept house to find his woman, mother of his children, climbing out of another man's car (morning or night) and not knock her clear out of her skin first and ask questions later. Not many men would cook breakfast for that same woman and listen with interest about the time she spent with a whore.

The rain fell all day long that day. The sky was a gray ceiling.

Bigelow children moved restlessly about the rooms of their homes, stared despondently through rain-streaked windows or bounced a ball impatiently against a wall.

Young lovers pulled each other closer, delighting in the patter of the raindrops and the colorless day that looked in at them. Old lovers would once again feel the fires of passion and desire take root and remain tangled in each other's arms until night fell.

The rain had that effect on people. And so did Sugar's presence.

They were both tired. Joe had hardly slept during the long train ride home. Pearl had been up since six that morning. They walked upstairs, arms linked, whispering instead of talking in normal tones. They each took turns washing up over the basin. Pearl washed her face and brushed her teeth twice. The Memphis Roll's homemade beer and the early morning breakfast had left a steely taste on her tongue.

Looking up from the basin, Pearl caught sight of herself in the mirror and laughed aloud, a light silly chuckle reserved for soft young mouths of school girls just discovering the magic and mystery of a boy's touch. She cast a guileful smile at the cotton gown that hung expectantly on the back of the bathroom door and her eyes moved back to the woman smiling in the mirror.

After a moment, she flicked the light switch off and walked stark naked from the bathroom to her bedroom.

In the gloomy gray morning light of the bedroom, Joe lay on his side. His mind was slowly being pulled into the darkness of slumber and he barely heard Pearl enter the room. He would marvel later at the absence of the swishing sound that usually accompanied Pearl's entrance and the giggle that replaced it. He would enjoy recalling how Pearl climbed in beside him and pressed herself hard against his back, her legs thrown across his own, her breath, heavy with lust, against his neck. He would lick his lips in retrospect on the exact moment her lips brushed against the nape of his shoulder while her hand found the slant opening in his boxer shorts. He would not know that at the exact moment he realized his wife was naked against him and demanding in hushed, heavy tones that he fuck her (those were her exact words) while she expertly guided his organ up and down between the soft palm and fingers of her hand, the memory of that moment would, for the rest of his life, dance across his mind causing a small smile to cross his face.

Chapter Sixteen

*T*HE first November morning was a warm sheath of fog that wrapped itself comfortably around Bigelow. People moved about cautiously, barely able to see their hands in front of their faces, much less an approaching car or person. The willow branches hung eerily over the main roads and brushed invisible against brown cheeks, causing women and some men to shriek at its touch. The sun was a dim lightbulb in the sky and the soil a deep wet brown that oozed beneath feet.

Summer had battled autumn and won and now it threatened to drag into war the approaching winter. Only the calendars that hung on kitchen walls and the daily newspaper confirmed that winter was quickly approaching. Thanksgiving would soon be upon them and frost had not yet replaced the morning dew that settled on the thin blade grass.

Talk about Sugar had not completely ceased, but had melted into a low hum. People had less of a reason to stop and point at Sugar. In fact, she had blended into the woven cloth that was Bigelow, like a small imperfection or crooked stitch. Brightly colored dresses, pedal pushers and cropped tops were slowly replaced with cool calm blues, whites and greens that hugged Sugar's figure more like an old friend than a lustful one-night stand.

She replaced the blonde and red wigs with subtle auburns

and ravens that complimented her face and brought attention to her eyes.

Joe and Pearl accompanied Sugar to the Memphis Roll practically every Saturday night now. The bartender, waitresses and quite a few of the customers called Joe and Pearl by name, and they even had their own table, center front. The more time Sugar spent with the Taylors, the less time she spent with Lappy Clayton. He'd cornered Sugar on one occasion, grabbing her roughly by the arm as she stepped down off the stage. "Where you been?" His breath was sour and his eyes bloodshot. Sugar snatched her arm away from him. "I been around," she said in disgust and started to walk away from him again. He stepped in front of her. "Yeah, you been around, but you ain't been with me." Sugar threw a quick look over his shoulder and saw Pearl's worried eyes looking back at her. Pearl's hand was resting on Joe's shoulder, pushing him gently back down into his seat.

"Look Lappy," Sugar said between clenched teeth, "this ain't the place or the time—"

"Yeah, it is the place and the right goddamn time!" Lappy was yelling, spit flew from his mouth and his eyes rolled in his head. "You ain't never home and when you here you with them." He turned and glowered at Joe and Pearl. His words were slurring and he stumbled back a step. "Who they to you now, huh? They your pimps now? Ma and Pa pimp!" He let out a reel of crazed laughter.

"You have had too much to drink, Lappy," Sugar said in a low voice. People were starting to look at them. "You need to go on home and sleep it off." She stepped around him and he turned and grabbed her again. This time Pearl could not keep Joe in his seat. He was up and on Lappy before Pearl could say a word.

"Problem?" Joe asked. He stood a full foot taller than Lappy and outweighed him by at least one hundred pounds. Lappy stepped backward and looked up into Joe's angry face. "I said, is there a problem?" Joe repeated himself and took a step toward Lappy. Lappy's hand fell from Sugar's arm.

"Naw, man. Ain't no problem here," Lappy responded in a

small voice that made Sugar turn her eyes away. Even though he didn't deserve her pity, Sugar still felt ashamed for him.

"You gonna pay," Lappy hissed at Sugar. Sugar rolled her eyes and dismissed his threat as drunken rhetoric.

Joe stood his ground until Sugar moved past him to the table and Lappy sulked his way out the front door, swearing vengeance.

Sugar sat beside them every Sunday in church. She understood the words Reverend Foster read from the large worn Bible that sat on his podium and little by little she began to apply them to her life. But her greatest joy, the thing that made her sit straight up in the pew, was the sometimes gentle and more often turbulent voices of the choir. They left her shaken, wet-eyed and weak with happiness. "You should join the choir," Pearl suggested this each and every Sunday. Sugar smiled and shook her head no, each and every time. Bigelow definitely was not ready to see her stand before them singing the Lord's praises.

Shirley, Minnie and Clair Bell offered Pearl short acknowledgments whenever they had the unfortunate pleasure to stumble across her path. Pearl told Sugar that they would eventually come around. Sugar knew they wouldn't, but agreed when she saw the slight sadness that misted Pearl's eyes as she stared at their swiftly retreating backs.

"Something's going to happen," Pearl said, mostly to herself. Her hands moved quickly, snapping the long firm green beans in half. She was halfway through the bowl and her eyes moved from her work to the window and back. She shook her head and mumbled to herself.

"What you say?" Sugar asked, lowering Sam Cook's crooning voice on the transistor radio.

"Nothing," Pearl said, and looked nervously back at the window. The fog was becoming denser, the humidity increased and the temperature rose by at least ten degrees. "Lord, Lord," Pearl uttered and quickly wiped her hands across her apron. She walked to the window and peered out into the solid gray. Unsatisfied, she moved to the front door and swung it open. Hesitatingly she stepped onto the porch and was swallowed by the smoky heather. She stepped back quickly and promptly shut the door.

"What in the world is wrong with you, Miss Pearl?" Sugar was less than concerned. By now she was used to Pearl's minor panic attacks, the way she got herself all worked up over the smallest things.

"It just ain't right," Pearl whispered as she walked back into the kitchen, throwing a worried look over her shoulder as she did. "I ain't never seen no fog like this in my whole life."

"It's just fog, Miss Pearl." Sugar's hand moved to turn the volume on the radio back up, but Pearl shook her head. Disgruntled, Sugar returned to cleaning the bucketful of chitlins that rested in the sink.

"Humph! Things just *ain't*, you hear me? Everything got a meaning and purpose. Ain't you learn that yet?" Pearl's eyes shone. Her words were felt like daggers in Sugar's heart. She rolled her eyes at the pig intestines, knowing full well that she could run from her past, but never hide.

Joe Jr. had called early in the week to advise his parents that once again, he would not be joining them for Thanksgiving. Maybe Christmas, he said, before hanging up. Pearl swallowed hard after she replaced the receiver. Joe said nothing, just cleared his throat and left the room, leaving Sugar and Pearl alone.

"Joe Jr. been gone near thirteen years now. Been home maybe three times. Jude's death shook him up a whole lot. He said the South ain't noplace for colored people. I told him colored people *are* the South. I know he's just scared, thinking the same thing might happen to him that happened to Jude. Can't blame him, really, but I sure do miss him." Her voice dripped with grief. "It's like I done lost two children instead of one."

"Well, why don't you and Joe go on up North and visit him, then?" Sugar voiced, her tone light and carefree. She wanted to try to avoid the melancholy she saw quickly enclosing Pearl.

"He ain't never invited us," Pearl said.

"Well, what about Seth?" Sugar smiled brightly. She sang her words instead of speaking them.

"Ain't heard from Seth for about four months. Who knows where that boy might be now. He always chasing his dreams and they never lead him home." She walked upstairs, her last word bouncing off the loneliness she felt, leaving Sugar alone.

The kitchen oozed cinnamon and nutmeg aromas; with each whip of the large wooden spoon through the sweet potato mixture, the smell became stronger. In between football quarters, Joe visited the women, looking over their shoulders and examining their progress. Pearl shooed him away like a bothersome child, but not before allowing him a taste of dressing or a fresh baked biscuit drenched with sweet butter. For the moment Pearl's attention was taken up by her work, the heavy fog outside her window forgotten.

The knock came late in the evening, just as Sugar was grabbing her sweater to go home. The day was done and the fog remained stubbornly in place like a cell block wall. Joe offered to walk Sugar to her door, but Sugar declined. "It's just across the way, Joe," she said in a bashful voice. She had only recently started calling him Joe, at his and Pearl's own urging.

"I'll get it," Sugar yelled out as her hand reached for the doorknob.

"No you won't, either!" Pearl was beside her before Sugar finished her sentence. She looked cautiously out the slim windows that framed the doorway. "You don't know who or what is out there in that fog," Pearl whispered. The knock came again, urgent now. Both women jumped. "Miss Pearl, you got me all spooked now," Sugar said in mild annoyance. She sucked her teeth and once again attempted to open the door. Pearl slapped her hand away. "Leave it alone. Joe." Pearl turned and called to Joe who was dozing in the living room. "Yeah, baby," he called back through a sleepy voice.

All three now stood at the door, Sugar and Pearl behind Joe as he swung the door open. The fog moved in first, long tentacles of mist that wrapped around their ankles. Pearl looked down and kicked at it, then she grabbed Joe's arm and began to shake.

"Someone there?" Joe said and took a step forward. "No, Joe!" Pearl screamed and pulled him backward almost toppling him to the floor. "Pe—" Someone or something jumped out of the fog. Sugar, in the middle of trying to steady Joe, caught sight of the form and fled. She was up the stairs before she was sure she'd seen anything at all. It seemed her legs were reacting on their own, without the help of her mind. Pearl had not released Joe, but dug her fingers in, locking her hold on his arm and squeezing her eyes shut against the horror that was sure to be standing before her. Joe reacted by bringing his free arm up and out, his fist making quick impact with the face of whatever it was that then lay groaning at his feet.

"Seth! Oh, my God, Seth!" Sugar heard Pearl's squeals of surprise and concern. Her trembling legs brought her slowly back down the stairs. "Oh Joe, look what you done!" Pearl and Joe stood huddled over the heap on the porch. Sugar saw Joe shake his head and then reach out to help the man up and then she heard a deep laugh. Pearl turned and Sugar saw that there were tears rolling down her face, but she was smiling. Closer still, she saw Seth's strong jawline, a nose that at the moment was bleeding, long thick eyelashes and wide-set eyes that were so dark and deep, she was sure that women had lost themselves in them forever.

She was staring at him, his long fingers and the strong large hands that she wanted to lay on top of her own. She shook her head against her thoughts.

"Sugar, this here is Seth." Pearl plucked him on the back of the head and went to retrieve the ice trays from the freezer. "Seth is my son and a fool!" she said with a laugh. "Seth, this here is my friend, our friend, Sugar Lacey."

His head was tilted back in order to thwart the flow of blood. He held a handkerchief to his nose that obstructed his view of her. "Hey," he said and raised his hand in a hello gesture.

"Hi," Sugar said and dropped her eyes.

"He is the biggest fool! Now what kinda person gonna jump outta nowhere like that? When you gonna grow up, Seth? I done told you over and over again that everything can't be a game.

Now suppose your daddy would have had the shotgun? You woulda been dead already!" She plucked him again on his head.

"Ow, Mamma! Daddy, tell her to quit!" Seth yelled in mock pain. Joe just chuckled and stood with his arms folded across his chest in fatherly admiration.

"Why didn't you call and tell us you were coming, Seth? We could've met you at the station." Pearl wrapped four blocks of ice in a new dishtowel with a red and yellow turkey on it and placed it on Seth's nose.

"I wanted to surprise ya'll and—"

"But how did you get here from the station? You get a lift? Oh, Seth, don't tell me you walked here, in this fog?"

"Mamma, no, I—"

"Well how did you get here then—"

"Pearl, would you let the boy talk," Joe firmly intervened. Pearl threw an exasperated look at him, but said nothing else.

"Thank you, Daddy. I drove here, Mamma."

Pearl did not seem to understand what Seth was saying.

"In a car," he added and shot Sugar a look of mild interest.

"A car? Whose car?" Pearl asked.

"My own. I done bought me a car, Mamma!" Seth was excited and looked at his beaming father for approval. Joe patted him firmly on the back.

"You did what!" Pearl screamed with glee, finally understanding what Seth was saying. "Oh, that's wonderful!" she said and kissed him on the cheek.

"It's right outside. I cut the engine when I was halfway up the street and coasted it the rest of the way, that's why you ain't hear me pull up."

"Sure 'nuff. My baby done bought himself a car. You doing okay then, huh? What else been going on with you, baby?" Pearl asked excitedly and pulled up a chair to sit next to her son.

Sugar listened for a while as Seth talked about New York and Harlem. He told them about the trains that moved hundreds of people all over the city and into Brooklyn, Queens and the Bronx. "Underneath the water?" Pearl said, her eyes wide with amazement.

Sugar was uncomfortable. She felt forgotten by the people who had, over the past few months, become more than friends, but family. "I gotta be going now," she whispered beneath the laughing and talking sounds that emanated from Seth and his parents, and moved quickly on tiptoe to the door. Once again, just as her hand was about to grasp the doorknob, Pearl's voice blocked her escape. "Sugar!"

She stopped cold. "Yes," she said, but did not make any attempt to turn around.

"Where do you think you're going?" Sugar knew the tone. She knew that Pearl was standing behind her, her hands placed firmly on her hips, her lips a straight line.

Sugar spoke to the door. "I got to go, Miss Pearl. Uhm. Things to do, you know?" Sugar felt the air move and then Pearl was beside her, speaking into her neck. "You said you wasn't gonna be doing *that* for a couple of days."

Sugar had agreed that she would not take in any work for the next week. She had enough money to live on, and anything she needed but couldn't afford, Pearl would supply. "I want you to stop this foolishness. You got other talents that don't require you to lay down and spread your legs." Sugar listened to Pearl and half heard her. She'd been told this before but all it got her was a small, big-teethed Jewish man chasing her around his desk, trying to take advantage of her.

Sugar knew it was useless to argue with Pearl. The energy involved was more than enough motivation for Sugar to just nod her head in agreement.

Pearl had asked Joe to ask around about other places in the county that offered what the Memphis Roll offered. To Pearl's surprise there were quite a few. But the places there were, were only willing to let Sugar sing for tips or were too high up on the chitlin circuit to consider an unknown.

"Don't worry, baby, you keep doing what you do at the Memphis Roll. Word gets around and those people who said no will be banging on your door begging you to come sing at their place." Sugar had wondered when Pearl moved from Bible-carrying Baptist to music industry mogul.

"I ain't doing *that*," Sugar hissed back now. "Ya'll don't need me around. I know you all want to catch up with one another."

"You stay right here. You are family now so you and Seth need to get acquainted." She grabbed Sugar firmly by the elbow, ignoring her rejections, and led her back to the kitchen where Seth and Joe were in deep conversation.

"Oh," Seth uttered. The smile that held his lips wavered, faded and then reluctantly reappeared. Sugar knew that look. It was the same look the good Bigelow women threw at her. A look that made it quite clear that she was not wanted or needed. A look that said: Clutch your children, watch your men and don't let your pocketbook hang too loose from your shoulder when she's around.

Those looks, the ones from the women, did not bother Sugar. She'd worn blinders against that sort of intimidation for far too long.

But from a man, from Seth Taylor, the look was wounding. Sugar staggered and almost doubled under the intensity of it. "Just wanted to say good-night," she said quickly and turned to rush out of the house.

"So mamma, what you got to eat?" Seth said, rubbing his palms together.

*T*he gray wall began to recede against the stubborn rays of the high morning sun. Slowly, slowly the thick rays of light sliced through it until it was nothing more than fine, thin strips of mist and then nothing at all.

Thanksgiving morning had ushered in a winter chill that took all by surprise and sent people scurrying to chop firewood for heat, squirrels scampering to gather food for the winter and Sugar wondering about her life in Bigelow.

Seth's reaction to her had haunted her for most of the night, causing her to twist and turn through small intervals of sleep, until finally her unrest sent her from the bed to the top drawer of her dresser and the joint that awaited her there. The marijuana muffled the noise in her head, fragmented the looming face of Seth Taylor and allowed her to sleep. But her sleep was filled with Jude. The haunting pictures of a child that looked so much like her. And Jude, as always, spoke to her from those black and white still lifes, pleaded with her to go away from Bigelow before a tear would fall from one almond-shaped eye and roll down the glossy photo finish, leaving blue and pink scars in its wake, finally falling off the rippled white border and into the vast darkness of Sugar's dream.

She woke with that very same tear in her own eye and wiped it quickly away. Why was Jude coming to her, asking her to leave? Was it jealousy? Sugar balled her hands into fists and beat at her head and yelled at the walls of her room, "What! What! What!"

It could be jealousy. A jealous spirit looking in from the great beyond. Pulling back the layers of time and space and seeing that her mother's pain had finally lifted. Sugar supposed that Jude's spirit felt threatened. If the pain had lessened and become a distant memory that brushed against your thoughts every blue moon, then a memory of a child taken could walk in pain's retreating footsteps.

Sugar was a fighter, had been all of her life, but how do you fight the soul of a dead child and her brother?

*I*f eating was a sin, then all that sat around the Taylor table would surely have been sentenced to hell. The table creaked beneath the weight of heavy ceramic bowls filled with sweet sausage dressing, collard greens, potato salad, macaroni salad, chitlins, candied yams and roasted potatoes. A turkey, baked to golden perfection, sat beside a glazed ham adorned with bright red cherries. Biscuits, so light and flaky they threatened to rise to the ceiling if not for the melting sweet butter that dripped and ran across their swollen bellies, restraining their flight. Music filled the background and the temporary voids that opened up when talk and laughter were put aside for a forkful of macaroni and cheese or a sip of plum wine.

Sugar smiled on top of the festivities, never quite feeling a part of them. No matter if she was quite often the subject of conversation. Seth and Joe retired full-bellied to the living room to watch the football game. Sugar and Pearl sat quietly at the table, picking at bits of sweet potato pie, their ears tuned in to the heavy male laughter a room away.

"Mamma, seeing that you cooked all this here food, I figure the least I can do is wash the dishes." Seth stood at the doorway, his arms expanded as wide as an eagle's wings. He yawned loudly. "If I don't do something, I'm gonna fall asleep." He smiled and walked toward the sink piled high with dishes. His eyes never touched Sugar.

"Joe asleep?" Pearl asked as she removed her apron. She didn't seem to notice Seth's apparent aversion to Sugar.

"You know he is." Seth laughed and twisted his hand up to his mouth in a drinking motion. "I think he had too much plum wine."

Pearl tied the apron around Seth's waist and kissed him lovingly on the cheek. "Well, then I will certainly take you up on the offer." She swatted him smartly on the behind and went to clear the remaining dishes and casseroles from the table.

"Miss Pearl, I'll take care of that," Sugar said and grabbed the plate from Pearl's hand. She didn't want to help. Would have been perfectly happy going home, running a bath and smoking a joint or having a tall glass of pike aid. But she wanted to show Seth that she was useful and not just a piece of garbage his mother had dragged in off the street.

"Well, okay," Pearl said with a wink. "I'm going to sit down and watch myself a little television."

At first the silence that surrounded the flowing water and clinking silverware was uncomfortable. Seth washed and Sugar dried. No talk. No eye contact. No brief smiles. Sugar reached to grab a plate from Seth and their fingers brushed, finally their eyes met and held. There was nothing for a long moment. Just a soundless circle around them. They could only hear the beating of their hearts. Not the rushing water or the static sounds of the television. Seth's lips moved and the sound came rushing back in. But it was warped and confusing and Sugar found herself leaning closer to Seth, desperately wanting to know what those lips were trying to communicate.

Seth's eyes widened and he pulled his head back. He too had been hurled into a zone of soundlessness. "What?" they both said in eager unison.

"You look a lot like Jude," Seth said. His eyes walked carefully across Sugar's face, pausing to examine her nose or to rest in the dip of her lip. Sugar returned to the table, answering him over her shoulder. "Yes. I know. I saw pictures."

"I guess that's why she likes you so much." Seth cut the water off and turned, leaning his back against the sink, crossing his arms over his chest. He watched her walk away, sway away. Her movements brought a slight smile to his face. "She talks about you all the time."

She smiled in spite of herself and was glad to hear the softness in his voice, the calm that for some unknown reason stirred and heated her insides. She did not respond; if she had her voice would have been light, her words a swirl of pink and white cotton candy on a May day. She couldn't risk the silly in her, answering for her.

"Daddy seems to like you too," Seth added and she heard his approaching footsteps. "Got my mamma to dye her hair and paint her fingernails," he noted in mild amusement. He was beside her now, looking down on her, through her. His eyes voicing so much more than his mouth was prepared to say.

Sugar nodded her response but kept her eyes lowered, staring hard at the table, as her hand continued wiping at the invisible crumbs.

"I like it." He leaned in and spoke close to her neck. She could feel his hot breath heavy with the scent of sweet potato pie. "I like it a lot. She looks twenty years younger. I think Daddy likes it too, although he probably ain't never said nothing to you about it. Just ain't his way." And then his breath was gone. Sugar closed her eyes and longed for its return.

"Mamma says you from Short Junction, but spent most of your time in St. Louis." He was sitting down, his long legs stretched

out before him, his hands crossed over his chest. He was looking at Sugar, wanting her to look back. "She says you a singer. Is
that so?"

"Why would your mamma tell you a lie?" It was out before
she could stop it. She almost slapped herself right there in that
kitchen. Right in front of Seth Taylor. Why couldn't she just answer the question like a normal human being? She was being ma-
licious for no reason. She raised her head to look at him, to
apologize. But then she remembered his reaction toward her the
night before and most of that afternoon, and decided he deserved it.

His eyebrows were hitched so high up on his forehead that
they were touching his hairline. Her lashing words had caught
him off guard. "W-well no, to the best of my knowledge, my
mamma ain't never told me a lie." His words were surrounded
by light laughter. He sparkled when he laughed. Sugar smiled.

"Oh, you something, ain't you?" He paused to consider his
next set of words. "So you sing. That's nice. Maybe you'll sing
for me before I go?" He winked at her and laughed again.

Sugar was still standing, but had dragged her hand from the
table, stopping the mechanical wiping movement her hand had
found comfort in. She stood there like a plank, her eyes darting
from Seth to the table and then back to Seth. She felt like an
idiot. She couldn't remember a time she was so uncomfortable
in front of a man. Too much of who she was was exposed to him.
She didn't have on a lot of makeup; just a little powder for the
shine and a bit of lipstick. The thought brought her hand up to
her face and she ran her fingers quickly across her cheek. Perhaps
it was the bulky sweater and faded ankle-cuffed denims. She felt
more naked in that than any of her skin-tight, low-cut dresses.
Maybe it was because she hadn't had a cigarette since she walked
in Pearl's house. She'd purposely left them at home and now she
questioned her decision.

"Ain't you tired? You and mamma done cooked up a storm
and ate up a bigger one. C'mon now, sit down." Seth moved the
chair out from beneath the table with his foot. "C'mon," he
coaxed and then flashed a smile.

"No, I gotta go," she said quickly. Her behind just brushed the plastic covering of the seat before she straightened up again. Too many weird thoughts and feelings were swirling around inside of her. She couldn't trust herself to be herself around Seth Taylor. Because at the very moment she wasn't sure who *herself* was. It was best she leave.

"Where?" he asked innocently.

"Home."

"Home?" Pearl walked in the kitchen and Sugar jumped like a child caught doing something wrong. "You going home now? I just talked Joe into a game of cards." Sugar detected the disappointment in Pearl's voice.

"I—I think I ate too much," Sugar said and tapped at her swollen belly. "I'm not feeling too hot," she lied and dropped her eyes.

"Oh no." Pearl's face filled with concern. "I think I got some seltzer around—"

"No," Sugar raised her hand in protest, "don't trouble yourself, Miss Pearl. I just need to lay down."

"You sure?"

"Uh-huh. I'll be fine. I'll see you tomorrow."

Sugar said good-night to Seth and went to wish a half-asleep Joe the same. Pearl and Seth met her at the front door. "Seth going to make sure you get home all right," Pearl said and gave Seth a little nudge. Sugar eyed mother and son suspiciously. "I just live right next door," she said, wondering if Pearl was going senile. She turned to face Seth, trying to gain some support. "You could spit the difference between here and there."

"I know where you live." Pearl rolled her eyes at Sugar's ignorance to the obvious. She was well aware of the attraction between the two. The previous evening Seth had asked a thousand questions about Sugar. He slipped them in the conversation, hoping Pearl would not notice his obvious interest in her neighbor. But she had. "Seth gonna see you home anyway. It's late and a lady shouldn't be out and about alone after dark."

No one had ever referred to her as a lady. It was a role she never thought she would play. She liked it. "Okay," Sugar surrendered.

The evening sky looked far above them. It was cobalt blue with a heavy dusting of tiny twinkling stars. Seth's and Sugar's breaths preceded them in tiny puffs of white that appeared and disappeared quickly. The temperature had dropped with the setting of the sun, and all around Bigelow fireplaces burned, sending billows of smoke up into the dark. Surrounded by silence, they walked the short distance down the road and to #10 Grove Street.

Sugar's mouth moved to say good-night when they reached the porch, but before she could utter one word his feet were already walking up her stairs, his body was settling down into her porch chair and his eyes were turned on the large Arkansas night sky that surrounded them. She moved hesitantly up the stairs and silently took a seat beside him on a beach chair made up of green and white strips of material wrapped around the metal frame. A Sears catalogue special that she'd seen and taken a fancy to. She would sit there and pretend that she was by a pool or on a beach, her feet lazing in the surf. It was her dreaming chair.

They sat there for a while, just staring at the sky and breathing in the new winter air. His voice startled her, although she had been waiting for it to come. "Short Junction is so close. You know, I ain't never been there? Been to most of these towns around here 'cept that one. I hear Short Junction smaller than Bigelow. Shoot, Bigelow ain't the size of nothing so Short Junction gotta be less than nothing." He laughed at his little joke. Sugar laughed too, and covered her mouth when she did.

"Daddy said you done woke something up in Mamma." The words came suddenly, his tone turned serious. Like his father, he spoke to his hands. "You know, after Jude died, she just went inside of herself, you know what I mean? It was like she was my mamma, but she wasn't. She was doing the same things she always done, after a while anyway. She took care of us and all, but her eyes were empty and she just stopped smiling altogether." A long time filled with quiet passed before he spoke again. "And then Joe Jr. went into the army. He wasn't doing nothing but running away. Still running I suppose. Me, I hung around for as long as I could, but couldn't stay here forever, not in Bigelow."

He looked around him as if he'd forgotten where he was. "Daddy say she smile all the time now and laughing too. Singing to herself in the kitchen and all! He say, he done got the woman he married back again."

Sugar was listening, enjoying the sound of his voice washing over her like a velvet wave. She didn't care what he said as long as he kept talking.

"Sugar." He was calling her name. Slow and then again, "Sugar?"

"Yes," she answered and turned to look into those deep brown eyes.

"I wanna thank you." Once again, his eyes finished his thoughts and Sugar found herself, as she knew she would, lost inside of them.

*T*he winter air left as quickly as it had arrived. The next morning's air and every morning after that was warm and brilliant. Children skipped happily to school and streaked home to finish homework and enjoy the remaining dwindling daylight. People smiled broadly and spoke loudly, needing to be heard over the tumultuous joy that entered Bigelow.

Sugar was caught up in that joy. She had become a living, breathing part of it. Seth had become another limb she never knew she needed. The hours she spent away from him were crippling and made it, if not impossible, extraordinarily difficult to hold a teacup or flick a light switch. He was a third lung. Her breathing was labored without him. He made it possible for Sugar to see the beauty she possessed inside and out.

She was Sugar Lacey, born in Short Junction, Arkansas, thirty years ago. Abandoned by her mother, father unknown, raised by three women who took pity on her and took her in, giving her their name and calling her their own. She was Sugar Lacey, St. Louis night club singer, come home.

That is what he had been told and that is what she was to him. No more. That's what his mamma told him, and that's what

Sugar had attested to. His mamma didn't lie, to the best of his knowledge. Life went on.

Pearl sat back in her rocking chair and watched Joe climb into his truck, back it out and head down the road. She waved good-bye and turned her attention to the November sky and silently thanked God for her life and the lives of her family and friends. Her lips moved soundlessly as she spoke to her Jude, as she often did now. Running down for her the events of the past five days.

"Jude, I know you know all about Sugar, what I done told you, and what you've seen for yourself. I believe you had a hand in guiding her here to me, and I thanks you. I guess you know that Seth is sweet on her, and she sweet on him too. He don't know what type of life she done led, the things she allowed men to do to her body, and I ain't gonna tell him. We all got our scars to bear, every single one of us. Sugar ain't spoiled, she just a little bruised, is all. Bruises can heal and fade away to nothing. He don't have to know.

"What good would it do? He's human like the rest of us, he's gonna automatically judge and that ain't for him to do. You know that, Jude, that's gotta be left to the Almighty.

"Seth likes Sugar for who she is now, and as far as he is concerned, she always been that person, no one else. Maybe when you sent her you ain't expect her to touch no one else but me. Maybe you ain't all for Seth and Sugar getting together, probably wasn't in your plan. But you gotta know that she done changed for the better, she halfway out of what she used to be. I think Seth can pull her out the rest of the way.

"I know he's your brother, but he's my son and a mother knows best. Seth done had his own hard times. A wife that ain't care about him. That Viola treated him like a dog. She wasn't no kinda wife for my Seth. I ain't never like that child, but I let Seth make his own decision and learn the hard way. And what happened? She crushed his little heart into dust and let it go on the first strong wind that passed by. Hurt him so bad, that he ain't never talked about another woman since then. Well, up until now. You see how his eyes light up when Sugar come around? You see how he just can't stop grinning at her? She make him

happy and he make her happy. He make her want to be re-
spectable.

"A man should have a wife, and a woman should have a husband. It ain't natural any other way. He need someone to love
and she need to be loved. I wants this to work! Lord knows I
wants this to work!"

Her face was wet with tears when she was done.

$\mathcal{S}$eth's time there was coming to an end. A few days more and
Sugar knew she would be standing alongside Pearl and Joe waving good-bye to Seth as his car cut through the road dust and
headed toward home. The thought disrupted the comfortable
happiness he'd brought to her. When things were bad, time had
a habit of taking its time to pass, making sure you experienced
every painful moment. When things were good and contentment abundant, time moved like the wind, hurrying precious
moments along and forcing things that normally require nurtur-
ing to grow and forge quickly.

Seth and Sugar's talk was light, supported by laughter and
hand holding. Seth told Sugar about his dreams and asked her
about her own. His hopes and dreams rolled effortlessly off his
tongue, like the dew off a leaf under the yellow heat of the sun.
She had very few dreams, and the few she had had only just blossomed within her, and they all included him. She shrugged her
shoulders. "I don't know, tell me more about yours."

"This old man I know, he's got a small diner up in Harlem.
Does all right business, I know I could make it do better. Anyway, his wife died some years ago, children all grown and gone.
He wants to come back South, live out the rest of his years in the
house he grew up in, says he'd sell me the diner. . . ." He trailed
off then, bending to pick a wildflower.

"You gonna buy it, right?" Sugar asked, her eyes wide.

"Want to." He placed the flower in Sugar's hair above her left
ear. Taking a moment to make sure it sat just right. His actions
always surprised her. They seemed so out of the ordinary to

Sugar. But Seth treated it like it was a part of everyday life. And maybe it was—Sugar never really had a normal everyday life against which to measure his actions.

"Well, it ain't that easy, takes money. I got some, but not enough."

"How much more you need?" she asked innocently. Not realizing that a man's business was his pride.

Seth raised his eyebrows. "Not too much, about five hundred, but more than I'll be able to get my hands on in the next month or so."

"Will he take less?" Sugar's mind was working. She had a little money left, not near five hundred, but almost two hundred. She would give it to him in a second. It was the least she could do for all he'd given to her during the past few days. Knowing Seth, though, he wouldn't take it.

Again his eyebrows rose and then he smiled. "Sure, probably."

Hodges Lake was a huge fluid mirror that the trees peered down into, witnessing their lush summer greens turn into deep reds and fiery oranges, until finally, unable to hang on any longer, they'd crumple. Dry and brittle, they'd float weightlessly down, littering the liquid spectrum.

Sugar thought, if not for Seth, she would have definitely felt uneasy. The tall looming trees, and weeds thick as branches, clasped tight around anything that stood still long enough. Birds moved suddenly and quickly from the treetops, their feathered bodies temporarily blocking out the small patches of blue that fought through the wooded canopy.

It was cold there. No one had informed the backwater woods that summer had decided to hang around a little bit longer. Sugar pulled her sweater closer to her body. An icy chill sliced through the thin blanket she and Seth shared, causing her to shake and her teeth to chatter. He wrapped his arm around her shoulder and pulled her close. "You cold?" he asked, the warmth in his eyes caressing her face.

"A little bit," she said and gave him a brief smile. They were alone for the first time since Thanksgiving night. No one in the next room or backseat. Just them. She was glad and nervous all at once.

"Me and Joe Jr. use to come here all the time and play when we was kids or fish alongside Daddy. Farther down," he pointed south, "the lake gets shallow. Daddy would let us swim there. We'd stay in the water so long that we'd look like raisins by the time we got home." He laughed at the memory. "Mamma would be mad. Fussing with Daddy about letting us stay in the water for so long."

"Was Jude with you?" Sugar asked. She was staring at the spot Seth pointed to and she could envision the three children, two boys, one girl, splashing happily around in the water.

"Sometimes," Seth said quietly. His mood was serious now. Sugar had felt it when she opened the door to his solemn face this morning. A massive change from the wonderful time they'd spent together the night before. They took in the new James Dean movie, *East of Eden*. Broward County held the only colored movie house in the state of Arkansas. It was a place where people could lose themselves to the imagination of the silver screen without having to be subjected to the confines of an over-crowded colored section of a white movie house balcony.

Sugar sat through the movie, barely conscious of what was going on in front of her. Seth's arm was wrapped around her, his hand softly, rhythmically stroking her shoulder. He gently guided her head to rest in the curve of his neck. Her heartbeat eventually slowed and her breathing evened, as she allowed her mind and body to become comfortable with his affection and tenderness. Seth's actions felt as foreign to her as another country. Afterward, when the movie was over and they filed out, blending amidst other black couples, he found her hand and held it tightly in his own. She could think of nothing else as they sped along the dark country roads, the moon lighting their way, Nat King Cole serenading them from the car radio. She wanted nothing more than to have him near her again, she wanted to return to the safe darkness of the movie theater, the drifting scents of buttered popcorn and the soft space between Seth's jawline and shoulder. And as if reading her thoughts, he pulled her to him once again.

Neither of them wanted the evening to end so they found

themselves in the sultry, sexy darkness of the Memphis Roll, hungry for passion but settling for two fried chicken plates and Cokes. She introduced him to some people, glad that he'd been absent from Arkansas and Bigelow long enough not to be familiar with more than two faces. Thankfully, two faces that she'd never known in the darkness of her bedroom. She took the stage to sing and although the Roll was filled to capacity, her songs were for Seth alone.

When the sun rose up to kiss the sky, Seth Taylor's own lips were brushing gently against Sugar's forehead. They said goodnight, even though morning was in full bloom, and went reluctantly smiling to their separate beds, holding themselves tightly until sleep slipped in and took them to the land of dreams.

Now they were seated close to the lake's edge, wanting so much to look directly at each other, to touch, but satisfied for now with the reflections that bounced off the deep blue belly of the lake.

"This lake mean a lot to me." Seth was speaking again. His tone was muddled, and made it more difficult for Sugar to decipher what he was feeling. She listened intently. "As a child I came here to play and then to mourn my sister's death. As a man, I loved here, asked Viola to be my wife and when it was over, I came here and tossed my wedding band into the water. I've come here to think things out, to be alone and to pray."

Sugar knew he was talking around what he really wanted to say. She knew that he was searching for the right words to express his real thoughts. If only she could look into his eyes, then she would know the truth. "What I'm saying is, this been the place where I make all my life's decisions, right here in this spot." He jabbed the ground with the piece of wood he'd been fiddling with. "Sugar, I ain't felt this way about a woman for a long time. I—I mean, you make me feel special and warm all over, you know?"

She did know, she was experiencing the same feelings. "I can't explain it. I feel like somebody done cast a spell on me or something." He laughed nervously. "What I means to say is, I'm heading back North the day after tomorrow and for the first time I don't wanna go, but I knows I gotta go, and what I wanna know is, well, will you come with me?" He said the last few words fast. His voice cracked like a pubescent boy, his hands shook.

Sugar's face was hurting. It was as if something was pulling the skin around her mouth in two different directions. It took a moment before she realized the wincing pain was from the wide smile that stretched across her face. Her heart exploded with joy and her soul sang hallelujah, but her mind dwelled on the truth of her life and she questioned her emotions.

His question shocked her mute, and she could not find her voice to answer, and if she could, she would have asked: *Why me?* Because happiness like this was not usually reserved for people like her and she knew it.

He read her face wrong, and assumed her smile meant yes. He embraced her and held her in his arms until she herself felt that yes could be the only right answer. She was going to take Pearl's advice, and stop looking behind her and set her eyesight straight ahead.

He kissed her, gently, timidly, on the lips. Unsure if he should, but unable to stop himself from doing so. His fingers found her scar and moved lovingly over it. She waited for him to ask about its origin, but he didn't. His hands slid down her back and branched off and up her sides, brushing innocently against the curve of her breasts, and then he pulled away suddenly, clearing his throat and averting his eyes. She felt it too, the fire and desire. For the first time in her life she *wanted* to give herself over to a man, and not because the rent had to be paid, or her stomach was touching her back, but because she loved him.

They walked, hand in hand, out of the woods and into the full bright light. The world looked so beautiful that she felt her life ahead couldn't be anything less than wonderful.

Chapter Seventeen

*S*UGAR'S mind was whirling as she moved quickly through the house, gathering what few things she owned and shoving them into her worn suitcase. They'd decided that they would tell Joe and Pearl tomorrow, the day before he was leaving—they were leaving.

Lunch was tough. Seth and Sugar were bursting with their secret and they couldn't help but grin stupidly every time their eyes met across the table. "What in the world is wrong with you two?" Pearl had inquired more than once. Joe just looked up from his cold chicken sandwich and shrugged.

"Ain't nothing wrong, Mamma, everything is all right," Seth answered, his mouth half full of food.

Pearl turned her eyes on Sugar. "Ya'll acting silly. Like a bunch of schoolchildren!"

"Leave it be, Bit," Joe said and winked at her. Pearl shrugged her shoulders in defeat. She changed the subject. "Ya'll going out tonight?"

"Yes ma'am, gonna go down to the Rib Shack and hang out down there for a while with them boys. Say my good-byes and all," Seth said and reached for the pitcher of lemonade.

A ghost of sadness crossed over Pearl's face. She didn't want her boy to go.

"Can't you stay a day longer?" she pleaded. "One more day, Seth."

"Mamma, I done stayed too long already. You want me to lose my job? I got's things to do, Mamma." Seth was smiling, trying to keep the mood jovial. " 'Sides, I'll be back before you know it!"

"Ask him not to go, Sugar," Pearl was demanding her. "Go'on, maybe he'll listen to you." She folded her arms stubbornly across her bosom.

Sugar shot Seth a look—she wanted to tell Pearl and Joe about their plans. It wasn't fair keeping their decision a secret; Pearl was gonna suffer all the more when she found out Sugar was going to be leaving with Seth. He shook his head no and looked at his father for help.

"Bit, c'mon now. The boy said he got's to get back to work. Do you want him to lose his job?" Joe intervened.

"He could always come back home to Bigelow, plenty of jobs 'round here."

"Like what? Working canning fish or cutting the white folks' lawns? He don't want that. He want better than that," Joe said and returned to his food.

His words made Sugar uneasy. "He want better than that." Was she part of the *better* he wanted? She quickly pushed the thought from her mind. Of course she was.

She helped Pearl wash and dry the dishes. Her mind was wrapped around so many things that she was getting a headache. She didn't have much to say and Pearl, overwhelmed with her own concerns about Seth's imminent departure, didn't notice.

"I'll be by to get you about nine." He was standing close, his hands enclosing hers, both of their hearts beating wildly. They wanted each other, but resisted. Sugar supposed that's what was called keeping it pure. He kissed her eyelids and the lobe of her ear then walked slowly home, looking back twice to make sure she was real and his.

The clothes she would take were packed. The others, the reminders of who she used to be, would be burned. She opened the small drawer to the nightstand by her bed, she didn't know why, and found herself looking at the small Bible Pearl had given her, a rosary and a wilted pack of Luckys. She stared at these things for a long moment until she finally picked up the Bible and opened it to the place that held her mother's picture. It had been a while since she looked at it and now she sat down and stared at the woman who'd given her life, as if it was the first time she was seeing her.

"I gotta man, Mamma. He say I make him feel happy. I'm gonna keep making him happy, Mamma. And maybe we'll get married and have us some babies."

The thought of having babies tickled her. She'd never imagined herself as a mother. But then she'd never imagined herself more than a whore.

"I ain't never gonna leave my babies, Mamma," she added and placed the picture safely back between the Bible pages.

She placed the Bible and the rosary on top of her clothes and closed the suitcase.

*S*he slipped twice running for the phone. Dripping wet, she left soggy footprints across the floor. "Hello?" she answered breathlessly, hoping it was Seth.

"Hey, baby!" The voice was low, haunting.

"Seth?" she said and pulled the towel around her.

"Naw, girl . . . it's your tootsie roll, your nigga . . . Lappy!"

Sugar stood stark still. She hadn't heard from him since he cornered her at the Memphis Roll more than a month ago.

"Yeah?" Her voice was granite.

"Baby, where you been? I been calling you but you ain't never home. I even drove by there the other night, knocked on your door, nothing. Started to go over to that old woman and ask her if you were still living, but it was late. You know I respect the elderly." He laughed a twisted laugh that caused the hair to stand up on Sugar's neck. "I got to bust a nut, girl. I been saving it just for you. Got a little weed, a little whiskey. What you say to that!"

The shaking started in her knees and rose quickly, until it was in her stomach churning like sour milk. She sat down and covered her mouth, trying to resist the urge to puke.

"Sugar?" His voice was like poison.

"No," she managed to say.

"No? C'mon, girl. You know uh, me and this cat named Lou figure maybe you can take us both. You know what I mean?"

"No!" She was screaming. "No! No! No!"

There was silence. Sugar thought the line was dead and then his voice came again like a coiled cobra poising to strike.

"You listen here, bitch, I'm the one who got you most of your customers. If it wasn't for me you would be blowing farm boys for fifty cents a pop. I'm the one that got you hooked up at the Roll! So don't you go telling me no. Because I don't much like that word. And people that done used it on me, ain't walking around to tell about it and neither are their old lady friends. You get what I'm saying?

"Now we both businesspeople, I ain't trying to come and get my goodies off for free. Naw, I'm willing to pay, just like always. Things been good for me and I'd like to share the wealth. Now we willing to pay you one hundred dollars for your time, now you know that's more than you make in a month. We'll be over there about ten, so if you ain't wash your ass, I suggest you do so."

Click.

The dial tone buzzed in her ear. She opened the nightstand drawer and pulled out the pack of Luckys.

*P*earl jumped as the front door slammed shut. "Oh, Lord! Seth is back!" Pearl squealed and scrambled from the bed.

"Bit, Seth is a grown man. He done been married his ownself, he know what married peoples do." Joe was laughing as he watched his wife run around the bedroom, her hefty behind jiggling madly as she rushed around picking up her bra and panties and trying anxiously to shove herself into them before her son made it to the top landing of the staircase.

"Yeah, but it's the middle of the day!" Pearl giggled in spite of herself and tossed the bra aside, opting to throw her house dress on over her bare breasts. Sex had become a daily routine with them. They found themselves breathlessly wrapped in each other's arms at least once a day. They had probably had more sex in the past two months then they did in the entire thirty or more years they'd been married. With each union, Pearl became less inhibited with her body and her actions toward Joe. It was wildly passionate, sometimes lasting for what seemed like hours, other times it was short, sweet and terribly satisfying, but right now it was interrupted.

Pearl rushed from the room and met Seth at the bottom of the stairs, practically slamming into him. "Oh, hello, baby," she said, her voice too high and sing-songy.

"Hey, Mamma," he responded. He noticed that her house dress was buttoned wrong, her hair tussled and her cheeks inflamed. "Where's Daddy?"

Pearl's hands came up to her face, brushing away the wild strands of hair from her eyes. Joe's scent lingered on her fingertips and caught her off guard. She quickly shoved her hands into the pockets of the dress.

"Uh, we was taking a . . . well, a nap."

"Uh-huh," Seth said and decided to return to the kitchen. It was obvious what was going on. He hadn't decided how to feel about his parents taking care of business as much as they did. Since he'd been home he'd heard the late-night groaning. The light tap, tap, tap of their headboard as it made insistent contact with his bedroom wall.

"You hungry. Want me to make you a sandwich?" Pearl spoke quickly, her movements swift and fluttery like a small bird.

"Okay, Mamma." Seth knew she needed to occupy herself.

They sat across from each other, enjoying the quiet mother and son moment. Pearl reached out and brushed her hand across his face, picking a piece of lint from his thick mass of hair or just rubbing the back of his resting hand. Seth talked a mile a minute; every other word was "Sugar." Pearl smiled. She knew by the way Sugar's name always seemed to find a place in his conversation, and how it rolled off his tongue like honey, that the two were smitten.

"You like her something awful, huh, Seth?"

"I likes her well enough," Seth said, still wanting to keep their announcement a secret until tomorrow.

"You likes her more than well enough," Pearl said as she removed his plate from the table.

"Well, to tell the truth, I thinks a man could do real well with a woman like that." Seth leaned back and rubbed his stomach heartily.

"Sure could," Pearl said, watching him sideways. Her heart was hopeful.

*A*t nine, Sugar heard Seth come up the porch steps and knock softly on the screen door. Everything he did was soft. Like how you'd expect a woman to be. Gentle. She heard him calling her name from beneath her bedroom window, over and over again. But she wouldn't answer. Couldn't answer. She just lay there enjoying the sound of her name in his mouth.

The shame of what she was about to do had taken her voice away, left her mute with remorse. She didn't know that at the time. Sugar thought she was doing it for Seth. Told herself the money would come in handy, help him to buy that business up in New York, help fulfill his dreams and make a better life for the both of them.

Then Sugar convinced herself that she was doing it for Pearl. Lappy wasn't a man to play with and he had told her that if Sugar didn't oblige him Pearl could be the one to suffer. She didn't want that.

But looking back, being open and real with herself, Sugar realized that she did it because of who she was and you can't change a person overnight or during a week home on holiday. What she was had been hammered into her.

The woman who Seth fell for, well, that wasn't Sugar. Not the real Sugar. The one he loved was a lie someone conjured up on the front porch of #10 Grove Street.

He would have found out sooner or later. Life is just that way, there's only so much you can do in the dark before it comes to light. If nothing else, Sugar learned that much. Who's to say his best friend in New York wasn't a customer of hers in St. Louis?

But that realization hadn't come yet. Even as she lay there and listened to Seth calling her name she still knew that she would let Lappy and his friend use her body one last time, and then she could just disappear. Their money in her pockets, Seth on her arm, the two of them burning up the road to New York, to a new life.

She heard Seth half walk, half run back to his house and she knew he was going to try and phone her. That phone rang a million times and then stopped and rang a million more times before he ran back and started banging on the door, Pearl and Joe with him this time. Six hands banging on her door. She thought she would go mad. But she lay there, sane as could be, still as the night.

Lappy Clayton's car pulled up and Pearl, Joe and Seth stopped calling her name.

She heard the car door slam, his footsteps as he left the car and approached the house and the breeze as it wrapped around the dogwoods.

"She ain't there," Seth said. He was mad that she ain't answer him. Mad that he didn't know if she was dead or alive. Mad that some high faluting, half breed nigger was walking up her front porch.

"C'mon, Seth. C'mon, now." Pearl's voice was scared. Sugar couldn't see what was happening, but she knew Pearl was pulling at him, coaxing him back over to the house. Last thing she wanted was her baby tussling with the likes of Lappy Clayton.

"Go on, son," Joe commanded him.

"Daddy, I'm trying to tell the man she ain't there! So he might as well head back to where he come from!"

Sugar whispered in the darkness: "Please, Seth."

Maybe she was talking to God. She didn't know. All she knew was didn't nobody step to Lappy Clayton and expect to walk away unmarked.

Lappy ain't said a thing. He didn't even take a moment to snuff at 'em. Didn't even look Seth over more than once. He just called Sugar's name out one time, loud and sharp, and there she was opening the door.

Seth's face changed instantly and his lips moved to form the question, why? Sugar didn't respond. How could she? She knew he was thinking all the wrong things, and whatever his thoughts were, were far better than the actual truth.

She wanted him to say her name one more time, not that it would have made a difference in the life she'd chosen to keep when she swung that door open for Lappy, but so she could feel something, for the last time.

*S*eth stood in the yard and watched as Lappy Clayton stepped into Sugar's home and closed the door behind him. Seth couldn't stop shaking his head. He couldn't stop clenching and unclenching his fists.

What had just happened?

"Lying bitch! If she had a man, why didn't she come out and say so?! Why!"

His parents stood behind him, saying nothing, not even breathing. Pearl's mouth hung open, and disbelief spread quickly across her face as she watched the scenario unfold before her. What the hell was Sugar doing?

Seth stormed past them and slammed into the house. By the time Pearl and Joe got up to the door of his room, half his clothes were already in his suitcase. His face was filled with anger.

"Seth." Pearl wouldn't cross the threshold. She felt that Seth's anger would surely blind him and possibly cause him to mistake her for someone else. "Seth?" she called again, above the slamming dresser drawers.

"Mamma." He answered between clenched teeth, then held up one hand and looked at her like she was the enemy.

Joe placed his hands firmly on her shoulders and backed her

away from the room. She turned questioning, concerned eyes on her husband. "He a man, let him deal with this as a man," Joe said. His words usually made sense to Pearl, but now they were meaningless bunches of letters.

"Seth, baby, please. What you doing? You ain't planning on leaving right now, tonight?"

Seth moved past them like the wind. Joe and Pearl followed. He was halfway out the door before his father's voice stopped him. *"Boy!"*

Seth's face was wet with angry hot tears. What he wanted was to just keep moving, let the cool air dry his face and maybe settle his soul. He wanted out of that house, away from Sugar, Bigelow, and all of the bad things that always seemed to happen there.

"You ain't gonna disrespect me and your mamma by just slamming out of this house and not saying good-bye, I don't care what's paining you." Joe knew his son was hurting, he felt the pain his son was experiencing. It spilled from Seth, infecting both of them.

He wiped at his tears, and turned to face his parents. His face was a pot of emotion, swirling and bubbling, threatening to boil over. He brushed his trembling lips against his mother's cheek, moving quickly away from her so as not to get caught in her embrace. He shook his father's hand. Pearl wept as Seth sat in his car, engine running, staring at the shadows that moved behind the thin curtains of Sugar's bedroom. He heard Lappy's laughter and then the lights went out. Seth's tires screamed against the black tarmac, and then he was gone.

Chapter Eighteen

*P*AIN was an unwanted friend of Sugar's. She couldn't seem to get away from it, no matter where she went. Sugar looked behind her and pain was there. Looked beside her and pain was there, looked ahead and pain was beckoning her to hurry and catch up.

From the moment Lappy entered her house, she knew he had been drinking and drugging for most of the day. His face was haggard and his eyes bloodshot. He smelled of booze and reefer. When Lappy lay down on top of Sugar, pain came and lay down on top of him, making Sugar's burden and misery greater. Sugar just pulled in as much air as her lungs would hold and let them both get on with what they had been destined to do.

She didn't ask where his friend was, or if she was gonna get the same amount of money for just doing him. She didn't want to speak because she was still hearing Seth's voice calling to her in the corner of her mind. It was a light echo that was quickly fading into the darkness that surrounded her and she strained to hear it over the creaking of the bedsprings and the howl of wind outside her window.

She looked up and over the shoulder of Lappy and caught sight of the dry leaves flying by like wingless birds. The cold that followed the morning gale was seeping in fast and all she could think of was, she should have lit the fireplace. But then she remembered she didn't have any firewood. And then she remembered she didn't have no Seth either.

"Who you think you are, huh? Who you!" He yelled and raised his hand as if to strike her. Sugar cringed and waited for the impact. "You bitch. I set you up at the Memphis Roll, I get you your customers and you treat me like some junkyard dog! Nah, baby, it don't work that way. You hear me, Sugar? I'm the man and you the bitch!" His words were hot and angry.

Lappy lowered his hand and turned Sugar roughly over, taking her from behind. She didn't even stop him when he began to get rough and scream obscenities at her. "You gonna learn your place. You hear me, you whoring bitch!"

She felt his hands on the back of her thighs and the only thing Sugar could think of were clusters of blackberries. She felt his tongue on her back and she saw the smooth stones that sat in the shallow part of Hodges Lake. With each of Lappy's thrusts Sugar could hear Seth calling her a lying bitch.

"Look up at me, gal," he says. "You embarrassed me. Made me look like a piece of shit. Everybody saw it. You and your *friends*." "Friends" came out wet and obscene. "Sitting up in the Roll like they own it. Like they had something to do with you being there." Lappy was breathing heavy like he needed air, sweating like the temperature just rose forty degrees instead of dropping twenty. He clutched his stomach as if in pain, but the smile that spread across his face said something different.

Sugar looked up past that mouth and into his eyes and there she saw what Jude saw fifteen years earlier, and she wasn't even scared.

Poor Sugar lay beneath Lappy waiting for the end, but realizing, after he began to speak, that she was just at the beginning. His words would have left her emotionally handicapped had it not been for the faith she did not know she possessed.

Lappy laughed with glee and began his tale where he should have climaxed. His voice was thick and he dribbled hot spit into the folds of Sugar's ear. His breath was like fire on her cheek and she could feel his heart beating so hard against her chest that she thought he would drop dead on top of her. But the more he spoke, the faster he slammed into her. It was as if the words alone motivated him, but Sugar was no more than a hole in the mattress by then. Her body had gone numb a lifetime ago.

He spoke of a car trip. A ride through the Arkansas countryside. Drunk and speeding down a lonely country road in an almost new 1936 Ford. He remembered the heat of the day and the sound of the car's engine as it suddenly shut down. Not knowing much about cars except how to drive them, he cussed most of the two miles he walked up the road in the hot sun toward Bigelow. He was just rounding a bend in the dirt road when he saw the ribbons, yellow and light, appearing for brief instances above the tall colorful wildflowers. Had the girl stopped jumping, the flowers would have hidden her completely from sight, but he saw the ribbons and evil propelled him toward her.

The girl smiled when she saw him coming, pushing the flowers aside and down, crushing them beneath his fine leather shoes. She wouldn't have been there, but she was supposed to meet a friend. A boy from Sunday school who'd passed her a note that said she was pretty and that he liked her. Liked her very much. She liked him too and had liked him for a good many years of her youth. She thought it was funny how they'd been in the same Sunday school class for years, and only this year had he finally noticed her.

Can't tell Mamma and Daddy, she'd thought as she stuffed the note into her brand-new white laced brassiere. She liked the way the paper felt against her budding breasts. "Knobs" her mother called them.

No, they would forbid it. "You don't meet no boy no wherever. A well-raised young man would come to your house, sit down with your family." She'd heard it a million times from her mamma's mouth and had never defied her, but today, today was different.

The girl wouldn't have been jumping up and down either, but she couldn't see the road over the flowers, couldn't see if he was coming along. She was too scared to stand too close to the road, too far out in the open, someone would see and tell her parents. So she stayed hidden in the thick field of flowers and jumped up every once in a while, snatching peeks at the road.

She smiled at Lappy because she was young and innocent. Nevertheless, her heart had jumped a bit at Lappy's approach and the smell of liquor that preceded him. The path through the flowers was a popular shortcut among the locals, but the girl did not find his face familiar. And if he was not familiar to her, then she was not familiar to him and he couldn't tell on her. And if he could, who would he tell? He didn't know whose child she was.

The thought of running like the wind did not even cross her mind until Lappy's heavy hand was crushing her windpipe.

Lappy's hands were closing hard around Sugar's own windpipe as he told her how Jude's scared eyes pleaded, how her knees buckled under his strength.

"She didn't die quick, you know," he said quietly, his eyes turned up, remembering his deed. His hand went slack around Sugar's throat; just enough to let a piece of air through. She gagged and felt her stomach turn over.

It was true, the girl's life stubbornly left her body in spastic jerks and twitches that rustled the long fragile stems of the flowers and drove her body deeper into the soft earth, soiling her white and yellow dress.

Lappy watched until death had replaced life and then he raised the child's dress above her waist and stared down at the clean white cotton panties that seemed to glow against her smooth brown skin. He reached into his pants pocket and pulled from it the switchblade he carried for protection and slowly cut the material away from her body. She was still a child and only barely a woman. Hair as light and sparse as the coat of a newborn cat covered the flesh that sheltered her womanhood.

Lappy lowered his face and inhaled her scent. He hurridly unzipped his pants and removed his penis. He tried to enter her, but her flesh was young and did not give enough to allow him inside. He cussed in frustration and spat in her face. His hand was up now, up over the girl, the blade glimmering in the high afternoon sun and then it was down, slicing through her skin, splintering her pelvis bone. Over and over again, until he'd separated her life-producing organs from her body.

Then he looked at her, lying there, her dress rolled up to her neck, a pool of blood covering her lower section, and he saw the eyes, wide open and staring. He saw himself in those eyes. He looked down at his life-taking hands and tried to shake away the murderous qualities they now possessed.

Lappy threw the young girl's vagina beside her, and walked away, looking back once only to see if anyone was witness to his crime before continuing down the road toward Bigelow.

He'd found out the girl's name a day later when the news of the murder spread like wildfire through ten towns.

Jude.

His hand tightened around Sugar's throat again and then loosened. He did not want to choke the life from her, he wanted to beat it out of her.

"I'ma do you just like I did her. This time though, it's gonna be sweeter 'cause you done gone and given me a reason to kill your ass!" He slapped her hard across her face and laughed.

It seemed as though the laughter went on for days. Sugar's ears were filled with it and then suddenly he stopped. His face changed and he leaned in close to her until their noses touched. "You know," he said with a slight look of wonder in his face, "you kinda look like her." They remained like that for some time. Noses touching. And then he laughed again and yelled, "Jude's waiting for you!"

Heavy-fisted blows rained down on Sugar's face until her nose spouted blood and her eyes swelled shut. His hands wrapped around her throat for the third time, stopping the passage of air, causing her chest to swell hot and the darkness behind her eyes to come forward and pull her in.

The howl of a wild animal is what yanked her back from death's grip and into the swirling gray room. Sugar could not open her mouth and she believed it must have been cut away from her face, because she felt nothingness there. The howling increased and held on until the pitch became unbearable and then it faded, only to gain momentum seconds later. She realized, after some time, that the howling was not that of a wild animal, but the combination of wind and wild man.

Fire gauged itself through her navel, long flaming fingers

reached out and ignited her womb so that no life would ever live there. The pain was a hurricane raging through her body seeking release in a scream that would never come.

She saw Jude's eyes. Those young wet eyes. Like buckets of water, looking down on her. Looking sad for her. She wanted death and asked for it out loud, "God please let me die!"

*P*earl saw Lappy leave beneath a black and mournful sky. The moon was hidden and not a star lent light. He left from the front door, same door he came through, except this time he didn't close it. He left it open, swinging hopelessly in the wind.

Pearl huffed and shook her head in disgust. She'd not slept. Not even one wink. First sadness kept her awake, then anger, then concern and finally dread. Joe would not leave her, and so he settled himself in the living room on the couch.

Pearl looked out the window again. Lappy's skin was glowing dim in the vast dark purple of the departing night. Red splattered his back, neck and hands, giving the illusion that *he* was wounded. Pearl watched, wondering if the lack of sleep was playing tricks on her eyes.

Lappy was whistling, his shirt thrown over one bare shoulder as he walked slowly toward his car. He stopped short of the driver's side door and bent over and puked. Pearl's hands came quickly to her mouth and her eyes widened. He turned around, feeling her presence, her watching eyes, and stared directly at the curtain that hid her. Puke dripped from the sides of his mouth and clung to his lower lip. His eyes seemed to glow, and the sight of them sent icy shivers up and down her spine. He smiled and then waved gaily at her.

Pearl's heart was beating so loud and fast, she thought she would faint right then and there. He looked up toward the silent second floor of Sugar's house and then climbed into his car and drove off.

Fear should have kept her welded to the spot behind the curtain. Fear should have sent her running to Joe's sleeping side, but instead fear sent her running from the safety of her home and straight through that open front door up to Sugar's room.

Pearl stood at the threshold of Sugar's bedroom as the pre-dawn light melted away the gray of the room. There was a smell like wet steel lingering in the air. Her heart began to sink, sink deep into her chest, trying to hide from the sight it was sure awaited. She stepped in, and a feeling so familiar and horrible took her by the hand and led her to a place she had been fifteen years earlier.

Among the crumpled, blood-soaked sheets lay Sugar. Pearl reached down to touch the purple, swollen face of her friend and it was 1940 all over again.

This time, however, Pearl's sanity was saved, by the grace of God, her sanity was saved. Sugar's eyes fluttered and then opened.

Her voice found her, after fifteen years her voice came and Pearl screamed until her throat closed up and Joe stood beside her, shotgun in hand.

*H*ours later, Sugar heard voices around her. "She needs to be in a hospital."

The voice came from above her. It was a stern disinfected voice. The sharp snap of rubber gloves followed the stringent words and then she heard Joe. "Well this here is the way we want it. No hospital, just home."

"She could set up an infection in any number of places on her body. Was the police notified?"

"Dr. Williams, maybe you've forgotten where you are. This here is Bigelow. The law don't care none about us and what we do to one another. It just don't make no sense getting them involved in something they could only make worse, now do it?" Joe's voice was calm, but his annoyance at the doctor's ignorance was evident.

Sugar could hear footsteps and the voices of Joe and Dr. Williams fading as they traveled down the stairs and out the front door. She felt a cool wet cloth move slowly across her forehead, a hand constantly brushing against her own and the sound of rapid prayers.

*S*he was alive. For some reason God had spared her. But Sugar would never look at it that way. She had asked God for only one thing in her entire life, and he had not granted it.

God had sent Sugar to the brink of death, dangled it before her and then snatched it away, hurling her back to Joe and Pearl Taylor. Three weeks and four days passed before Sugar was able to stand. Lappy had done a job on her. Cutting deep into her stomach, but somehow missing her vital organs. Bruised purple fingerprints remained wrapped around Sugar's throat, broken skin around her cheekbones and the soft underside of her eyes would heal and scar blacker than her midnight skin.

She dropped down in weight, unwilling or unable to eat. She did not speak or let her eyes wander across the soft faces of her saviors. Joe's strong arms lifted her from her bed and carried her gently from the room and into the bathroom. He sat her on the toilet, holding her body erect as Pearl undressed her, before he placed her into the warm soapy water of the bathtub. They washed her together. Husband and wife. Father and mother. They washed her as if she belonged to them.

They took turns feeding her or speaking small words of hope, faith and encouragement. The hugs came often accompanied by quiet easy kisses on the slope of her cheek and the brim of her head lulling her to sleep or waking her to the breaking day.

Time's seamlessness enwrapped her and when the blue haze of hopelessness finally faded away into the morning mist of the twentieth day, Sugar decided that her time in Bigelow had come to an end.

"Miss Pearl." Sugar's words were not spoken, but seemed to be a part of a weary breath taken years earlier. Pearl turned slowly toward the dark living room and her heart stopped and started again with the first step she managed into the room.

"S-Sugar?" she said warily. "What you doing out of bed child." She tried to make her tone light and rushed as if she had better things to do, but would take the time anyway. "C'mon, back to bed, you ain't near well enough to be—"

"Pearl, please." Sugar's words came stronger now. "You look worse than me." Pearl half-laughed, and moved into the small light that spilled in from the hallway. The swelling had gone down in Sugar's face but it was easy to see it had been used as a punching bag. Her brown eyes were nothing more than brown pools of water. Her lips were puffed and black.

"You, well, you and Joe have done all you can for me. Look at you, here all day every day. All night every night. You got your own to worry about." She coughed and Pearl took a step toward her. Sugar raised her hand to keep her away. "Stop, Pearl. You been doing for me for a long time. I don't even know how long, but I knows it been a while. I want to thank you." Her voice cracked. "Ain't many people would have taken the time to care for the likes of me, and at first I gotta say that I was mad at ya'll for doing it. Dead was the only place I wanted to be, but in time I realized that no matter how much I wanted it, I wasn't getting it. Life's funny like that sometime. I also wanna thank you for keeping the law outta this. It would have made no sense, really. Lappy like to be the devil himself, reporting what he done to me could only bring more harm than good. Thank you."

She moved slowly to the couch and sat down, leaning forward briefly to put out her cigarette. Pearl was shaking. She had wanted with all her heart to call the police. She wanted Lappy Clayton to be hung from the nearest tree and his body left to whatever would have him. But Sugar had whispered no in her ear so many times after Pearl found her that she'd dreamed the word dancing around her for two nights straight. And so she did nothing, but hoped that Sugar, after she healed, would think differently and want justice to be done.

"I'm better now, not good as new, but I ain't never been new, just borrowed, lent and given like secondhand things usually are. I am who I am, Miss Pearl, can't no amount of soap and water change that."

"Sugar." Pearl felt despair clogging her throat, forcing tears from her eyes.

"I ain't deserve a lot of what I got here in Bigelow," Sugar continued. "I mean the good things, the things that made me smile, laugh and sing. I ain't do much good for people in my life and so I really don't know why so much good has come to me." She shook her head in disbelief. "But I suppose that will all end now, seeing what I went and done to Seth." Sugar found it hard to say his name now. Saying it was like a blade being dragged across her heart. "I ain't get a chance to say sorry." Her voice choked with emotion.

"You planning on leaving. To go where?" Pearl asked, trying to sound casual, to masquerade the panic that was growing inside of her. She wiped at her tears and forced a smile.

"Don't know yet."

"When you thinking about going?"

"Soon."

Pearl looked around her. She tried to imagine herself without Sugar. She didn't know who that might be, the person that existed before Sugar's arrival was buried deep into the hard, dry memory of Bigelow next to the rotting bones of her baby girl. How could she be anything more with the loss of two in her life now?

It would do no good to beg against Sugar's decision. Just as it had done no good to force Sugar into a role that she was unprepared for. Look at the damage that had been done already. Pearl could have kept Sugar close and not changed a thing about her, she was really fine as she was. Dark, loud and full of energy and song. Who said she had to be demure, low-key, with an unpainted face and a Christian clean soul? Does that make a good human being, a good and decent friend?

They would all have to learn to live with the misjudgment they'd made.

Sugar had another burden to bear, another secret to hide. Every time she looked at Joe or Pearl she heard Lappy's words echoing in the forefront of her mind. Her decision had been made as soon as the words rolled out of Lappy's mouth. If she lived she would never tell. Telling would only open old wounds that were still healing. Pearl and Joe didn't deserve that kind of pain.

Jude was there all the time now, popping up beside her, hiding behind her eyelids and inviting herself into her dreams. The mirror reflecting her face, sometimes with those sad eyes, sometimes just her sweet face with deep black holes where her eyes should have been.

She was always there. A piece of lint on the blanket, a moon ray on the wall. Just there, floating and waiting. Taunting Sugar with her presence.

Sugar didn't know whether she was trying to get her to stay or push her away.

"What!" she would yell. "What do you want from me!"

Those sad, wet eyes just stared back at her.

Sugar sat slumped on the bed. Staring at nothing in particular. Her sight was turned inward. Every once in a while her body would quiver and tremble, but just for a moment. And then her head would lift and she'd survey the room with quick darting eyes. She was afraid to take too much of it in at one time. The room where she carried out the business of pleasure, the room where Lappy Clayton had tried to carry out the business of killing. She blinked back the memory and shuddered.

It was during one of those episodes that she spotted the box. Small, wrapped in brown paper, resting on the dresser. Probably brought in by Pearl or Joe during one of their vigils. She walked over and examined it. It was a package, delivered through the mail. Her name and address was scrawled on top:

Sugar Lacey
#10 Grove Street
Bigelow, Arkansas

In the far corner, the return address was written:

> *Mae Lacey*
> *Duncan Road*
> *Short Junction, Arkansas*

Sugar stood there for a moment, not sure if she should open it or not. She cocked her head sideways, trying to help her mind tell her what to do next.

She felt the room cool. The wind suddenly died outside her window, but she felt a breeze pick up around her ankles. It swirled slowly, almost lovingly around her calves, edging its way up her thighs, hips and waist, until finally she was enwrapped.

"Mama?" Sugar muttered and then jumped at her own voice. Her hands went up to her mouth and her fingers touched her lips in awe.

With trembling hands she tore at the brown paper that secured the box. Tore through its many layers—layers that at times seemed like skin—until she reached the lid. She removed the top and her nose was accosted with the scent of lavender. Dozens of aged yellow envelopes that carried her name in delicate, fading black ink lay before her.

She removed the envelopes, one by one, first bringing them close to her nose and smelling the lavender, then moving them across her cheek and down her neck. She could feel her mother. For the first time she could really feel her mother. She laughed, a tearful sorrowful laugh as she opened the letters.

Each envelope held thin sheets of paper that carried words so unbelievable, yet so believable that there would be no decision for her to make. It had been made while she lingered in her mother's womb, a wisp of balled flesh, a secret not yet known.

They all began the same: "My dear sweet child."

And closed simply: "Mother."

The letters revealed a life filled with suffering. They told of a sliver of time when Bertie took love for herself beneath the watchful eye of the moon and her glowing children. It explained her choice to abandon a perfect ebony child because of her fear of inherited madness and the cancerous guilt that manifested itself into the tumor that consumed her body and finally extinguished her life.

". . . He knows nothing about you and I hope he never will."

Sugar's hands trembled violently as she held each letter and read aloud the life of a woman she never knew. She hoped her father's name would be revealed to her among the words that spilled out in jagged black ink. But it never was and then she came upon the picture.

There was her mother, young and beautiful, her hair pulled back, her skin glowing, a shy smile across her face, nothing like the sadness that blanketed her in the first picture Sugar had. A young man stood bashfully beside her, tall, dark and incredibly handsome. Their bodies didn't touch as they posed awkwardly for the camera. Sugar pulled the picture closer to her face, even though it was quite evident who the man was. She saw her own features sketched in his face. She saw Seth's features in his face. She turned the picture around and her mother's handwriting confirmed what she already knew to be true: *Me and Joe 1924.*

*D*ays later, Sugar set her bags just inside the entrance of the church doors. Visible for all to see. She wanted them to know that they'd won. Their God had heard their prayers. She was leaving.

"On the eve of our Lord's birth." That's what the Reverend called it, and that's the way Sugar would always remember it.

Pearl looked up in surprise when Sugar appeared beside her. She nudged Joe to scoot down some so as to make room for Sugar in the pew. Even when the space was made Sugar stood staring at them for a good long while. Her focus moved slowly from Pearl to Joe, resting on him for some time before it moved back to Pearl.

She looked as she did when she waltzed into Bigelow behind the crazed winter of '54–'55, except her skin was the color of what flames leave behind after they danced across the walls of a poor man's house. Her eyes, never much to sparkle, were now black holes.

Pearl's hands went up and across her mouth. Sugar looked so vulnerable and at that moment she looked more like Jude than ever before.

Whispers filled the spaces between the Reverend's words as the people of Bigelow muttered under their breath. Word had gotten out about the attack, and no one was up in arms about it. Who was Sugar? Certainly not a Jude. She belonged to no one and nowhere. A whore.

At the height of the Reverend's sermon, Sugar stood up. Tiny waterfalls of sweat spilled down his face and his voice rose to a holler while his hands gripped the sides of the podium, steadying his Jesus jumping. He caught sight of her and stopped dead. The congregation was thrown and turned to see what he was looking at. Sugar was walking now. Straight toward him. Her feet hit the floorboards hard and with great intent. The Reverend had taken more than a few steps backward. His heart raced. His thoughts filled with the memories of the wicked, stolen pleasures he'd shared with the woman that was now in his face. He held his breath and felt the blood drain from his head down to his feet.

Sugar was looking at the Reverend, but not seeing him. She turned on the congregation. A combined breath was taken and for a moment, there was no sound at all. Sugar looked down on the people of Bigelow and they looked back at her. Waiting.

Then suddenly, like a fledgling breeze before an approaching storm, whispers rose up from the pews, filling the emptiness until the church walls groaned and the whispers became a raging gale of shouts and screams.

"Sit down, girl!"

"You done lost your mind? The Reverend is preachin'!"

"Lord, she ain't got the good sense God gave her."

Sugar stood before the congregation, her head hanging heavy on the stick that was her neck. And then she spoke with a voice that betrayed her grief and disguised the hopelessness that was eating away at her senses.

"Ain't but two of ya'll in this church ever made me feel welcomed here," Sugar began. She raised her hand and pointed a shaking finger toward Joe and Pearl.

Clair Bell, Minnie and Shirley twisted uncomfortably in their seats, and pulled at the collars of their dresses. "I'm leavin' here tonight," she continued, "but not without sayin' some things that need to be said."

The men who'd laid down with her squeezed their legs shut and scratched at the spaces behind their ears and beneath their chins, bracing themselves against the truths they thought she would tell.

"I wanna say to Joe"—she raised her head high and looked directly at him—"and Miss Pearl, that ya'll been like family to me. I appreciate you looking on me with warm eyes, talkin' to me like I was somebody, treatin' me like I was your own." She choked on "your own," giving it all the meaning it deserved. The sound of those two words placed together caught some people's attention as they slipped from her mouth.

Sugar's eyes did not welcome those faces into view. Her eyes rested solely on her Joe and Pearl. Her words were meant for those two only. "I wanna say sorry for the things I did and the things I didn't do and I wanna thank you, for everything."

Anna Lee smiled and turned her head to exchange a triumphant glance with Fayline.

Sugar walked slowly down the aisle, away from the pulpit and toward the door.

A quiet peace had settled over Sugar. A peace she had never known in all her years. Even as she walked past the sad staring eyes of Joe and Pearl, the good-riddance looks from the Bigelow women and the forlorn glances of the Bigelow men, she was not fazed. Her hurt had been replaced with tranquility. The anger that had laid heavy in her heart for so many years was no longer present in her mind and soul. It had dissolved with each step she took toward the pulpit and each word she spoke to those who cared for her.

Pearl willed herself to stay seated. She kept telling herself, "She ain't yours. Let her go." She repeated these words over and over in her mind until they escaped from her mouth in a moan. She dug her fingers deep into the soft underside of Joe's arm and rocked herself back and forth.

Joe's eyes teared for the third time in his adult life. The first time was when he promised himself to his wife. The second time, when he lifted the cold, dead body of his baby girl, and now. He could not give reason as to why he felt so impassioned. It would be one year later before he would understand why his heart had opened and allowed his emotions to slip down his face.

Pearl was losing another one. Only this time, she would not have to bend over a pine box to say a final good-bye.

No, this was worse.

This time the sound would come like a flood. It started deep in Pearl's belly and rose in her throat like lava; hot and steaming. Fifteen years of loss. Fifteen years of grief. Fifteen years of anguish finally spewed forth and shook the church's insides and everyone who had the misfortune of being there.

Black John braced himself. He did not have the comfort of his straw hat. His hands moved around his lap, searching for consolation, until finally clasping on to those of his neighbor.

*S*ugar, already out the door, never heard the great wail of emotion released at her back. If she had, the depth alone of Pearl's sorrow would have spun her around.

Sugar barely noticed the biting cold and brutal wind that had its way with her as she walked down the path that led from the church to the street that would place her firmly back onto the familiar road of her life.

One step forward, two steps backward. Two steps backward. One step forward.

$\mathscr{A}$FTER

FALL 1956

"*I* GOT some people from over in Carnery wanna come on over here and check out the house." A white man with a beet-red face and a tan plaid jacket looked in at Pearl through the screen door. It was barely ten o'clock and the temperature had already soared to eighty degrees. "They told me that you all got the keys to the place," he continued.

Pearl couldn't tell if the heat was making him uncomfortable or the fact that he was talking to a black woman with a blank face. She looked him over and without a word, turned and walked away.

"Ma'am?" The white man was confused. He took out his paper and looked down at the name and address again. He was at the right place. He cussed under his breath and was about to turn to go back to his car when Joe came to the screen door. The white man was short, so he had to tilt his head way back to meet Joe's eyes.

"You need the keys to number ten?" Joe pushed the door open a crack.

"Uh, yes," the man said, scratching his head.

"Just a minute." Joe let the screen door close again. When he came back he had one lone silver key in hand. "Lemme come on over there with you, the lock is a little funny, you gotta jiggle it just right."

The white man nodded and pulled his handkerchief out of his back pocket to wipe at his forehead and the back of his neck. He had to half run and half walk to keep up with Joe's long strides. He finally caught up and stuck out his hand. "Tommy Cathers," he said. Joe considered his sweaty palm and then took it into his own. "Joe Taylor."

"Uh, this house been up for near a year now. We just got this listing two weeks ago. You had a lotta people out here looking at it?"

"A few." Joe hesitated before he took the steps up to #10.

"Really. You know the people that usta live here?"

Joe didn't answer; he was jiggling the lock. He hadn't been in the house for almost as long as Sugar had been gone. A month after she left someone came and placed a FOR SALE sign in the front yard.

The door was open and Joe stepped back to let the man in.

"Thanks . . . Joe," the man said and hesitantly stepped into the house.

Joe stood, peering into the dusty emptiness. He half expected Sugar to come swaggering around a corner or down the stairs. He closed his eyes and wished it hard, because Sugar had taken part of his wife with her. But when he opened them all he saw was the white man's red face staring back at him. "You okay?" the man asked, genuine concern in his voice. That's all he needed was this colored man to pass out or drop dead with no witnesses. Not with all of the civil rights stuff going on down there; he didn't want to be blamed for anything.

"Yeah," Joe said and turned to leave.

He was halfway back to his house when the white man came out to the porch, calling to him. Joe looked down and realized that he still had the key clutched tightly in his hand. "Probably want to keep it," he thought to himself and turned back toward #10.

The white man was grinning and holding something in his hand.

"It was laying on the floor near the fireplace. Burnt a little 'round the edges, but still clear." The white man's voice was excited. "I almost threw it in the trash, but I looked at it and realized it was you."

Joe sighed. The heat and this man's babbling were toying with his patience. He took the picture from the man and stared at it. His heart skipped a beat. His breath shortened and then he turned and sat heavily down on the stairs.

It was him. Him and Bertie Mae.

"That's you, ain't it?" the man bellowed and slapped his knee in triumph.

Joe stared long and hard at the picture. Stared into the truth he'd tried to avoid the whole time Sugar was there. He didn't need a picture of him and Bertie Mae to see that she was a clear product of the two of them—he'd thought it the first time he saw her, but had convinced himself otherwise. Now he stood, his stature a bit stooped, and placed the picture safely in the breast pocket of his shirt.

He took the first step toward home, where he would speak the first word of an age-old story and ask, for the first time in his life, for forgiveness from his wife.

Bernice L. McFadden

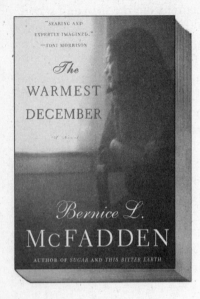

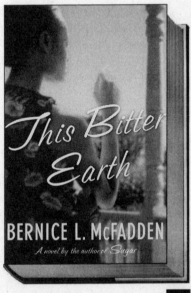